Children of the Tenements

Jacob A. Riis

ISBN: 1981637192

ISBN-13: 978-1981637195

Table of Contents

THE RENT BABY

Adam Grunschlag sat at his street stand in a deep brown study. He heeded not the gathering twilight, or the snow that fell in great white flakes, as yet with an appreciable space between, but with the promise of a coming storm in them. He took no notice of the bustle and stir all about that betokened the approaching holiday. The cries of the huckster hawking oranges from his cart, of the man with the crawling toy, and of the pedler of colored Christmas candles passed him by unheard. Women with big baskets jostled him, stopped and fingered his cabbages; he answered their inquiries mechanically. Adam's mind was not in the street, at his stand, but in the dark back basement where his wife Hansche was lying, there was no telling how sick. They could not afford a doctor. Of course, he might send to the hospital for one, but he would be sure to take her away, and then what would become of little Abe? Besides, if they had nothing else in the whole world, they had yet each other. When that was no longer the case—Adam would have lacked no answer to the vexed question if life were then worth living.

Troubles come not singly, but in squads, once the bag be untied. It was not the least sore point with Adam that he had untied it himself. They were doing well enough, he and his wife, in their home in Leinbach, Austria, keeping a little grocery store, and living humbly but comfortably, when word of the country beyond the sea where much money was made, and where every man was as good as the next, made them uneasy and discontented. In the end they gave up the grocery and their little home, Hansche not without some tears; but she dried them quickly at the thought of the good times that were waiting. With these ever before them they bore the hardships of the steerage, and in good season reached Hester Street and the longed-for haven, only to find—this. A rear basement, dark and damp and unwholesome, for which the landlord, along with the privilege of keeping a stand in the street, which was not his to give, made them pay twelve dollars a month. Truly, much money was made in America, but not by those who paid the rent. It was all they could do, working early and late, he with his push-cart and at his stand, she with the needle, slaving for the sweater, to get the rent together and keep a roof over the head of little Abe.

Five years they had kept that up, and things had gone from bad to worse. The police blackmail had taken out of it what little profit there was in the push-cart business. Times had grown harder than they ever were in Hester Street. To cap it all, two weeks ago gas had begun to leak into the basement from somewhere, and made Hansche sick, so that she dropped down at her work. Adam had complained to the landlord, and he had laughed at him. What did he want for twelve dollars, anyway? If the basement wasn't good enough for him, why didn't he hire an upstairs flat? The landlord did not tell him that he could do that for the same rent he paid for the miserable hole he burrowed in. He had a good thing and he knew it. Adam Grunschlag knew nothing of the Legal Aid Society, that is there to help such as he. He was afraid to appeal to the police. He was just a poor, timid Jew, of a race that has been hunted for centuries to make sport and revenue for the great and mighty. When he spoke of moving and the landlord said that he would forfeit the twenty dollars deposit that he had held back all these years, and which was all the capital the pedler had, he thought that was the law, and was silent. He could not afford to lose it, and yet he must find some way of making a change, for the sake of little Abe as well as his wife, and the child.

At the thought of the child, the pedler gave a sudden start and was wide awake on the instant. Little Abe was their own, and though he had come in the gloom of that dismal basement, he had been the one ray of sunshine that had fallen into their dreary lives. But the child was a rent baby. In the crowded tenements of New York the lodger serves the same purpose as the Irishman's pig; he helps to pay the rent. "The child"—it was never called anything else—was a lodger. Flotsam from Rivington Street, after the breaking up of a family there, it had come to them, to perish "if the Lord so willed it" in that basement. "Infant slaughter houses" the Tenement House Commission had called their kind. The father paid seventy-five cents a week for its keep, pending the disclosure of the divine purpose with the baby. The Grunschlags, all unconscious of the partnership that was thus thrust upon them, did their best for it, and up to the time the trouble with the gas began it was a disgracefully healthy baby. Since then it had sickened with the rest. But now, if the worst came to the worst, what was to become of the child?

The pedler was not given long to debate this new question. Even as he sat staring dumbly at nothing in his perplexity, little Abe crawled out of the yard with the news that "mamma was most deaded;" and though it was not so bad as that, it was made clear to her husband when he found her in one of her bad fainting spells, that things had come to a pass where something had to be done. There followed a last ineffectual interview with the landlord, a tearful leave-taking, and as the ambulance rolled away with Hansche to the hospital, where she would be a hundred times better off than in Hester Street, the pedler took little Abe by the hand, and, carrying the child, set out to deliver it over to its rightful owners. If he were rid of it, he and Abe might make a shift to get along. It was a case, emphatically; in which two were company and three a crowd.

He spied the father in Stanton Street where he was working, but when he saw Adam he tried to run away. Desperation gave the pedler both strength and speed, however, and he overhauled him despite his handicaps, and thrust the baby upon him. But the father would have none of it.

"Aber, mein Gott," pleaded the pedler, "vat I do mit him? He vas your baby."

"I don't care what you do with her," said the hard-hearted father. "Give her away—anything. I can't keep her."

And this time he really escaped. Left alone with his charge, the pedler bethought himself of a friend in Pitt Street who had little children. Where so many fed, there would be easily room for another. To Pitt Street he betook himself, only to meet with another setback. They didn't want any babies there; had enough of their own. So he went to a widow in East Broadway who had none, to be driven forth with hard words. What did a widow want with a baby? Did he want to disgrace her? Adam Grunschlag visited in turn every countryman he knew of on the East Side, and proposed to each of them to take the baby off his hands, without finding a single customer for it. Either because it was hurt by such treatment, or because it thought it time for Hansche's attentions, the child at length set up a great cry. Little Abe, who had trotted along bravely upon his four-years-old legs, wrapped in a big plaid shawl, lost his grip at that and joined in, howling dolefully that he was hungry.

Adam Grunschlag gave up at last and sat down on the curb, helpless and hopeless. Hungry! Yes, and so was he. Since morning he had not eaten a morsel, and been on his feet incessantly. Two hungry mouths to fill beside his own and not a cent with which to buy bread. For the first time he felt a pang of bitterness as he saw the shoppers hurry by with filled baskets to homes where there was cheer and plenty. From the window of a tenement across the way shone the lights of a Christmas tree, lighted as in old-country fashion on the Holy Eve. Christmas! What had it ever meant to him and his but hatred and persecution? There was a shout from across the street and voices raised in laughter and song. The children could be seen dancing about the tree, little room though there was.

Ah, yes! Let them make merry upon their holiday while two little ones were starving in the street. A colder blast than ordinary came up from the river and little Abe crept close to him, wailing disconsolate within his shawl.

"Hey, what's this?" said a rough, but not unkindly voice at his elbow. "Campin' out, shepherd fashion, Moses? Bad for the kids; these ain't the hills of Judea."

It was the policeman on the beat stirring the trio gently with his club. The pedler got up without a word, to move away, but little Abe, from fright or hunger, set up such a howl that the policeman made him stop to explain. While he did so, telling as briefly as he could about the basement and Hansche and the baby that was not his, a silver quarter found its way mysteriously into little Abe's fist, to the utter upsetting of all that "kid's" notions of policemen and their functions. When the pedler had done, the officer directed him to Police Headquarters where they would take the baby, he need have no fear of that.

"Better leave this one there, too," was his parting counsel. Little Abe did not understand, but he took a firmer grip on his papa's hand, and never let go all the way up the three long flights of stairs to the police nursery where the child at last found peace and a bottle. But when the matron tried to coax him to stay also, he screamed and carried on so that they were glad to let him go lest he wake everybody in the building. Though proverbially Police Headquarters never sleeps, yet it does not like to be disturbed in its midnight nap, as it were. It is human with the rest of us, that is how.

Down in the marble-tiled hall little Abe and his father stopped irresolute. Outside it was dark and windy; the snow, that had ceased falling in the evening, was swept through the streets on the northern blast. They had nowhere to go. The doorman was called downstairs just then to the telegraph office. When he came up again he found father and son curled up on the big mat by the register, sound asleep. It was against the regulations entirely, and he was going to wake them up and put them out, when he happened to glance through the glass doors at the storm without, and remembered that it was Christmas Eve. With a growl he let them sleep, trusting to luck that the inspector wouldn't come out. The doorman, too, was human.

So it came about that the newspaper boys who ran with messages to the reporters' offices across the street, found them there and held a meeting over them. Rudie, the smartest of them, declared that his "fingers just itched for that sheeny's whiskers," but the others paid little attention to him. Even reporters' messengers are not so bad as they like to have others believe them, sometimes. The year before, in their rough sport in the alley, the boys had upset old Mary, so that she fell and broke her arm. That finished old Mary's scrubbing, for the break never healed. Ever since this, bloodthirsty Rudie had been stealing down Mulberry Street to the old woman's attic on pay-day and sharing his meagre wages with her, paying, beside, the insurance premium that assured her of a decent burial; though he denied it hotly if charged with it. So when Rudie announced that he would like to pull the pedler's whiskers, it was taken as a motion that he be removed to the reporters' quarters and made comfortable there, and the motion was carried unanimously. Was it not Christmas Eve?

Little Abe was carried across Mulberry Street, sleeping soundly, and laid upon Rudie's cot. The dogs, Chief and Trilby, that run things in Mulberry Street when the boys are away, snuggled down by him to keep him warm, taking him at once under their protection. The father took off his shoes, and curling up by the stove, slept, tired out, but not until he had briefly told the boys the story he had once that evening gone over with the policeman. They heard it in silence, but one or two made notes which, could he have seen them, would have spoiled one Hester Street landlord's Christmas. When the pedler was asleep, they took them across the street and consulted with the inspector about it.

Father and son slept soundly yet when, the morning papers having gone to press, the boys came down into the office with the night-gang of reporters to spend the dog-watch, according to their wont, in a game of ungodly poker. They were flush, for it had been pay-day in the afternoon, and under the reckless impulse of the holiday the jack-pot, ordinarily modest enough for cause, grew to unheard-of proportions. It contained nearly fifteen dollars when Rudie opened it at last. Amid breathless silence, he then and there made the only public speech of his life.

"The pot," he said, "goes to the sheeny and his kid for their Christmas, or my name is mud."

Wild applause followed the speech. It awakened the pedler and little Abe. They sat up and rubbed their eyes, while Chief and Trilby barked their welcome. The morning was struggling through the windows. The snow had ceased falling and the sky was clear.

"Mornin'," said Rudie, with mock deference, "will yer worships have yer breakfast now, or will ye wait till ye get it?"

The pedler looked about him in bewilderment. "I hab kein blam' cent," he said, feeling hopelessly in his pockets.

A joyous yell greeted him. "Ikey has more nor you," shouted the boys, showing the quarter which little Abe had held fast to in his sleep. "And see this."

They swept the jack-pot into his lap, handfuls of shining silver. The pedler blinked at the sight.

"Good morning and Merry Christmas," they shouted. "We just had Bellevue on the 'phone, and Hansche is all right. She will be out to-day. The gas poisoned her, that was all. For that the police will settle with the landlord, or we will. You go back there and get your money back, and go and hire a flat. This is Christmas, and don't you forget it!"

And they pushed the pedler and little Abe, made fast upon a gorgeous sled that suddenly appeared from somewhere, out into the street, and gave them a rousing cheer as they turned the corner going east, Adam dragging the sled and little Abe seated on his throne, perfectly and radiantly happy.

A STORY OF BLEECKER STREET

Mrs. Kane had put the baby to bed. The regular breathing from two little cribs in different corners told her that her day's work was nearing its end. She paused at the window in the middle of her picking-up to look out at the autumn evening. The house stood on the bank of the East River near where the Harlem joins it. Below ran the swift stream, with the early twilight stealing over it from the near shore; across the water the myriad windows in the Children's Hospital glowed red in the sunset. From the shipyard, where men were working overtime, came up the sound of hammering and careless laughter.

The peacefulness of the scene rested the tired woman. She stood absorbed, without noticing that the door behind her was opened swiftly and that some one came in. It was only when the baby, wakening, sat up in bed and asked with wide, wondering eyes, "Who is that?" that she turned to see.

Just inside the door stood a strange woman. A glance at her dress showed her to be an escaped prisoner. A number of such from the Island were employed under guard in the adjoining hospital, and Mrs. Kane saw them daily. Her first impulse was to call to the men working below, but something in the stranger's look and attitude checked her. She went over to the child's bed and stood by it.

"How did you get out?" she asked, confronting the woman. The question rose to her lips mechanically.

The woman answered with a toss of her head toward the hospital. She was young yet, but her face was old. Debauchery had left deep scars upon it. Her black hair hung in disorder.

"They'll be after me," she said hurriedly. Her voice was hoarse; it kept the promise of the face. "Don't let them. Hide me there—anywhere." She glanced uneasily from the open closet to the door of the inner room.

Mrs. Kane's face hardened. The stranger was a convict, a thief perhaps. Why should she—A door slammed below, and there were excited voices in the hall, the tread of heavy steps on the stairs. The fugitive listened.

"That's them," she said. "Quick! lemme get in! O God!" she pleaded with desperate entreaty, as Mrs. Kane stood coldly unresponsive, "you have your baby. I haven't seen mine in seven months, and they never wrote. I'll never have the chance again."

The steps had halted in the second-floor hall. They were on the last flight of stairs now. The mother's heart relented.

"Here," she said, "go in."

The bedroom door had barely closed upon the fugitive when a man in a prison-keeper's garb stuck his head in from the hall. He saw only the mother and the baby in its crib.

"Hang the woman!" he growled. "Did yez—"

A voice called from the lower hall: "Hey, Billy! she ain't in there. She give us the slip, sure."

The keeper withdrew his head, growling. In the street the hue and cry was raised; a prisoner had escaped.

When all was quiet, Mrs. Kane opened the bedroom door. She had a dark wrapper and an old gray shawl on her arm.

"Go," she said, not unkindly, and laid them on the bed; "Go to your child."

The woman caught at her hand with a sob, but she withdrew it hastily and went back to her baby's crib.

The moon shone upon the hushed streets, when a woman, hooded in a gray shawl, walked rapidly down Fifth Street, eying the tenements with a searching look as she passed. On the stoop of one, a knot of mothers were discussing their household affairs, idling a bit after the day's work. The woman halted in front of the group, and was about to ask a question, when one of the women arose with the exclamation:—

"Mother of God! it's Mame."

"Well," said the woman, testily, "and what if it is? Am I a spook that ye need stare at me so? Ye knowed me well enough before. Where is Will?"

There was no answer. The women looked at one another irresolutely. None of them seemed to know what to say. It was the newcomer who broke the silence again.

"Can't ye speak?" she said, in a voice in which anger and rising apprehension were struggling. "Where's the boy? Kate, what is it?"

She had caught hold of the rail, as if in fear of falling. The woman addressed said hesitatingly:—

"Did ye never hear, Mame? Ain't no one tole ye?"

"Tole me what?" cried the other, shrilly. "They tole me nothing. What's wrong? Good God! 'tain't nothin' with the child?" She shook the other in sudden anger. "Speak, Kate, can't you?"

"Will is dead," said Kate, slowly, thus urged. "It's nine weeks come Sunday that he fell out o' the winder and was kilt. They buried him from the Morgue. We thought you knowed."

Stunned by the blow, the woman had sunk upon the lowest step and buried her face in her hands. She sat there with her shawl drawn over her head, as one by one the neighbors went inside. One lingered; it was the one they had called Kate.

"Mame," she said, when the last was gone, touching her on the shoulder—"Mame!"

An almost imperceptible movement of the head under its shawl testified that she heard.

"Mebbe it was for the best," said Kate, irresolutely; "he might have took after—Tim—you know."

The shrouded figure sat immovable, Kate eyed it in silence, and went her way.

The night wore on. The streets were deserted and the stores closed. Only the saloon windows blazed with light. But the figure sat there yet. It had not stirred. Then it rose, shook out the shawl, and displayed the face of the convict woman who had sought refuge in Mrs. Kane's flat. The face was dry-eyed and hard.

The policeman on the beat rang the bell of the Florence Mission at two o'clock on Sunday morning, and waited until Mother Pringle had unbolted the door. "One for you," he said briefly, and pointed toward the bedraggled shape that crouched in the corner. It was his day off, and he had no time to trouble with prisoners. The matron drew a corner of the wet shawl aside and took one cold hand. She eyed it attentively; there was a wedding ring upon it.

"Why, child," she said, "you'll catch your death of cold. Come right in. Girls, give a hand."

Two of the women inmates half led, half carried her in, and the bolts shut out Bleecker Street once more. They led her to the dormitory, where they took off her dress and shawl, heavy with the cold rain. The matron came bustling in; one of the girls spoke to her aside. She looked sharply at the newcomer.

"Mamie Anderson!" she said. "Well, of all things! Where have you been all this while? Yes, I know," she added soothingly, as the stranger made a sign to speak. "Never mind; we'll talk about it to-morrow. Go to sleep now and get over it."

But though bathed and fed and dosed with bromide,—bromide is a standard prescription at the Florence Mission,—Mamie Anderson did not get over it. Bruised and sore from many blows, broken in body and spirit, she told the girls who sat by her bed through the night such fragments of her story as she could remember. It began, the part of it that took account of Bleecker Street, when her husband was sent to State's Prison for robbery, and, to live, she took up with a scoundrel from whom she kept the secret of her child. With such of her earnings as she could steal from her tormentor she had paid little Willie's board until she was arrested and sent to the Island.

What had happened in the three days since she escaped from the hospital, where she had been detailed with the scrubbing squad, she recalled only vaguely and with long lapses. They had been days and nights of wild carousing. She had come to herself at last, lying beaten and bound in a room in the house where her child was killed, so she said. A neighbor had heard her groans, released her, and given her car fare to go down town. So she had come and sat in the doorway of the Mission to die.

How much of this story was the imagining of a disordered mind, the police never found out.

Upon her body were marks as of ropes that had made dark bruises, but at the inquest they were said to be of blows. Toward morning, when the girls had lain down to snatch a moment's sleep, she called one of them, whom she had known before, and asked for a drink of water. As she took it with feeble hand, she asked:—

"Lil', can you pray?"

For an answer the girl knelt by her bed and prayed. When she had ended, Mamie Anderson fell asleep.

She was still sleeping when the others got up. They noticed after a while that she lay very quiet and white, and one of them going to see, found her dead.

That is the story of Mamie Anderson, as Bleecker Street told it to me. Out on Long Island there is, in a suburban cemetery, a lovely shaded spot where I sometimes sit by our child's grave. The green hillside slopes gently under the chestnuts, violets and buttercups spring from the sod, and the robin sings its jubilant note in the long June twilights. Halfway down the slope, six or eight green mounds cluster about a granite block in which are hewn the words:—

These are they which came out of great tribulation, and have washed their robes, and made them white in the blood of the Lamb.

It is the burial-plot of the Florence Mission. Under one of the mounds lies all that was mortal of Mamie Anderson.

THE KID HANGS UP HIS STOCKING

The clock in the West Side Boys' Lodging-house ticked out the seconds of Christmas eve as slowly and methodically as if six fat turkeys were not sizzling in the basement kitchen against the morrow's spread, and as if two-score boys were not racking their brains to guess what kind of pies would go with them. Out on the avenue the shopkeepers were barring doors and windows, and shouting "Merry Christmas!" to one another across the street as they hurried to get home. The drays ran over the pavement with muffled sounds; winter had set in with a heavy snow-storm. In the big hall the monotonous click of checkers on the board kept step with the clock. The smothered exclamations of the boys at some unexpected, bold stroke, and the scratching of a little fellow's pencil on a slate, trying to figure out how long it was yet till the big dinner, were the only sounds that broke the quiet of the room. The superintendent dozed behind his desk.

A door at the end of the hall creaked, and a head with a shock of weather-beaten hair was stuck cautiously through the opening.

"Tom!" it said in a stage-whisper. "Hi, Tom! Come up an' git on ter de lay of de Kid."

A bigger boy in a jumper, who had been lounging on two chairs by the group of checker players, sat up and looked toward the door. Something in the energetic toss of the head there aroused his instant curiosity, and he started across the room. After a brief whispered conference the door closed upon the two, and silence fell once more on the hall.

They had been gone but a little while when they came back in haste. The big boy shut the door softly behind him and set his back against it.

"Fellers," he said, "what d'ye t'ink? I'm blamed if de Kid ain't gone an' hung up his sock fer Chris'mas!"

The checkers dropped, and the pencil ceased scratching on the slate, in breathless suspense.

"Come up an' see," said Tom, briefly, and led the way.

The whole band followed on tiptoe. At the foot of the stairs their leader halted.

"Yer don't make no noise," he said, with a menacing gesture. "You, Savoy!"—to one in a patched shirt and with a mischievous twinkle,—"you don't come none o' yer monkey-shines. If you scare de Kid you'll get it in de neck, see!"

With this admonition they stole upstairs. In the last cot of the double tier of bunks a boy much smaller than the rest slept, snugly tucked in the blankets. A tangled curl of yellow hair strayed over his baby face. Hitched to the bedpost was a poor, worn little stocking, arranged with much care so that Santa Claus should have as little trouble in filling it as possible. The edge of a hole in the knee had been drawn together and tied with a string to prevent anything falling out. The boys looked on in amazed silence. Even Savoy was dumb.

Little Willie, or, as he was affectionately dubbed by the boys, "the Kid," was a waif who had drifted in among them some months before. Except that his mother was in the hospital, nothing was known about him, which was regular and according to the rule of the house. Not as much was known about most of its patrons; few of them knew more themselves, or cared to remember. Santa Claus had never been anything to them but a fake to make the colored supplements sell. The revelation of the Kid's simple faith struck them with a kind of awe. They sneaked quietly downstairs.

"Fellers," said Tom, when they were all together again in the big room,—by virtue of his length, which had given him the nickname of "Stretch," he was the speaker on all important occasions,—"ye seen it yerself. Santy Claus is a-comin' to this here joint to-night. I wouldn't 'a' believed it. I ain't never had no dealin's wid de ole guy. He kinder forgot I was around, I guess. But de Kid says he is a-comin' to-night, an' what de Kid says goes."

Then he looked round expectantly. Two of the boys, "Gimpy" and Lem, were conferring aside in an undertone. Presently Gimpy, who limped, as his name indicated, spoke up.

"Lem says, says he—"

"Gimpy, you chump! you'll address de chairman," interrupted Tom, with severe dignity, "or you'll get yer jaw broke, if yer leg *is* short, see!"

"Cut it out, Stretch," was Gimpy's irreverent answer. "This here ain't no regular meetin', an' we ain't goin' to have none o' yer rot. Lem he says, says he, let's break de bank an' fill de Kid's sock. He won't know but it wuz ole Santy done it."

A yell of approval greeted the suggestion. The chairman, bound to exercise the functions of office in season and out of season, while they lasted, thumped the table.

"It is regular motioned an' carried," he announced, "that we break de bank fer de Kid's Chris'mas. Come on, boys!"

The bank was run by the house, with the superintendent as paying teller. He had to be consulted, particularly as it was past banking hours; but the affair having been succinctly put before him by a committee, of which Lem and Gimpy and Stretch were the talking members, he readily consented to a reopening of business for a scrutiny of the various accounts which represented the boys' earnings at selling papers and blacking boots, minus the cost of their keep and of sundry surreptitious flings at "craps" in secret corners. The inquiry developed an available surplus of three dollars and fifty cents. Savoy alone had no account; the run of craps had recently gone heavily against him. But in consideration of the season, the house voted a credit of twenty-five cents to him. The announcement was received with cheers. There was an immediate rush for the store, which was delayed only a few minutes by the necessity of Gimpy and Lem stopping on the stairs to "thump" one another as the expression of their entire satisfaction.

The procession that returned to the lodging-house later on, after wearing out the patience of several belated storekeepers, might have been the very Santa's supply-train itself. It signalized its advent by a variety of discordant noises, which were smothered on the stairs by Stretch, with much personal violence, lest they wake the Kid out of season. With boots in hand and bated breath, the midnight band stole up to the dormitory and looked in. All was safe. The Kid was dreaming, and smiled in his sleep. The report roused a passing suspicion that he was faking, and Savarese was for pinching his toe to find out. As this would inevitably result in disclosure, Savarese and his proposal were scornfully sat upon. Gimpy supplied the popular explanation.

"He's a-dreamin' that Santy Claus has come," he said, carefully working a base-ball bat past the tender spot in the stocking.

"Hully Gee!" commented Shorty, balancing a drum with care on the end of it, "I'm thinkin' he ain't far out. Looks's ef de hull shop'd come along."

It did when it was all in place. A trumpet and a gun that had made vain and perilous efforts to join the bat in the stocking leaned against the bed in expectant attitudes. A picture-book with a pink Bengal tiger and a green bear on the cover peeped over the pillow, and the bedposts and rail were festooned with candy and marbles in bags. An express-wagon with a high seat was stabled in the gangway. It carried a load of fir branches that left no doubt from whose livery it hailed. The last touch was supplied by Savoy in the shape of a monkey on a yellow stick, that was not in the official bill of lading.

"I swiped it fer de Kid," he said briefly in explanation.

When it was all done the boys turned in, but not to sleep. It was long past midnight before the deep and regular breathing from the beds proclaimed that the last had succumbed.

The early dawn was tinging the frosty window panes with red when from the Kid's cot there came a shriek that roused the house with a start of very genuine surprise.

"Hello!" shouted Stretch, sitting up with a jerk and rubbing his eyes. "Yes, sir! in a minute. Hello, Kid, what to—"

The Kid was standing barefooted in the passageway, with a base-ball bat in one hand and a trumpet and a pair of drumsticks in the other, viewing with shining eyes the wagon and its cargo, the gun and all the rest. From every cot necks were stretched, and grinning faces watched the show. In the excess of his joy the Kid let out a blast on the trumpet that fairly shook the building. As if it were a signal, the boys jumped out of bed and danced a breakdown about him in their shirt-tails, even Gimpy joining in.

"Holy Moses!" said Stretch, looking down, "if Santy Claus ain't been here an' forgot his hull kit, I'm blamed!"

THE SLIPPER-MAKER'S FAST

Isaac Josephs, slipper-maker, sat up on the fifth floor of his Allen Street tenement, in the gray of the morning, to finish the task he had set himself before Yom Kippur. Three days and three nights he had worked without sleep, almost without taking time to eat, to make ready the two dozen slippers that were to enable him to fast the fourth day and night for conscience' sake, and now they were nearly done. As he saw the end of his task near, he worked faster and faster while the tenement slept.

Three years he had slaved for the sweater, stinted and starved himself, before he had saved enough to send for his wife and children, awaiting his summons in the city by the Black Sea. Since they came they had slaved and starved together; for wages had become steadily less, work more grinding, and hours longer and later. Still, of that he thought little. They had known little else, there or here; they were together now. The past was dead; the future was their own, even in the Allen Street tenement, toiling night and day at starvation wages. To-morrow was the feast, their first Yom Kippur since they had come together again,—Esther, his wife, and Ruth and little Ben,—the feast when, priest and patriarch of his own house, he might forget his bondage and be free. Poor little Ben! The hand that smoothed the soft leather on the last took a tenderer, lingering touch as he glanced toward the stool where the child had sat watching him work till his eyes grew small. Brave little Ben, almost a baby yet, but so patient, so wise, and so strong!

The deep breathing of the sleeping children reached him from their crib. He smiled and listened, with the half-finished slipper in his hand. As he sat thus, a great drowsiness came upon him. He nodded once, twice; his hands sank into his lap, his head fell forward upon his chest. In the silence of the morning he slept, worn out with utter weariness.

He awoke with a guilty start to find the first rays of the dawn struggling through his window, and his task yet undone. With desperate energy he seized the unfinished slipper to resume his work. His unsteady hand upset the little lamp by his side, upon which his burnishing-iron was heating. The oil blazed up on the floor and ran toward the nearly finished pile of work. The cloth on the table caught fire. In a fever of terror and excitement, the slipper-maker caught it in his hands, wrung it, and tore at it to smother the flames. His hands were burned, but what of that? The slippers, the slippers! If they were burned, it was ruin. There would be no Yom Kippur, no feast of Atonement, no fast—rather, no end of it; starvation for him and his.

He beat the fire with his hands and trampled it with his feet as it burned and spread on the floor. His hair and his beard caught fire: With a despairing shriek he gave it up and fell before the precious slippers, barring, the way of the flames to them with his body.

The shriek woke his wife. She sprang out of bed, snatched up a blanket, and threw it upon the fire. It went out, was smothered under the blanket. The slipper-maker sat up, panting and grateful. His Yom Kippur was saved.

The tenement awoke to hear of the fire in the morning, when all Jew town was stirring with preparations for the feast. The slipper-maker's wife was setting the house to rights for the holiday then. Two half-naked children played about her knees, asking eager questions about it. Asked if her husband had often to work so hard, and what he made by it, she shrugged her shoulders and said, "The rent and a crust."

And yet all this labor and effort to enable him to fast one day according to the old dispensation, when all the rest of the days he fasted according to the new!

DEATH COMES TO CAT ALLEY

The dead-wagon stopped at the mouth of Cat Alley. Its coming made a commotion among the children in the block, and the Chief of Police looked out of his window across the street, his attention arrested by the noise. He saw a little pine coffin carried into the alley under the arm of the driver, a shoal of ragged children trailing behind. After a while the driver carried it out again, shoved it in the wagon, where there were other boxes like it, and, slamming the door, drove off.

A red-eyed woman watched it down the street until it disappeared around the corner. Then she wiped her eyes with her apron and went in.

It was only Mary Welsh's baby that was dead, but to her the alley, never cheerful on the brightest of days, seemed hopelessly desolate to-day. It was all she had. Her first baby died in teething.

Cat Alley is a back-yard illustration of the theory of evolution. The fittest survive, and the Welsh babies were not among them. It would be strange if they were. Mike, the father, works in a Crosby Street factory when he does work. It is necessary to put it that way, for, though he has not been discharged, he had only one day's work this week and none at all last week. He gets one dollar a day, and the one dollar he earned these last two weeks his wife had to draw to pay the doctor with when the baby was so sick. They have had nothing else coming in, and but for the wages of Mrs. Welsh's father, who lives with them, there would have been nothing in the house to eat.

The baby came three weeks ago, right in the hardest of the hard times. It was never strong enough to nurse, and the milk bought in Mulberry Street is not for babies to grow on who are not strong enough to stand anything. Little John never grew at all. He lay upon his pillow this morning as white and wan and tiny as the day he came into a world that didn't want him.

Yesterday, just before he died, he sat upon his grandmother's lap and laughed and crowed for the first time in his brief life, "just like he was talkin' to me," said the old woman, with a smile that struggled hard to keep down a sob. "I suppose it was a sort of inward cramp," she added—a mother's explanation of baby laugh in Cat Alley.

The mother laid out the little body on the only table in their room, in its only little white slip, and covered it with a piece of discarded lace curtain to keep off the flies. They had no ice, and no money to pay an undertaker for opening the little grave in Calvary, where their first baby lay. All night she sat by the improvised bier, her tears dropping silently.

When morning came and brought the woman with the broken arm from across the hall to sit by her, it was sadly evident that the burial of the child must be hastened. It was not well to look at the little face and the crossed baby hands, and even the mother saw it.

"Let the trench take him, in God's name; He has his soul," said the grandmother, crossing herself devoutly.

An undertaker had promised to put the baby in the grave in Calvary for twelve dollars and take two dollars a week until it was paid. But how can a man raise two dollars a week, with only one coming in in two weeks, and that gone to the doctor? With a sigh Mike Welsh went for the "lines" that must smooth its way to the trench in the Potter's Field, and then to Mr. Blake's for the dead-wagon. It was the hardest walk of his life.

And so it happened that the dead-wagon halted at Cat Alley and that little John took his first and last ride. A little cross and a number on the pine box, cut in the lid with a chisel, and his brief history was closed, with only the memory of the little life remaining to the Welshes to help them fight the battle alone.

In the middle of the night, when the dead-lamp burned dimly at the bottom of the alley, a policeman brought to Police Headquarters a wailing child, an outcast found in the area of a Lexington Avenue house by a citizen, who handed it over to the police. Until its cries were smothered in the police nursery upstairs with the ever ready bottle, they reached the bereaved mother in Cat Alley and made her tears drop faster. As the dead-wagon drove away with its load in the morning, Matron Travers came out with the now sleeping waif in her arms. She, too, was bound for Mr. Blake's.

The two took their ride on the same boat—the living child, whom no one wanted, to Randall's Island, to be enlisted with its number in the army of the city's waifs, strong and able to fight its way; the dead, for whom a mother's heart yearns, to its place in the great ditch.

A PROPOSAL ON THE ELEVATED

The sleeper on the 3.35 a.m. elevated train from the Harlem bridge was awake for once. The sleeper is the last car in the train, and has its own set that snores nightly in the same seats, grunts with the fixed inhospitality of the commuter at the intrusion of a stranger, and is on terms with Conrad, the German conductor, who knows each one of his passengers and wakes him up at his station. The sleeper is unique. It is run for the benefit of those who ride in it, not for the company's. It not only puts them off properly; it waits for them, if they are not there. The conductor knows that they will come. They are men, mostly, with small homes beyond the bridge, whose work takes them down town to the markets, the Post-office, and the busy marts of the city long before cockcrow. The day begins in New York at all hours.

Usually the sleeper is all that its name implies, but this morning it was as far from it as could be. A party of young people, fresh from a neighboring hop, had come on board and filled the rear end of the car. Their feet tripped yet to the dance, and snatches of the latest waltz floated through the train between peals of laughter and little girlish shrieks. The regulars glared, discontented, in strange seats, unable to go to sleep. Only the railroad yardmen dropped off promptly as they came in. Theirs was the shortest ride, and they could least afford to lose time. Two old Irishmen, flanked by their dinner-pails, gravely discussed the Henry George campaign.

Across the passage sat a group of three apart—a young man, a girl, and a little elderly woman with lines of care and hard work in her patient face. She guarded carefully three umbrellas, a very old and faded one, and two that were new and of silk, which she held in her lap, though it had not rained for a month. He was a likely young fellow, tall and straight, with the thoughtful eye of a student. His dark hair fell nearly to his shoulders, and his coat had a foreign cut. The girl was a typical child of the city, slight and graceful of form, dressed in good taste, and with a bright, winning face. The two chatted confidentially together, forgetful of all else, while mamma, between them, nodded sleepily in her seat.

A sudden burst of white light flooded the car.

"Hey! Ninety-ninth Street!" called the conductor, and rattled the door. The railroad men tumbled out pell-mell, all but one. Conrad shook him, and he went out mechanically, blinking his eyes.

"Eighty-ninth next!" from the doorway.

The laughter at the rear end of the car had died out. The young people, in a quieter mood, were humming a popular love-song. Presently above the rest rose a clear tenor:—

Oh, promise me that some day you and I
Will take our love together to some sky
Where we can be alone and faith renew—

The clatter of the train as it flew over a switch drowned the rest. When the last wheel had banged upon the frog, I heard the young student's voice, in the soft accents of southern Europe:—

"Wenn ich in Wien war—" He was telling her of his home and his people in the language of his childhood. I glanced across. She sat listening with kindling eyes. Mamma slumbered sweetly; her worn old hands clutched unconsciously the umbrellas in her lap. The two Irishmen, having settled the campaign, had dropped to sleep, too. In the crowded car the two were alone. His hand sought hers and met it halfway.

"Forty-seventh!" There was a clatter of tin cans below. The contingent of milkmen scrambled out of their seats and off for the depot. In the lull that followed their going, the tenor rose from the last seat:—

Those first sweet violets of early spring,
Which come in whispers, thrill us both, and sing
Of love unspeakable that is to be,
Oh, promise me! Oh, promise me!

The two young people faced each other. He had thrown his hat upon the seat beside him and held her hand fast, gesticulating with his free hand as he spoke rapidly, eloquently, eagerly of his prospects and his hopes. Her own toyed nervously with his coat-lapel, twisting and twirling a button as he went on. What he said might have been heard to the other end of the car, had there been anybody to listen. He was to live here always; his uncle would open a business in New York, of which he was to have charge, when he had learned to know the country and its people. It would not be long now, and then—and then—

"Twenty-third Street!"

There was a long stop after the levy for the ferries had left. The conductor went out on the platform and consulted with the ticket-chopper. He was scrutinizing his watch for the second time, when the faint jingle of an east-bound car was heard.

"Here she comes!" said the ticket-chopper. A shout, and a man bounded up the steps, three at a time. It was an engineer who, to make connection with his locomotive at Chatham Square, must catch that train.

"Hullo, Conrad! Nearly missed you," he said as he jumped on the car, breathless.

"All right, Jack." And the conductor jerked the bell-rope. "You made it, though." The train sped on.

Two lives, heretofore running apart, were hastening to a union. The lovers had seen nothing, heard nothing but each other. His eyes burned as hers met his and fell before them. His head bent lower until his face almost touched hers. His dark hair lay against her blond curls. The ostrich-feather on her hat swept his shoulder.

"Mögtest Du mich haben?" he entreated.

Above the grinding of the wheels as the train slowed up for the station a block ahead, pleaded the tenor:—

Oh, promise me that you will take my hand,
The most unworthy in this lonely land—

Did she speak? Her face was hidden, but the blond curls moved with a nod so slight that only a lover's eye could see it. He seized her disengaged hand. The conductor stuck his head into the car.

"Fourteenth Street!"

A squad of stout, florid men with butchers' aprons started for the door. The girl arose hastily.

"Mamma!" she called, "steh' auf! Es ist Fourteenth Street."

The little woman woke up, gathered the umbrellas in her arms, and bustled after the marketmen, her daughter leading the way. He sat as one dreaming.

"Ach!" he sighed, and ran his hand through his dark hair, "so rasch!"

And he went out after them.

LITTLE WILL'S MESSAGE

"It is that or starve, Captain. I can't get a job. God knows I've tried, but without a recommend, it's no use. I ain't no good at beggin'. And—and—there's the childer."

There was a desperate note in the man's voice that made the Captain turn and look sharply at him. A swarthy, strongly built man in a rough coat, and with that in his dark face which told that he had lived longer than his years, stood at the door of the Detective Office. His hand that gripped the door handle shook so that the knob rattled in his grasp, but not with fear. He was no stranger to that place. Black Bill's face had looked out from the Rogues' Gallery longer than most of those now there could remember. The Captain looked him over in silence.

"You had better not, Bill," he said. "You know what will come of it. When you go up again it will be the last time. And up you go, sure."

The man started to say something, but choked it down and went out without a word. The Captain got up and rang his bell.

"Bill, who was here just now, is off again," he said to the officer who came to the door. "He says it is steal or starve, and he can't get a job. I guess he is right. Who wants a thief in his pay? And how can I recommend him? And still I think he would keep straight if he had the chance. Tell Murphy to look after him and see what he is up to."

The Captain went out, tugging viciously at his gloves. He was in very bad humor. The policeman at the Mulberry Street door got hardly a nod for his cheery "Merry Christmas" as he passed.

"Wonder what's crossed him," he said, looking down the street after him.

The green lamps were lighted and shone upon the hurrying six o'clock crowds from the Broadway shops. In the great business buildings the iron shutters were pulled down and the lights put out, and in a little while the reporters' boys that carried slips from Headquarters to the newspaper offices across the street were the only tenants of the block. A stray policeman stopped now and then on the corner and tapped the lamp-post reflectively with his club as he looked down the deserted street and wondered, as his glance rested upon the Chief's darkened windows, how it felt to have six thousand dollars a year and every night off. In the Detective Office the Sergeant who had come in at roll-call stretched himself behind the desk and thought of home. The lights of a Christmas tree in the abutting Mott Street tenement shone through his window, and the laughter of children mingled with the tap of the toy drum. He pulled down the sash in order to hear better. As he did so, a strong draught swept his desk. The outer door slammed. Two detectives came in bringing a prisoner between them. A woman accompanied them.

The Sergeant pulled the blotter toward him mechanically and dipped his pen.

"What's the charge?" he asked.

"Picking pockets in Fourteenth Street. This lady is the complainant, Mrs. ——"

The name was that of a well-known police magistrate. The Sergeant looked up and bowed. His glance took in the prisoner, and a look of recognition came into his face.

"What, Bill! So soon?" he said.

The prisoner was sullenly silent. He answered the questions put to him briefly, and was searched. The stolen pocket-book, a small paper package, and a crumpled letter were laid upon the desk. The Sergeant saw only the pocket-book.

"Looks bad," he said with wrinkled brow.

"We caught him at it," explained the officer. "Guess Bill has lost heart. He didn't seem to care. Didn't even try to get away."

The prisoner was taken to a cell. Silence fell once more upon the office. The Sergeant made a few red lines in the blotter and resumed his reveries. He was not in a mood for work. He hitched his chair nearer the window and looked across the yard. But the lights there were put out, the children's laughter had died away. Out of sorts at he hardly knew what, he leaned back in his chair, with his hands under the back of his head. Here it was Christmas Eve, and he at the desk instead of being out with the old woman buying things for the children. He thought with a sudden pang of conscience of the sled he had promised to get for Johnnie and had forgotten. That was hard luck. And what would Katie say when—

He had got that far when his eye, roaming idly over the desk, rested upon the little package taken from the thief's pocket. Something about it seemed to move him with sudden interest. He sat up and reached for it. He felt it carefully all over. Then he undid the package slowly and drew forth a woolly sheep. It had a blue ribbon about its neck, with a tiny bell hung on it.

The Sergeant set the sheep upon the desk and looked at it fixedly for better than a minute. Having apparently studied out its mechanism, he pulled its head and it baa-ed. He pulled it once more, and nodded. Then he took up the crumpled letter and opened it.

This was what he read, scrawled in a child's uncertain hand:—

"Deer Sante Claas—Pease wont yer bring me a sjeep wat bas. Aggie had won wonst. An Kate wants a dollie offul. In the reere 718 19th Street by the gas house. Your friend Will."

The Sergeant read it over twice very carefully and glanced over the page at the sheep, as if taking stock and wondering why Kate's dollie was not there. Then he took the sheep and the letter and went over to the Captain's door. A gruff "Come in!" answered his knock. The Captain was pulling off his overcoat. He had just come in from his dinner.

"Captain," said the Sergeant, "we found this in the pocket of Black Bill who is locked up for picking Mrs. ——'s pocket an hour ago. It is a clear case. He didn't even try to give them the slip," and he set the sheep upon the table and laid the letter beside it.

"Black Bill?" said the Captain, with something of a start; "the dickens, you say!" And he took up the letter and read it. He was not a very good penman, was little Will. The Captain had even a harder time of it than the Sergeant had had making out his message.

Three times he went over it, spelling out the words, and each time comparing it with the woolly exhibit that was part of the evidence, before he seemed to understand. Then it was in a voice that would have frightened little Will very much could he have heard it, and with a black look under his bushy eyebrows, that he bade the Sergeant "Fetch Bill up here!" One might almost have expected the little white lamb to have taken to its heels with fright at having raised such a storm, could it have run at all. But it showed no signs of fear. On the contrary it baa-ed quite lustily when the Sergeant should have been safely out of earshot. The hand of the Captain had accidentally rested upon the woolly head in putting down the letter. But the Sergeant was not out of earshot. He heard it and grinned.

An iron door in the basement clanged and there were steps in the passageway. The doorman brought in Bill. He stood by the door, sullenly submissive. The Captain raised his head. It was in the shade.

"So you are back, are you?" he said.

The thief nodded.

The Captain bent his brows upon him and said with sudden fierceness, "You couldn't keep honest a month, could you?"

"They wouldn't let me. Who wants a thief in his pay? And the children were starving."

It was said patiently enough, but it made the Captain wince all the same. They were his own words. But he did not give in so easily.

"Starving?" he repeated harshly. "And that's why you got this, I suppose," and he pushed the sheep from under the newspaper that had fallen upon it by accident and covered it up.

The thief looked at it and flushed to the temples. He tried to speak but could not. His face worked, and he seemed to be strangling. In the middle of his fight to master himself he saw the child's crumpled message on the desk. Taking a quick step across the room he snatched it up, wildly, fiercely.

"Captain," he gasped, and broke down utterly. The hardened thief wept like a woman.

The Captain rang his bell. He stood with his back to the prisoner when the doorman came in. "Take him down," he commanded. And the iron door clanged once more behind the prisoner.

Ten minutes later the reporters were discussing across the way the nature of "the case" which the night promised to develop. They had piped off the Captain and one of his trusted men leaving the building together, bound east. Could they have followed them all the way, they would have seen them get off the car at Nineteenth Street, and go toward the gas house, carefully scanning the numbers of the houses as they went. They found one at last before which they halted. The Captain searched in his pocket and drew forth the baby's letter to Santa Claus, and they examined the number under the gas lamp. Yes, that was right. The door was open, and they went right through to the rear.

Up in the third story three little noses were flattened against the window pane, and three childish mouths were breathing peep-holes through which to keep a lookout for the expected Santa Claus. It was cold, for there was no fire in the room, but in their fever of excitement the children didn't mind that. They were bestowing all their attention upon keeping the peep-holes open.

"Do you think he will come?" asked the oldest boy—there were two boys and a girl—of Kate.

"Yes, he will. I know he will come. Papa said so," said the child in a tone of conviction.

"I'se so hungry, and I want my sheep," said Baby Will.

"Wait and I'll tell you of the wolf," said his sister, and she took him on her lap. She had barely started when there were steps on the stairs and a tap on the door. Before the half-frightened children could answer it was pushed open. Two men stood on the threshold. One wore a big fur overcoat. The baby looked at him in wide-eyed wonder.

"Is you Santa Claus?" he asked.

"Yes, my little man, and are you Baby Will?" said a voice that was singularly different from the harsh one Baby Will's father had heard so recently in the Captain's office, and yet very like it.

"See. This is for you, I guess," and out of the big roomy pocket came the woolly sheep and baa-ed right off as if it were his own pasture in which he was at home. And well might any sheep be content nestling at a baby heart so brimful of happiness as little Will's was then, child of a thief though he was.

"Papa spoke for it, and he spoke for Kate, too, and I guess for everybody," said the bogus Santa Claus, "and it is all right. My sled will be here in a minute. Now we will just get to work and make ready for him. All help!"

The Sergeant behind the desk in the Detective Office might have had a fit had he been able to witness the goings-on in that rear tenement in the next hour; and then again he might not. There is no telling about those Sergeants. The way that poor flat laid itself out of a sudden was fairly staggering. It was not only that a fire was made and that the pantry filled up in the most extraordinary manner; but a real Christmas tree sprang up, out of the floor, as it were, and was found to be all besprinkled with gold and stars and cornucopias with sugarplums. From the top of it, which was not higher than Santa Claus could easily reach, because the ceiling was low, a marvellous doll, with real hair and with eyes that could open and shut, looked down with arms wide open to take Kate to its soft wax heart. Under the branches of the tree browsed every animal that went into and came out of Noah's Ark, and there were glorious games of Messenger Boy and Three Bad Bears, and honey-cakes and candy apples, and a little yellow-bird in a cage, and what not? It was glorious. And when the tea-kettle began to sing, skilfully manipulated by Santa Claus's assistant, who nominally was known in Mulberry Street as Detective Sergeant Murphy, it was just too lovely for anything. The baby's eyes grew wider and wider, and Kate's were shining with happiness, when in the midst of it all she suddenly stopped and said:—

"But where is papa? Why don't he come?"

Santa Claus gave a little start at the sudden question, but pulled himself together right away.

"Why, yes," he said, "he must have got lost. Now you are all right we will just go and see if we can find him. Mrs. McCarthy here next door will help you keep the kettle boiling and the lights burning till we come back. Just let me hear that sheep baa once more. That's right! I bet we'll find papa." And out they went.

An hour later, while Mr. ——, the Magistrate, and his good wife were viewing with mock dismay the array of little stockings at their hearth in their fine up-town house, and talking of the adventure of Mrs. —— with the pickpocket, there came a ring at the door-bell and the Captain of the detectives was ushered in. What he told them I do not know, but this I do know, that when he went away the honorable Magistrate went with him, and his wife waved good-by to them from the stoop with wet eyes as they drove away in a carriage hastily ordered up from a livery stable. While they drove down town, the Magistrate's wife went up to the nursery and hugged her sleeping little ones, one after the other, and tear-drops fell upon their warm cheeks that had wiped out the guilt of more than one sinner before, and the children smiled in their sleep. They say among the simple-minded folk of far-away Denmark that then they see angels in their dreams.

The carriage stopped in Mulberry Street, in front of Police Headquarters, and there was great scurrying among the reporters, for now they were sure of their "case." But no "prominent citizen" came out, made free by the Magistrate, who opened court in the Captain's office. Only a rough-looking man with a flushed face, whom no one knew, and who stopped on the corner and looked back as one in a dream and then went east, the way the Captain and his man had gone on their expedition personating no less exalted a personage than Santa Claus himself.

That night there was Christmas, indeed, in the rear tenement "near the gas house," for papa had come home just in time to share in its cheer. And there was no one who did it with a better will, for the Christmas evening that began so badly was the luckiest night in his life. He had the promise of a job on the morrow in his pocket, along with something to keep the wolf from the door in the holidays. His hard days were over, and he was at last to have his chance to live an honest life. And it was the baby's letter to Santa Claus and the baa sheep that did it all, with the able assistance of the Captain and the Sergeant. Don't let us forget the Sergeant.

LOST CHILDREN

I am not thinking now of theological dogmas or moral distinctions. I am considering the matter from the plain every-day standpoint of the police office. It is not my fault that the one thing that is lost more persistently than any other in a large city is the very thing you would imagine to be safest of all in the keeping of its owner. Nor do I pretend to explain it. It is simply one of the contradictions of metropolitan life. In twenty years' acquaintance with the police office, I have seen money, diamonds, coffins, horses, and tubs of butter brought there and pass into the keeping of the property clerk as lost or strayed. I remember a whole front stoop, brownstone, with steps and iron railing all complete, being put up at auction, unclaimed. But these were mere representatives of a class which as a whole kept its place and the peace. The children did neither. One might have been tempted to apply the old inquiry about the pins to them but for another contradictory circumstance: rather more of them are found than lost.

The Society for the Prevention of Cruelty to Children keeps the account of the surplus. It has now on its books half a score Jane Does and twice as many Richard Roes, of whom nothing more will ever be known than that they were found, which is on the whole, perhaps, best—for them certainly. The others, the lost, drift from the tenements and back, a host of thousands year by year. The two I am thinking of were of these, typical of the maelstrom.

Yette Lubinsky was three years old when she was lost from her Essex Street home, in that neighborhood where once the police commissioners thought seriously of having the children tagged with name and street number, to save trotting them back and forth between police station and Headquarters. She had gone from the tenement to the corner where her father kept a stand, to beg a penny, and nothing more was known of her. Weeks after, a neighbor identified one of her little frocks as the match of one worn by a child she had seen dragged off by a rough-looking man. But though Max Lubinsky, the pedler, and Yette's mother camped on the steps of Police Headquarters early and late, anxiously questioning every one who went in and out about their lost child, no other word was heard of her. By and by it came to be an old story, and the two were looked upon as among the fixtures of the place. Mulberry Street has other such.

They were poor and friendless in a strange land, the very language of which was jargon to them, as theirs was to us, timid in the crush, and they were shouldered out. It was not inhumanity; at least, it was not meant to be. It was the way of the city, with every one for himself; and they accepted it, uncomplaining. So they kept their vigil on the stone steps, in storm and fair weather, every night taking turns to watch all who passed. When it was a policeman with a little child, as it was many times between sunset and sunrise, the one on the watch would start up the minute they turned the corner, and run to meet them, eagerly scanning the little face, only to return, disappointed but not cast down, to the step upon which the other slept, head upon knees, waiting the summons to wake and watch.

Their mute sorrow appealed to me, then doing night duty in the newspaper office across the way, and I tried to help them in their search for the lost Yette. They accepted my help gratefully, trustfully, but without loud demonstration. Together we searched the police records, the hospitals, the morgue, and the long register of the river's dead. She was not there. Having made sure of this, we turned to the children's asylums. We had a description of Yette sent to each and every one, with the minutest particulars concerning her and her disappearance, but no word came back in response. A year passed, and we were compelled at last to give over the search. It seemed as if every means of finding out what had become of the child had been exhausted, and all alike had failed.

During the long search, I had occasion to go more than once to the Lubinskys' home. They lived up three flights, in one of the big barracks that give to the lower end of Essex Street the appearance of a deep black cañon with cliff-dwellers living in tiers all the way up, their watch-fires showing like so many dull red eyes through the night. The hall was pitch-dark, and the whole building redolent of the slum; but in the stuffy little room where the pedler lived there was, in spite of it all, an atmosphere of home that set it sharply apart from the rest. One of these visits I will always remember. I had stumbled in, unthinking, upon their Sabbath-eve meal. The candles were lighted, and the children gathered about the table; at its head, the father, every trace of the timid, shrinking pedler of Mulberry Street laid aside with the week's toil, was invoking the Sabbath blessing upon his house and all it harbored. I saw him turn, with a quiver of the lip, to a vacant seat between him and the mother, and it was then that I noticed the baby's high chair, empty, but kept ever waiting for the little wanderer. I understood; and in the strength of domestic affection that burned with unquenched faith in the dark tenement after the many months of weary failure I read the history of this strange people that in every land and in every day has conquered even the slum with the hope of home.

It was not to be put to shame here, either. Yette returned, after all, and the way of it came near being stranger than all the rest. Two long years had passed, and the memory of her and hers had long since faded out of Mulberry Street, when, in the overhauling of one of the children's homes we thought we had canvassed thoroughly, the child turned up, as unaccountably as she had been lost. All that I ever learned about it was that she had been brought there, picked up by some one in the street, probably, and, after more or less inquiry that had failed to connect with the search at our end of the line, had been included in their flock on some formal commitment, and had stayed there. Not knowing her name,—she could not tell it herself, to be understood,—they had given her one of their own choosing; and thus disguised, she might have stayed there forever but for the fortunate chance that cast her up to the surface once more, and gave the clew to her identity at last. Even then her father had nearly as much trouble in proving his title to his child as he had had in looking for her, but in the end he made it good. The frock she had worn when she was lost proved the missing link. The mate of it was still carefully laid away in the tenement. So Yette returned to fill the empty chair at the Sabbath board, and the pedler's faith was justified.

My other chip from the maelstrom was a lad half grown. He dropped into my office as if out of the clouds, one long and busy day, when, tired and out of sorts, I sat wishing my papers and the world in general in Halifax. I had not heard the knock, and when I looked up, there stood my boy, a stout, square-shouldered lad, with heavy cowhide boots and dull, honest eyes—eyes that looked into mine as if with a question they were about to put, and then gave it up, gazing straight ahead, stolid, impassive. It struck me that I had seen that face before, and I found out immediately where. The officer of the Children's Aid Society who had brought him explained that Frands—that was his name—had been in the society's care five months and over. They had found him drifting in the streets, and, knowing whither that drift set, had taken him in charge and sent him to one of their lodging-houses, where he had been since, doing chores and plodding about in his dull way. That was where I had met him. Now they had decided that he should go to Florida, if he would, but first they would like to find out something about him. They had never been able to, beyond the fact that he was from Denmark. He had put his finger on the map in the reading-room, one day, and shown them where he came from: that was the extent of their information on that point. So they had sent him to me to talk to him in his own tongue and see what I could make of him.

I addressed him in the politest Danish I was master of, and for an instant I saw the listening, questioning look return; but it vanished almost at once, and he answered in monosyllables, if at all. Much of what I said passed him entirely by. He did not seem to understand. By slow stages I got out of him that his father was a farm-laborer; that he had come over to look for his cousin, who worked in Passaic, New Jersey, and had found him,—Heaven knows how!—but had lost him again. Then he had drifted to New York, where the society's officers had come upon him. He nodded when told that he was to be sent far away to the country, much as if I had spoken of some one he had never heard of. We had arrived at this point when I asked him the name of his native town.

The word he spoke came upon me with all the force of a sudden blow. I had played in the old village as a boy; all my childhood was bound up in its memories. For many years now I had not heard its name—not since boyhood days—spoken as he spoke it. Perhaps it was because I was tired: the office faded away, desk, Headquarters across the street, boy, officer, business, and all. In their place were the brown heath I loved, the distant hills, the winding wagon track, the peat stacks, and the solitary sheep browsing on the barrows. Forgotten the thirty years, the seas that rolled between, the teeming city! I was at home again, a child. And there he stood, the boy, with it all in his dull, absent look. I read it now as plain as the day.

"Hua er et no? Ka do ett fostó hua a sejer?"

It plumped out of me in the broad Jutland dialect I had neither heard nor spoken in half a lifetime, and so astonished me that I nearly fell off my chair. Sheep, peat-stacks, cairn, and hills all vanished together, and in place of the sweet heather there was the table with the tiresome papers. I reached out yearningly after the heath; I had not seen it for such a long time,—how long it did seem!—and—but in the same breath it was all there again in the smile that lighted up Frands's broad face like a glint of sunlight from a leaden sky.

"Joesses, jou," he laughed, "no ka a da saa grou godt."[1]

It was the first honest Danish word he had heard since he came to this bewildering land. I read it in his face, no longer heavy or dull; saw it in the way he followed my speech—spelling the words, as it were, with his own lips, to lose no syllable; caught it in his glad smile as he went on telling me about his journey, his home, and his homesickness for the heath, with a breathless kind of haste, as if now that at last he had a chance, he were afraid it was all a dream, and that he would presently wake up and find it gone. Then the officer pulled my sleeve.

He had coughed once or twice, but neither of us had heard him. Now he held out a paper he had brought, with an apologetic gesture. It was an agreement Frands was to sign, if he was going to Florida. I glanced at it. Florida? Yes, to be sure; oh, yes, Florida. I spoke to the officer, and it was in the Jutland dialect. I tried again, with no better luck. I saw him looking at me queerly, as if he thought it was not quite right with me, either, and then I recovered myself, and got back to the office and to America; but it was an effort. One does not skip across thirty years and two oceans, at my age, so easily as that.

And then the dull look came back into Frands's eyes, and he nodded stolidly. Yes, he would go to Florida. The papers were made out, and off he went, after giving me a hearty hand-shake that warranted he would come out right when he became accustomed to the new country; but he took something with him which it hurt me to part with.

Frands is long since in Florida, growing up with the country, and little Yette is a young woman. So long ago was it that the current which sucked her under cast her up again, that there lives not in the whole street any one who can recall her loss. I tried to find one only the other day, but all the old people were dead or had moved away, and of the young, who were very anxious to help me, scarcely one was born at that time. But still the maelstrom drags down its victims; and far away lies my Danish heath under the gray October sky, hidden behind the seas.

PAOLO'S AWAKENING

Paolo sat cross-legged on his bench, stitching away for dear life. He pursed his lips and screwed up his mouth into all sorts of odd shapes with the effort, for it was an effort. He was only eight, and you would scarcely have imagined him over six, as he sat there sewing like a real little tailor; only Paolo knew but one seam, and that a hard one. Yet he held the needle and felt the edge with it in quite a grown-up way, and pulled the thread just as far as his short arm would reach. His mother sat on a stool by the window, where she could help him when he got into a snarl,—as he did once in a while, in spite of all he could do,—or when the needle had to be threaded. Then she dropped her own sewing, and, patting him on the head, said he was a good boy.

Paolo felt very proud and big then, that he was able to help his mother, and he worked even more carefully and faithfully than before, so that the boss should find no fault. The shouts of the boys in the block, playing duck-on-a-rock down in the street, came in through the open window, and he laughed as he heard them. He did not envy them, though he liked well enough to romp with the others. His was a sunny temper, content with what came; besides, his supper was at stake, and Paolo had a good appetite. They were in sober earnest, working for dear life—Paolo and his mother.

"Pants" for the sweater in Stanton Street was what they were making; little knickerbockers for boys of Paolo's own age. "Twelve pants for ten cents," he said, counting on his fingers. The mother brought them once a week—a big bundle which she carried home on her head—to have the buttons put on, fourteen on each pair, the bottoms turned up, and a ribbon sewed fast to the back seam inside. That was called finishing. When work was brisk—and it was not always so since there had been such frequent strikes in Stanton Street—they could together make the rent money, and even more, as Paolo was learning and getting a stronger grip on the needle week by week. The rent was six dollars a month for a dingy basement room, in which it was twilight even on the brightest days, and a dark little cubbyhole where it was always midnight, and where there was just room for a bed of old boards, no more. In there slept Paolo with his uncle; his mother made her bed on the floor of the "kitchen," as they called it.

The three made the family. There used to be four; but one stormy night in winter Paolo's father had not come home. The uncle came alone, and the story he told made the poor home in the basement darker and drearier for many a day than it had yet been. The two men worked together for a padrone on the scows. They were in the crew that went out that day to the dumping-ground, far outside the harbor. It was a dangerous journey in a rough sea. The half-frozen Italians clung to the great heaps like so many frightened flies, when the waves rose and tossed the unwieldy scows about, bumping one against the other, though they were strung out in a long row behind the tug, quite a distance apart. One sea washed entirely over the last scow and nearly upset it. When it floated even again, two of the crew were missing, one of them Paolo's father. They had been washed away and lost, miles from shore. No one ever saw them again.

The widow's tears flowed for her dead husband, whom she could not even see laid in a grave which the priest had blessed. The good father spoke to her of the sea as a vast God's acre, over which the storms are forever chanting anthems in His praise to whom the secrets of its depths are revealed; but she thought of it only as the cruel destroyer that had robbed her of her husband, and her tears fell faster. Paolo cried, too: partly because his mother cried; partly, if the truth must be told, because he was not to have a ride to the cemetery in the splendid coach. Giuseppe Salvatore, in the corner house, had never ceased talking of the ride he had when his father died, the year before. Pietro and Jim went along, too, and rode all the way behind the hearse with black plumes. It was a sore subject with Paolo, for he was in school that day.

And then he and his mother dried their tears and went to work. Henceforth there was to be little else for them. The luxury of grief is not among the few luxuries which Mott Street tenements afford. Paolo's life, after that, was lived mainly with the pants on his hard bench in the rear tenement. His routine of work was varied by the household duties, which he shared with his mother. There were the meals to get, few and plain as they were. Paolo was the cook, and not infrequently, when a building was being torn down in the neighborhood, he furnished the fuel as well. Those were his off days, when he put the needle away and foraged with the other children, dragging old beams and carrying burdens far beyond his years.

The truant officer never found his way to Paolo's tenement to discover that he could neither read nor write, and, what was more, would probably never learn. It would have been of little use, for the public schools thereabouts were crowded, and Paolo could not have got into one of them if he had tried. The teacher from the Industrial School, which he had attended for one brief season while his father was alive, called at long intervals, and brought him once a plant, which he set out in his mother's window-garden and nursed carefully ever after. The "garden" was contained within an old starch box, which had its place on the window-sill since the policeman had ordered the fire-escape to be cleared. It was a kitchen-garden with vegetables, and was almost all the green there was in the landscape. From one or two other windows in the yard there peeped tufts of green; but of trees there was none in sight—nothing but the bare clothes-poles with their pulley-lines stretching from every window.

Beside the cemetery plot in the next block there was not an open spot or breathing-place, certainly not a playground, within reach of that great teeming slum that harbored more than a hundred thousand persons, young and old. Even the graveyard was shut in by a high brick wall, so that a glimpse of the greensward over the old mounds was to be caught only through the spiked iron gates, the key to which was lost, or by standing on tiptoe and craning one's neck. The dead there were of more account, though they had been forgotten these many years, than the living children who gazed so wistfully upon the little paradise through the barred gates, and were chased by the policeman when he came that way. Something like this thought was in Paolo's mind when he stood at sunset and peered in at the golden rays falling athwart the green, but he did not know it. Paolo was not a philosopher, but he loved beauty and beautiful things, and was conscious of a great hunger which there was nothing in his narrow world to satisfy.

Certainly not in the tenement. It was old and rickety and wretched, in keeping with the slum of which it formed a part. The whitewash was peeling from the walls, the stairs were patched, and the door-step long since worn entirely away. It was hard to be decent in such a place, but the widow did the best she could. Her rooms were as neat as the general dilapidation would permit. On the shelf where the old clock stood, flanked by the best crockery, most of it cracked and yellow with age, there was red and green paper cut in scallops very nicely. Garlic and onions hung in strings over the stove, and the red peppers that grew in the starch-box at the window gave quite a cheerful appearance to the room. In the corner, under a cheap print of the Virgin Mary with the Child, a small night-light in a blue glass was always kept burning. It was a kind of illumination in honor of the Mother of God, through which the widow's devout nature found expression. Paolo always looked upon it as a very solemn show. When he said his prayers, the sweet, patient eyes in the picture seemed to watch him with a mild look that made him turn over and go to sleep with a sigh of contentment. He felt then that he had not been altogether bad, and that he was quite safe in their keeping.

Yet Paolo's life was not wholly without its bright spots. Far from it. There were the occasional trips to the dump with Uncle Pasquale's dinner, where there was always sport to be had in chasing the rats that overran the place, fighting for the scraps and bones the trimmers had rescued from the scows. There were so many of them, and so bold were they, that an old Italian who could no longer dig, was employed to sit on a bale of rags and throw things at them, lest they carry off the whole establishment. When he hit one, the rest squealed and scampered away; but they were back again in a minute, and the old man had his hands full pretty nearly all the time. Paolo thought that his was a glorious job, as any boy might, and hoped that he would soon be old, too, and as important. And then the men at the cage—a great wire crate into which the rags from the ash barrels were stuffed, to be plunged into the river, where the tide ran through them and carried some of the loose dirt away. That was called washing the rags. To Paolo it was the most exciting thing in the world. What if some day the crate should bring up a fish, a real fish, from the river? When he thought of it he wished that he might be sitting forever on that string-piece, fishing with the rag-cage, particularly when he was tired of stitching and turning over, a whole long day.

Besides, there were the real holidays, when there was a marriage, a christening, or a funeral in the tenement, particularly when a baby died whose father belonged to one of the many benefit societies. A brass band was the proper thing then, and the whole block took a vacation to follow the music and the white hearse out of their ward into the next. But the chief of all the holidays came once a year, when the feast of St. Rocco—the patron saint of the village where Paolo's parents had lived—was celebrated. Then a really beautiful altar was erected at one end of the yard, with lights and pictures on it. The rear fire-escapes in the whole row were decked with sheets, and made into handsome balconies,—reserved seats, as it were,—on which the tenants sat and enjoyed it.

A band in gorgeous uniforms played three whole days in the yard, and the men in their holiday clothes stepped up, bowed, and crossed themselves, and laid their gifts on the plate which St. Rocco's namesake, the saloon-keeper in the block, who had got up the celebration, had put there for them. In the evening they set off great strings of fire-crackers in the street in the saint's honor, until the police interfered once and forbade that. Those were great days for Paolo always.

But the fun Paolo loved best of all was when he could get in a corner by himself, with no one to disturb him, and build castles and things out of some abandoned clay or mortar, or wet sand if there was nothing better. The plastic material took strange shapes of beauty under his hands. It was as if life had been somehow breathed into it by his touch, and it ordered itself as none of the other boys could make it. His fingers were tipped with genius, but he did not know it, for his work was only for the hour. He destroyed it as soon as it was made, to try for something better. What he had made never satisfied him—one of the surest proofs that he was capable of great things, had he only known it. But, as I said, he did not.

The teacher from the Industrial School came upon him one day, sitting in the corner by himself, and breathing life into the mud. She stood and watched him awhile, unseen, getting interested, almost excited, as he worked on. As for Paolo, he was solving the problem that had eluded him so long, and had eyes or thought for nothing else. As his fingers ran over the soft clay, the needle, the hard bench, the pants, even the sweater himself, vanished out of his sight, out of his life, and he thought only of the beautiful things he was fashioning to express the longing in his soul, which nothing mortal could shape. Then, suddenly, seeing and despairing, he dashed it to pieces, and came back to earth and to the tenement.

But not to the pants and the sweater. What the teacher had seen that day had set her to thinking, and her visit resulted in a great change for Paolo. She called at night and had a long talk with his mother and uncle through the medium of the priest, who interpreted when they got to a hard place. Uncle Pasquale took but little part in the conversation. He sat by and nodded most of the time, assured by the presence of the priest that it was all right. The widow cried a good deal, and went more than once to take a look at the boy, lying snugly tucked in his bed in the inner room, quite unconscious of the weighty matters that were being decided concerning him. She came back the last time drying her eyes, and laid both her hands in the hand of the teacher. She nodded twice and smiled through her tears, and the bargain was made. Paolo's slavery was at an end.

His friend came the next day and took him away, dressed up in his best clothes, to a large school where there were many children, not of his own people, and where he was received kindly. There dawned that day a new life for Paolo, for in the afternoon trays of modelling-clay were brought in, and the children were told to mould in it objects that were set before them. Paolo's teacher stood by, and nodded approvingly as his little fingers played so deftly with the clay, his face all lighted up with joy at this strange kind of a school-lesson.

After that he had a new and faithful friend, and, as he worked away, putting his whole young soul into the tasks that filled it with radiant hope, other friends, rich and powerful, found him out in his slum. They brought better-paying work for his mother than sewing pants for the sweater, and Uncle Pasquale abandoned the scows to become a porter in a big shipping-house on the West Side. The little family moved out of the old home into a better tenement, though not far away. Paolo's loyal heart clung to the neighborhood where he had played and dreamed as a child, and he wanted it to share in his good fortune, now that it had come. As the days passed, the neighbors who had known him as little Paolo came to speak of him as one who some day would be a great artist and make them all proud. He laughed at that, and said that the first bust he would hew in marble should be that of his patient, faithful mother; and with that he gave her a little hug, and danced out of the room, leaving her to look after him with glistening eyes, brimming over with happiness.

But Paolo's dream was to have another awakening. The years passed and brought their changes. In the manly youth who came forward as his name was called in the academy, and stood modestly at the desk to receive his diploma, few would have recognized the little ragamuffin who had dragged bundles of fire-wood to the rookery in the alley, and carried Uncle Pasquale's dinner-pail to the dump. But the audience gathered to witness the commencement exercises knew it all, and greeted him with a hearty welcome that recalled his early struggles and his hard-won success. It was Paolo's day of triumph. The class honors and the medal were his. The bust that had won both stood in the hall crowned with laurel—an Italian peasant woman, with sweet, gentle face, in which there lingered the memories of the patient eyes that had lulled the child to sleep in the old days in the alley. His teacher spoke to him, spoke of him, with pride in voice and glance; spoke tenderly of his old mother of the tenement, of his faithful work, of the loyal manhood that ever is the soul and badge of true genius. As he bade him welcome to the fellowship of artists who in him honored the best and noblest in their own aspirations, the emotion of the audience found voice once more. Paolo, flushed, his eyes filled with happy tears, stumbled out, he knew not how, with the coveted parchment in his hand.

Home to his mother! It was the one thought in his mind as he walked toward the big bridge to cross to the city of his home—to tell her of his joy, of his success. Soon she would no longer be poor. The day of hardship was over. He could work now and earn money, much money, and the world would know and honor Paolo's mother as it had honored him. As he walked through the foggy winter day toward the river, where delayed throngs jostled one another at the bridge entrance, he thought with grateful heart of the friends who had smoothed the way for him. Ah, not for long the fog and slush! The medal carried with it a travelling stipend, and soon the sunlight of his native land for him and her. He should hear the surf wash on the shingly beach and in the deep grottos of which she had sung to him when a child. Had he not promised her this? And had they not many a time laughed for very joy at the prospect, the two together?

He picked his way up the crowded stairs, carefully guarding the precious roll. The crush was even greater than usual. There had been delay—something wrong with the cable; but a train was just waiting, and he hurried on board with the rest, little heeding what became of him so long as the diploma was safe. The train rolled out on the bridge, with Paolo wedged in the crowd on the platform of the last car, holding the paper high over his head, where it was sheltered safe from the fog and the rain and the crush.

Another train backed up, received its load of cross humanity, and vanished in the mist. The damp, gray curtain had barely closed behind it, and the impatient throng was fretting at a further delay, when consternation spread in the bridge-house. Word had come up from the track that something had happened. Trains were stalled all along the route. While the dread and uncertainty grew, a messenger ran up, out of breath. There had been a collision. The last train had run into the one preceding it, in the fog. One was killed, others were injured. Doctors and ambulances were wanted.

They came with the police, and by and by the partly wrecked train was hauled up to the platform. When the wounded had been taken to the hospital, they bore from the train the body of a youth, clutching yet in his hand a torn, blood-stained paper, tied about with a purple ribbon. It was Paolo. The awakening had come. Brighter skies than those of sunny Italy had dawned upon him in the gloom and terror of the great crash. Paolo was at home, waiting for his mother.

THE LITTLE DOLLAR'S CHRISTMAS JOURNEY

"It is too bad," said Mrs. Lee, and she put down the magazine in which she had been reading of the poor children in the tenements of the great city that know little of Christmas joys; "no Christmas tree! One of them shall have one, at any rate. I think this will buy it, and it is so handy to send. Nobody would know that there was money in the letter." And she enclosed a coupon in a letter to a professor, a friend in the city, who, she knew, would have no trouble in finding the child, and had it mailed at once. Mrs. Lee was a widow whose not too great income was derived from the interest on some four per cent government bonds which represented the savings of her husband's life of toil, that was none the less hard because it was spent in a counting-room and not with shovel and spade. The coupon looked for all the world like a dollar bill, except that it was so small that a baby's hand could easily cover it. The United States, the printing on it said, would pay on demand to the bearer one dollar; and there was a number on it, just as on a full-grown dollar, that was the number of the bond from which it had been cut.

The letter travelled all night, and was tossed and sorted and bunched at the end of its journey in the great gray beehive that never sleeps, day or night, and where half the tears and joys of the land, including this account of the little dollar, are checked off unceasingly as first-class matter or second or third, as the case may be. In the morning it was laid, none the worse for its journey, at the professor's breakfast plate. The professor was a kindly man, and he smiled as he read it. "To procure one small Christmas tree for a poor tenement," was its errand.

"Little dollar," he said, "I think I know where you are needed." And he made a note in his book. There were other notes there that made him smile again as he saw them. They had names set opposite them. One about a Noah's ark was marked "Vivi." That was the baby; and there was one about a doll's carriage that had the words "Katie, sure," set over against it. The professor eyed the list in mock dismay.

"How ever will I do it?" he sighed, as he put on his hat.

"Well, you will have to get Santa Claus to help you, John," said his wife, buttoning his greatcoat about him. "And, mercy! the duckses' babies! don't forget them, whatever you do. The baby has been talking about nothing else since he saw them at the store, the old duck and the two ducklings on wheels. You know them, John?"

But the professor was gone, repeating to himself as he went down the garden walk, "The duckses' babies, indeed!" He chuckled as he said it, why I cannot tell. He was very particular about his grammar, was the professor, ordinarily. Perhaps it was because it was Christmas eve.

Down town went the professor; but instead of going with the crowd that was setting toward Santa Claus's headquarters, in the big Broadway store, he turned off into a quieter street, leading west. It took him to a narrow thoroughfare, with five-story tenements frowning on either side, where the people he met were not so well dressed as those he had left behind, and did not seem to be in such a hurry of joyful anticipation of the holiday. Into one of the tenements he went, and, groping his way through a pitch-dark hall, came to a door way back, the last one to the left, at which he knocked. An expectant voice said, "Come in," and the professor pushed open the door.

The room was very small, very stuffy, and very dark, so dark that a smoking kerosene lamp that burned on a table next the stove hardly lighted it at all, though it was broad day. A big, unshaven man, who sat on the bed, rose when he saw the visitor, and stood uncomfortably shifting his feet and avoiding the professor's eye. The latter's glance was serious, though not unkind, as he asked the woman with the baby if he had found no work yet.

"No," she said, anxiously coming to the rescue, "not yet; he was waitin' for a recommend." But Johnnie had earned two dollars running errands, and, now there was a big fall of snow, his father might get a job of shovelling. The woman's face was worried, yet there was a cheerful note in her voice that somehow made the place seem less discouraging than it was. The baby she nursed was not much larger than a middle-sized doll. Its little face looked thin and wan. It had been very sick, she explained, but the doctor said it was mending now. That was good, said the professor, and patted one of the bigger children on the head.

There were six of them, of all sizes, from Johnnie, who could run errands, down. They were busy fixing up a Christmas tree that half filled the room, though it was of the very smallest. Yet, it was a real Christmas tree, left over from the Sunday-school stock, and it was dressed up at that. Pictures from the colored supplement of a Sunday newspaper hung and stood on every branch, and three pieces of colored glass, suspended on threads that shone in the smoky lamplight, lent color and real beauty to the show. The children were greatly tickled.

"John put it up," said the mother, by way of explanation, as the professor eyed it approvingly. "There ain't nothing to eat on it. If there was, it wouldn't be there a minute. The childer be always a-searchin' in it."

"But there must be, or else it isn't a real Christmas tree," said the professor, and brought out the little dollar. "This is a dollar which a friend gave me for the children's Christmas, and she sends her love with it. Now, you buy them some things and a few candles, Mrs. Ferguson, and then a good supper for the rest of the family. Good night, and a Merry Christmas to you. I think myself the baby is getting better." It had just opened its eyes and laughed at the tree.

The professor was not very far on his way toward keeping his appointment with Santa Claus before Mrs. Ferguson was at the grocery laying in her dinner. A dollar goes a long way when it is the only one in the house; and when she had everything, including two cents' worth of flitter-gold, four apples, and five candles for the tree, the grocer footed up her bill on the bag that held her potatoes—ninety-eight cents. Mrs. Ferguson gave him the little dollar.

"What's this?" said the grocer, his fat smile turning cold as he laid a restraining hand on the full basket. "That ain't no good."

"It's a dollar, ain't it?" said the woman, in alarm. "It's all right. I know the man that give it to me."

"It ain't all right in this store," said the grocer, sternly. "Put them things back. I want none o' that."

The woman's eyes filled with tears as she slowly took the lid off the basket and lifted out the precious bag of potatoes. They were waiting for that dinner at home. The children were even then camping on the door-step to take her in to the tree in triumph. And now—

For the second time a restraining hand was laid upon her basket; but this time it was not the grocer's. A gentleman who had come in to order a Christmas turkey had overheard the conversation, and had seen the strange bill.

"It is all right," he said to the grocer. "Give it to me. Here is a dollar bill for it of the kind you know. If all your groceries were as honest as this bill, Mr. Schmidt, it would be a pleasure to trade with you. Don't be afraid to trust Uncle Sam where you see his promise to pay."

The gentleman held the door open for Mrs. Ferguson, and heard the shout of the delegation awaiting her on the stoop as he went down the street.

"I wonder where that came from, now," he mused. "Coupons in Bedford Street! I suppose somebody sent it to the woman for a Christmas gift. Hello! Here are old Thomas and Snowflake. Now, wouldn't it surprise her old stomach if I gave her a Christmas gift of oats? If only the shock doesn't kill her! Thomas! Oh, Thomas!"

The old man thus hailed stopped and awaited the gentleman's coming. He was a cartman who did odd jobs through the ward, so picking up a living for himself and the white horse, which the boys had dubbed Snowflake in a spirit of fun. They were a well-matched old pair, Thomas and his horse. One was not more decrepit than the other.

There was a tradition along the docks, where Thomas found a job now and then, and Snowflake an occasional straw to lunch on, that they were of an age, but this was denied by Thomas.

"See here," said the gentleman, as he caught up with them; "I want Snowflake to keep Christmas, Thomas. Take this and buy him a bag of oats. And give it to him carefully, do you hear?—not all at once, Thomas. He isn't used to it."

"Gee whizz!" said the old man, rubbing his eyes with his cap, as his friend passed out of sight, "oats fer Christmas! G'lang, Snowflake; yer in luck."

The feed-man put on his spectacles and looked Thomas over at the strange order. Then he scanned the little dollar, first on one side, then on the other.

"Never seed one like him," he said. "'Pears to me he is mighty short. Wait till I send round to the hockshop. He'll know, if anybody."

The man at the pawnshop did not need a second look. "Why, of course," he said, and handed a dollar bill over the counter. "Old Thomas, did you say? Well, I am blamed if the old man ain't got a stocking after all. They're a sly pair, he and Snowflake."

Business was brisk that day at the pawnshop. The door-bell tinkled early and late, and the stock on the shelves grew. Bundle was added to bundle. It had been a hard winter so far. Among the callers in the early afternoon was a young girl in a gingham dress and without other covering, who stood timidly at the counter and asked for three dollars on a watch, a keepsake evidently, which she was loath to part with. Perhaps it was the last glimpse of brighter days. The pawnbroker was doubtful; it was not worth so much. She pleaded hard, while he compared the number of the movement with a list sent in from Police Headquarters.

"Two," he said decisively at last, snapping the case shut—"two or nothing." The girl handed over the watch with a troubled sigh. He made out a ticket and gave it to her with a handful of silver change.

Was it the sigh and her evident distress, or was it the little dollar? As she turned to go, he called her back.

"Here, it is Christmas!" he said. "I'll run the risk." And he added the coupon to the little heap.

The girl looked at it and at him questioningly.

"It is all right," he said; "you can take it; I'm running short of change. Bring it back if they won't take it. I'm good for it." Uncle Sam had achieved a backer.

In Grand Street the holiday crowds jammed every store in their eager hunt for bargains. In one of them, at the knit-goods counter, stood the girl from the pawnshop, picking out a thick, warm shawl. She hesitated between a gray and a maroon-colored one, and held them up to the light.

"For you?" asked the salesgirl, thinking to aid her. She glanced at her thin dress and shivering form as she said it.

"No," said the girl; "for mother; she is poorly and needs it." She chose the gray, and gave the salesgirl her handful of money.

The girl gave back the coupon.

"They don't go," she said; "give me another, please."

"But I haven't got another," said the girl, looking apprehensively at the shawl. "The— Mr. Feeney said it was all right. Take it to the desk, please, and ask."

The salesgirl took the bill and the shawl, and went to the desk. She came back, almost immediately, with the storekeeper, who looked sharply at the customer and noted the number of the coupon.

"It is all right," he said, satisfied apparently by the inspection; "a little unusual, only. We don't see many of them. Can I help you, miss?" And he attended her to the door.

In the street there was even more of a Christmas show going on than in the stores. Pedlers of toys, of mottoes, of candles, and of knickknacks of every description stood in rows along the curb, and were driving a lively trade. Their push-carts were decorated with fir branches—even whole Christmas trees. One held a whole cargo of Santa Clauses in a bower of green, each one with a cedar-bush in his folded arms, as a soldier carries his gun. The lights were blazing out in the stores, and the hucksters' torches were flaring at the corners. There was Christmas in the very air and Christmas in the storekeeper's till. It had been a very busy day. He thought of it with a satisfied nod as he stood a moment breathing the brisk air of the winter day, absently fingering the coupon the girl had paid for the shawl. A thin voice at his elbow said: "Merry Christmas, Mr. Stein! Here's yer paper."

It was the newsboy who left the evening papers at the door every night. The storekeeper knew him, and something about the struggle they had at home to keep the roof over their heads. Mike was a kind of protégé of his. He had helped to get him his route.

"Wait a bit, Mike," he said. "You'll be wanting your Christmas from me. Here's a dollar. It's just like yourself: it is small, but it is all right. You take it home and have a good time."

Was it the message with which it had been sent forth from far away in the country, or what was it? Whatever it was, it was just impossible for the little dollar to lie still in the pocket while there was want to be relieved, mouths to be filled, or Christmas lights to be lit. It just couldn't, and it didn't.

Mike stopped around the corner of Allen Street, and gave three whoops expressive of his approval of Mr. Stein; having done which, he sidled up to the first lighted window out of range to examine his gift. His enthusiasm changed to open-mouthed astonishment as he saw the little dollar. His jaw fell. Mike was not much of a scholar, and could not make out the inscription on the coupon; but he had heard of shinplasters as something they "had in the war," and he took this to be some sort of a ten-cent piece. The policeman on the block might tell. Just now he and Mike were hunk. They had made up a little difference they'd had, and if any one would know, the cop surely would. And off he went in search of him.

Mr. McCarthy pulled off his gloves, put his club under his arm, and studied the little dollar with contracted brow. He shook his head as he handed it back, and rendered the opinion that it was "some dom swindle that's ag'in' the law." He advised Mike to take it back to Mr. Stein, and added, as he prodded him in an entirely friendly manner in the ribs with his locust, that if it had been the week before he might have "run him in" for having the thing in his possession. As it happened, Mr. Stein was busy and not to be seen, and Mike went home between hope and fear, with his doubtful prize.

There was a crowd at the door of the tenement, and Mike saw, before he had reached it, running, that it clustered about an ambulance that was backed up to the sidewalk. Just as he pushed his way through the throng it drove off, its clanging gong scattering the people right and left. A little girl sat weeping on the top step of the stoop. To her Mike turned for information.

"Susie, what's up?" he asked, confronting her with his armful of papers. "Who's got hurted?"

"It's papa," sobbed the girl. "He ain't hurted. He's sick, and he was took that bad he had to go, an' to-morrer is Christmas, an'—oh, Mike!"

It is not the fashion of Essex Street to slop over. Mike didn't. He just set his mouth to a whistle and took a turn down the hall to think. Susie was his chum. There were seven in her flat; in his only four, including two that made wages. He came back from his trip with his mind made up.

"Suse," he said, "come on in. You take this, Suse, see! an' let the kids have their Christmas. Mr. Stein give it to me. It's a little one, but if it ain't all right I'll take it back and get one that is good. Go on, now, Suse, you hear?" And he was gone.

There was a Christmas tree that night in Susie's flat, with candles and apples and shining gold, but the little dollar did not pay for it. That rested securely in the purse of the charity visitor who had come that afternoon, just at the right time, as it proved. She had heard the story of Mike and his sacrifice, and had herself given the children a one-dollar bill for the coupon. They had their Christmas, and a joyful one, too, for the lady went up to the hospital and brought back word that Susie's father would be all right with rest and care, which he was now getting. Mike came in and helped them "sack" the tree when the lady was gone. He gave three more whoops for Mr. Stein, three for the lady, and three for the hospital doctor to even things up. Essex Street was all right that night.

"Do you know, professor," said that learned man's wife, when, after supper, he had settled down in his easy-chair to admire the Noah's ark and the duckses' babies and the rest, all of which had arrived safely by express ahead of him and were waiting to be detailed to their appropriate stockings while the children slept—"do you know, I heard such a story of a little newsboy to-day. It was at the meeting of our district charity committee this evening. Miss Linder, our visitor, came right from the house." And she told the story of Mike and Susie.

"And I just got the little dollar bill to keep. Here it is." She took the coupon out of her purse and passed it to her husband.

"Eh! what?" said the professor, adjusting his spectacles and reading the number. "If here isn't my little dollar come back to me! Why, where have you been, little one? I left you in Bedford Street this morning, and here you come by way of Essex. Well, I declare!" And he told his wife how he had received it in a letter in the morning.

"John," she said, with a sudden impulse,—she didn't know, and neither did he, that it was the charm of the little dollar that was working again,—"John, I guess it is a sin to stop it. Jones's children won't have any Christmas tree, because they can't afford it. He told me so this morning when he fixed the furnace. And the baby is sick. Let us give them the little dollar. He is here in the kitchen now."

And they did; and the Joneses, and I don't know how many others, had a Merry Christmas because of the blessed little dollar that carried Christmas cheer and good luck wherever it went. For all I know, it may be going yet. Certainly it is a sin to stop it, and if any one has locked it up without knowing that he locked up the Christmas dollar, let him start it right out again. He can tell it easily enough. If he just looks at the number, that's the one.

THE KID

He was an every-day tough, bull-necked, square-jawed, red of face, and with his hair cropped short in the fashion that rules at Sing Sing and is admired of Battle Row. Any one could have told it at a glance. The bruised and wrathful face of the policeman who brought him to Mulberry Street, to be "stood up" before the detectives in the hope that there might be something against him to aggravate the offence of beating an officer with his own club, bore witness to it. It told a familiar story. The prisoner's gang had started a fight in the street, probably with a scheme of ultimate robbery in view, and the police had come upon it unexpectedly. The rest had got away with an assortment of promiscuous bruises. The "Kid" stood his ground, and went down with two "cops" on top of him after a valiant battle, in which he had performed the feat that entitled him to honorable mention henceforth in the felonious annals of the gang. There was no surrender in his sullen look as he stood before the desk, his hard face disfigured further by a streak of half-dried blood, reminiscent of the night's encounter. The fight had gone against him—that was all right. There was a time for getting square. Till then he was man enough to take his medicine, let them do their worst.

It was there, plain as could be, in his set jaws and dogged bearing as he came out, numbered now and indexed in the rogues' gallery, and started for the police court between two officers. It chanced that I was going the same way, and joined company. Besides, I have certain theories concerning toughs which my friend the sergeant says are rot, and I was not averse to testing them on the Kid.

But the Kid was a bad subject. He replied to my friendly advances with a muttered curse, or not at all, and upset all my notions in the most reckless way. Conversation had ceased before we were halfway across to Broadway. He "wanted no guff," and I left him to his meditations respecting his defenceless state. At Broadway there was a jam of trucks, and we stopped at the corner to wait for an opening.

It all happened so quickly that only a confused picture of it is in my mind till this day. A sudden start, a leap, and a warning cry, and the Kid had wrenched himself loose. He was free. I was dimly conscious of a rush of blue and brass; and then I saw—the whole street saw—a child, a toddling baby, in the middle of the railroad track, right in front of the coming car. It reached out its tiny hand toward the madly clanging bell and crowed. A scream rose wild and piercing above the tumult; men struggled with a frantic woman on the curb, and turned their heads away—

And then there stood the Kid, with the child in his arms, unhurt. I see him now, as he set it down, gently as any woman, trying with lingering touch to unclasp the grip of the baby hand upon his rough finger. I see the hard look coming back into his face as the policeman, red and out of breath, twisted the nipper on his wrist, with a half-uncertain aside to me, "Them toughs there ain't no depending on, nohow." Sullen, defiant, planning vengeance, I see him led away to jail. Ruffian and thief! The police blotter said so.

But, even so, the Kid had proved that my theories about toughs were not rot. Who knows but that, like sergeants, the blotter may be sometimes mistaken?

WHEN THE LETTER CAME

"To-morrow it will come," Godfrey Krueger had said that night to his landlord. "To-morrow it will surely come, and then I shall have money. Soon I shall be rich, richer than you can think."

And the landlord of the Forsyth Street tenement, who in his heart liked the gray-haired inventor, but who had rooms to let, grumbled something about a to-morrow that never came.

"Oh, but it will come," said Krueger, turning on the stairs and shading the lamp with his hand, the better to see his landlord's good-natured face; "you know the application has been advanced. It is bound to be granted, and to-night I shall finish my ship."

Now, as he sat alone in his room at his work, fitting, shaping, and whittling with restless hands, he had to admit to himself that it was time it came. Two whole days he had lived on a crust, and he was starving. He had worked and waited thirteen hard years for the success that had more than once been almost within his grasp, only to elude it again. It had never seemed nearer and surer than now, and there was need of it. He had come to the jumping-off place. All his money was gone, to the last cent, and his application for a pension hung fire in Washington unaccountably. It had been advanced to the last stage, and word that it had been granted might be received any day. But the days slipped by and no word came. For two days he had lived on faith and a crust, but they were giving out together. If only—

Well, when it did come, what with his back pay for all those years, he would have the means to build his ship, and hunger and want would be forgotten. He should have enough. And the world would know that Godfrey Krueger was not an idle crank.

"In six months I shall cross the ocean to Europe in twenty hours in my air-ship," he had said in showing the landlord his models, "with as many as want to go. Then I shall become a millionnaire and shall make you one, too." And the landlord had heaved a sigh at the thought of his twenty-seven dollars, and doubtingly wished it might be so.

Weak and famished, Krueger bent to his all but finished task. Before morning he should know that it would work as he had planned. There remained only to fit the last parts together. The idea of building an air-ship had come to him while he lay dying with scurvy, as they thought, in a Confederate prison, and he had never abandoned it. He had been a teacher and a student, and was a trained mathematician. There could be no flaw in his calculations. He had worked them out again and again. The energy developed by his plan was great enough to float a ship capable of carrying almost any burden, and of directing it against the strongest head winds. Now, upon the threshold of success, he was awaiting merely the long-delayed pension to carry his dream into life. To-morrow would bring it, and with it an end to all his waiting and suffering.

One after another the lights went out in the tenement. Only the one in the inventor's room burned steadily through the night. The policeman on the beat noticed the lighted window, and made a mental note of the fact that some one was sick. Once during the early hours he stopped short to listen. Upon the morning breeze was borne a muffled sound, as of a distant explosion. But all was quiet again, and he went on, thinking that his senses had deceived him. The dawn came in the eastern sky, and with it the stir that attends the awakening of another day. The lamp burned steadily yet behind the dim window pane.

The milkmen came, and the push-cart criers. The policeman was relieved, and another took his place. Lastly came the mail-carrier with a large official envelope marked, "Pension Bureau, Washington." He shouted up the stairway:—

"Krueger! Letter!"

The landlord came to the door and was glad. So it had come, had it?

"Run, Emma," he said to his little daughter, "run and tell Mr. Godfrey his letter has come."

The child skipped up the steps gleefully. She knocked at the inventor's door, but no answer came. It was not locked, and she pushed it open. The little lamp smoked yet on the table. The room was strewn with broken models and torn papers that littered the floor. Something there frightened the child. She held to the banisters and called faintly:—

"Papa! Oh, papa!"

They went in together on tiptoe without knowing why, the postman with the big official letter in his hand. The morrow had kept its promise. Of hunger and want there was an end. On the bed, stretched at full length, with his Grand Army hat flung beside him, lay the inventor, dead. A little round hole in the temple, from which a few drops of blood had flowed, told what remained of his story. In the night disillusion had come, with failure.

THE CAT TOOK THE KOSHER MEAT

The tenement No. 76 Madison Street had been for some time scandalized by the hoidenish ways of Rose Baruch, the little cloak maker on the top floor. Rose was seventeen, and boarded with her mother in the Pincus family. But for her harum-scarum ways she might, in the opinion of the tenement, be a nice girl and some day a good wife; but these were unbearable.

For the tenement is a great working hive in which nothing has value unless exchangeable for gold. Rose's animal spirits, which long hours and low wages had no power to curb, were exchangeable only for wrath in the tenement. Her noisy feet on the stairs when she came home woke up all the tenants, and made them swear at the loss of the precious moments of sleep which were their reserve capital. Rose was so Americanized, they said impatiently among themselves, that nothing could be done with her.

Perhaps they were mistaken. Perhaps Rose's stout refusal to be subdued even by the tenement was their hope, as it was her capital. Perhaps her spiteful tread upon the stairs heralded the coming protest of the free-born American against slavery, industrial or otherwise, in which their day of deliverance was dawning. It may be so. They didn't see it. How should they? They were not Americanized; not yet.

However that might be, Rose came to the end that was to be expected. The judgment of the tenement was, for the time, borne out by experience. This was the way of it:—

Rose's mother had bought several pounds of kosher meat and put it into the ice-box—that is to say, on the window-sill of their fifth-floor flat. Other ice-box these East Side sweaters' tenements have none. And it does well enough in cold weather, unless the cat gets around, or, as it happened in this case, it slides off and falls down. Rose's breakfast and dinner disappeared down the air-shaft, seventy feet or more, at 10.30 p.m.

There was a family consultation as to what should be done. It was late, and everybody was in bed, but Rose declared herself equal to the rousing of the tenants in the first floor rear, through whose window she could climb into the shaft for the meat. She had done it before for a nickel. Enough said. An expedition set out at once from the top floor to recover the meat. Mrs. Baruch, Rose, and Jake, the boarder, went in a body.

Arrived before the Knauff family's flat on the ground floor, they opened proceedings by a vigorous attack on the door. The Knauffs woke up in a fright, believing that the house was full of burglars. They were stirring to barricade the door, when they recognized

Rose's voice and were calmed. Let in, the expedition explained matters, and was grudgingly allowed to take a look out of the window in the air-shaft. Yes! there was the meat, as yet safe from rats. The thing was to get it.

The boarder tried first, but crawled back frightened. He couldn't reach it. Rose jerked him impatiently away.

"Leg go!" she said. "I can do it. I was there wunst. You're no good."

And she bent over the window-sill, reaching down until her toes barely touched the floor, when all of a sudden, before they could grab her skirts, over she went, heels over head, down the shaft, and disappeared.

The shrieks of the Knauffs, of Mrs. Baruch, and of Jake, the boarder, were echoed from below. Rose's voice rose in pain and in bitter lamentation from the bottom of the shaft. She had fallen fully fifteen feet, and in the fall had hurt her back badly, if, indeed, she had not injured herself beyond repair. Her cries suggested nothing less. They filled the tenement, rising to every floor and appealing at every bedroom window.

In a minute the whole building was astir from cellar to roof. A dozen heads were thrust out of every window, and answering wails carried messages of helpless sympathy to the once so unpopular Rose. Upon this concert of sorrow the police broke in with anxious inquiry as to what was the matter.

When they found out, a second relief expedition was organized. It reached Rose through the basement coal-bin, and she was carried out and sent to the Gouverneur Hospital. There she lies, unable to move, and the tenement wonders what is amiss that it has lost its old spirits. It has not even anything left to swear at.

The cat took the kosher meat.

NIBSY'S CHRISTMAS

It was Christmas Eve over on the East Side. Darkness was closing in on a cold, hard day. The light that struggled through the frozen windows of the delicatessen store and the saloon on the corner, fell upon men with empty dinner-pails who were hurrying homeward, their coats buttoned tightly, and heads bent against the steady blast from the river, as if they were butting their way down the street.

The wind had forced the door of the saloon ajar, and was whistling through the crack; but in there it seemed to make no one afraid. Between roars of laughter, the clink of glasses and the rattle of dice on the hardwood counter were heard out in the street. More than one of the passers-by who came within range was taken with an extra shiver in which the vision of wife and little ones waiting at home for his coming was snuffed out, as he dropped in to brace up. The lights were long out when the silent streets reëchoed his unsteady steps toward home, where the Christmas welcome had turned to dread.

But in this twilight hour they burned brightly yet, trying hard to pierce the bitter cold outside with a ray of warmth and cheer. Where the lamps in the delicatessen store made a mottled streak of brightness across the flags, two little boys stood with their noses flattened against the window. The warmth inside, and the lights, had made little islands of clear space on the frosty pane, affording glimpses of the wealth within, of the piles of smoked herring, of golden cheese, of sliced bacon and generous, fat-bellied hams; of the rows of odd-shaped bottles and jars on the shelves that held there was no telling what good things, only it was certain that they must be good from the looks of them.

And the heavenly smell of spices and things that reached the boys through the open door each time the tinkling bell announced the coming or going of a customer! Better than all, back there on the top shelf the stacks of square honey-cakes, with their frosty coats of sugar, tied in bundles with strips of blue paper.

The wind blew straight through the patched and threadbare jackets of the lads as they crept closer to the window, struggling hard by breathing on the pane to make their peep-holes bigger, to take in the whole of the big cake with the almonds set in; but they did not heed it.

"Jim!" piped the smaller of the two, after a longer stare than usual; "hey, Jim! them's Sante Claus's. See 'em?"

"Sante Claus!" snorted the other, scornfully, applying his eye to the clear spot on the pane. "There ain't no ole duffer like dat. Them's honey-cakes. Me 'n' Tom had a bite o' one wunst."

"There ain't no Sante Claus?" retorted the smaller shaver, hotly, at his peep-hole. "There is, too. I seen him myself when he cum to our alley last—"

"What's youse kids a-scrappin' fur?" broke in a strange voice.

Another boy, bigger, but dirtier and tougher looking than either of the two, had come up behind them unobserved. He carried an armful of unsold "extras" under one arm. The other was buried to the elbow in the pocket of his ragged trousers.

The "kids" knew him, evidently, and the smallest eagerly accepted him as umpire.

"It's Jim w'at says there ain't no Sante Claus, and I seen him—"

"Jim!" demanded the elder ragamuffin, sternly, looking hard at the culprit; "Jim! yere a chump! No Sante Claus? What're ye givin' us? Now, watch me!"

With utter amazement the boys saw him disappear through the door under the tinkling bell into the charmed precincts of smoked herring, jam, and honey-cakes. Petrified at their peep-holes, they watched him, in the veritable presence of Santa Claus himself with the fir-branch, fish out five battered pennies from the depths of his pocket and pass them over to the woman behind the jars, in exchange for one of the bundles of honey-cakes tied with blue. As if in a dream they saw him issue forth with the coveted prize.

"There, kid!" he said, holding out the two fattest and whitest cakes to Santa Claus's champion; "there's yer Christmas. Run along, now, to yer barracks; and you, Jim, here's one for you, though yer don't desarve it. Mind ye let the kid alone."

"This one'll have to do for me grub, I guess. I ain't sold me 'Newses,' and the ole man'll kick if I bring 'em home."

Before the shuffling feet of the ragamuffins hurrying homeward had turned the corner, the last mouthful of the newsboy's supper was smothered in a yell of "Extree!" as he shot across the street to intercept a passing stranger.

As the evening wore on, it grew rawer and more blustering still. Flakes of dry snow that stayed where they fell, slowly tracing the curb-lines, the shutters, and the door-steps of the tenements with gathering white, were borne up on the storm from the water. To the right and left stretched endless streets between the towering barracks, as beneath frowning cliffs pierced with a thousand glowing eyes that revealed the watch-fires within—a mighty city of cave-dwellers held in the thraldom of poverty and want.

Outside there was yet hurrying to and fro. Saloon doors were slamming, and bare-legged urchins, carrying beer-jugs, hugged the walls close for shelter. From the depths of a blind alley floated out the discordant strains of a vagabond brass band "blowing in" the yule of the poor. Banished by police ordinance from the street, it reaped a scant harvest of pennies for Christmas cheer from the windows opening on the back yard. Against more than one pane showed the bald outline of a forlorn little Christmas tree, some stray branch of a hemlock picked up at the grocer's and set in a pail for "the childer" to dance around, a dime's worth of candy and tinsel on the boughs.

From the attic over the way came, in spells between, the gentle tones of a German song about the Christ-child. Christmas in the East Side tenements begins with the sunset on the "Holy Eve," except where the name is as a threat or a taunt. In a hundred such homes the whir of many sewing-machines, worked by the sweater's slaves with weary feet and aching backs, drowned every feeble note of joy that struggled to make itself heard above the noise of the great treadmill.

To these what was Christmas but the name for suffering, reminder of lost kindred and liberty, of the slavery of eighteen hundred years, freedom from which was purchased only with gold. Ay, gold! The gold that had power to buy freedom yet, to buy the good-will, ay, and the good name, of the oppressor, with his houses and land. At the thought the tired eye glistened, the aching back straightened, and to the weary foot there came new strength to finish the long task while the city slept.

Where a narrow passageway put in between two big tenements to a ramshackle rear barrack, Nibsy, the newsboy, halted in the shadow of the doorway and stole a long look down the dark alley.

He toyed uncertainly with his still unsold papers—worn dirty and ragged as his clothes by this time—before he ventured in, picking his way between barrels and heaps of garbage; past the Italian cobbler's hovel, where a tallow dip, stuck in a cracked beer-glass, before a picture of the "Mother of God," showed that even he knew it was Christmas and liked to show it; past the Sullivan flat, where blows and drunken curses mingled with the shriek of women, as Nibsy had heard many nights before this one.

He shuddered as he felt his way past the door, partly with a premonition of what was in store for himself, if the "old man" was at home, partly with a vague, uncomfortable feeling that somehow Christmas Eve should be different from other nights, even in the alley; down to its farthest end, to the last rickety flight of steps that led into the filth and darkness of the tenement. Up this he crept, three flights, to a door at which he stopped and listened, hesitating, as he had stopped at the entrance to the alley; then, with a sudden, defiant gesture, he pushed it open and went in.

A bare and cheerless room; a pile of rags for a bed in the corner, another in the dark alcove, miscalled bedroom; under the window a broken candle and an iron-bound chest, upon which sat a sad-eyed woman with hard lines in her face, peeling potatoes in a pan; in the middle of the room a rusty stove, with a pile of wood, chopped on the floor alongside. A man on his knees in front fanning the fire with an old slouch hat. With each breath of draught he stirred, the crazy old pipe belched forth torrents of smoke at every joint. As Nibsy entered, the man desisted from his efforts and sat up, glaring at him—a villanous ruffian's face, scowling with anger.

"Late ag'in!" he growled; "an' yer papers not sold. What did I tell yer, brat, if ye dared—"

"Tom! Tom!" broke in the wife, in a desperate attempt to soothe the ruffian's temper. "The boy can't help it, an' it's Christmas Eve. For the love o'—"

"The devil take yer rot and yer brat!" shouted the man, mad with the fury of passion. "Let me at him!" and, reaching over, he seized a heavy knot of wood and flung it at the head of the boy.

Nibsy had remained just inside the door, edging slowly toward his mother, but with a watchful eye on the man at the stove. At the first movement of his hand toward the woodpile he sprang for the stairway with the agility of a cat, and just dodged the missile. It struck the door, as he slammed it behind him, with force enough to smash the panel.

Down the three flights in as many jumps he went, and through the alley, over barrels and barriers, never stopping once till he reached the street, and curses and shouts were left behind.

In his flight he had lost his unsold papers, and he felt ruefully in his pocket as he went down the street, pulling his rags about him as much from shame as to keep out the cold.

Four pennies were all he had left after his Christmas treat to the two little lads from the barracks; not enough for supper or for a bed; and it was getting colder all the time.

On the sidewalk in front of the notion store a belated Christmas party was in progress. The children from the tenements in the alley and across the way were having a game of blind-man's-buff, groping blindly about in the crowd to catch each other. They hailed Nibsy with shouts of laughter, calling to him to join in.

"We're having Christmas!" they yelled.

Nibsy did not hear them. He was thinking, thinking, the while turning over his four pennies at the bottom of his pocket. Thinking if Christmas was ever to come to him, and the children's Santa Claus to find his alley where the baby slept within reach of her father's cruel hand. As for him, he had never known anything but blows and curses. He could take care of himself. But his mother and the baby—And then it came to him with shuddering cold that it was getting late, and that he must find a place to sleep.

He weighed in his mind the merits of two or three places where he was in the habit of hiding from the "cops" when the alley got to be too hot for him.

There was the hay barge down by the dock, with the watchman who got drunk sometimes, and so gave the boys a chance. The chances were at least even of its being available on Christmas Eve, and of Santa Claus having thus done him a good turn after all.

Then there was the snug berth in the sand-box you could curl all up in. Nibsy thought with regret of its being, like the hay barge, so far away and to windward, too.

Down by the printing-offices there were the steam gratings, and a chance corner in the cellars, stories and stories underground, where the big presses keep up such a clatter from midnight till far into the day.

As he passed them in review, Nibsy made up his mind with sudden determination, and, setting his face toward the south, made off down town.

*** **

The rumble of the last departing news-wagon over the pavement, now buried deep in snow, had died away in the distance, when, from out of the bowels of the earth there issued a cry, a cry of mortal terror and pain that was echoed by a hundred throats.

From one of the deep cellar-ways a man ran out, his clothes and hair and beard afire; on his heels a breathless throng of men and boys; following them, close behind, a rush of smoke and fire.

The clatter of the presses ceased suddenly, to be followed quickly by the clangor of hurrying fire-bells. With hooks and axes the firemen rushed in; hose was let down through the manholes, and down there in the depths the battle was fought and won.

The building was saved; but in the midst of the rejoicing over the victory there fell a sudden silence. From the cellar-way a grimy, helmeted figure arose, with something black and scorched in his arms. A tarpaulin was spread upon the snow and upon it he laid his burden, while the silent crowd made room and word went over to the hospital for the doctor to come quickly.

Very gently they lifted poor little Nibsy—for it was he, caught in his berth by a worse enemy than the "cop" or the watchman of the hay barge—into the ambulance that bore him off to the hospital cot, too late.

Conscious only of a vague discomfort that had succeeded terror and pain, Nibsy wondered uneasily why they were all so kind. Nobody had taken the trouble to as much as notice him before. When he had thrust his papers into their very faces they had pushed him roughly aside.

Nibsy, unhurt and able to fight his way, never had a show. Sick and maimed and sore, he was being made much of, though he had been caught where the boys were forbidden to go. Things were queer, anyhow, and—

The room was getting so dark that he could hardly see the doctor's kindly face, and had to grip his hand tightly to make sure that he was there; almost as dark as the stairs in the alley he had come down in such a hurry.

There was the baby now—poor baby—and mother—and then a great blank, and it was all a mystery to poor Nibsy no longer. For, just as a wild-eyed woman pushed her way through the crowd of nurses and doctors to his bedside, crying for her boy, Nibsy gave up his soul to God.

*** **

It was very quiet in the alley. Christmas had come and gone. Upon the last door a bow of soiled crape was nailed up with two tacks. It had done duty there a dozen times before, that year.

Upstairs, Nibsy was at home, and for once the neighbors, one and all, old and young, came to see him.

Even the father, ruffian that he was, offered no objection. Cowed and silent, he sat in the corner by the window farthest from where the plain little coffin stood, with the lid closed down.

A couple of the neighbor-women were talking in low tones by the stove, when there came a timid knock at the door. Nobody answering, it was pushed open, first a little, then far enough to admit the shrinking form of a little ragamuffin, the smaller of the two who had stood breathing peep-holes on the window pane of the delicatessen store the night before when Nibsy came along.

He dragged with him a hemlock branch, the leavings from some Christmas tree at the grocery.

"It's from Sante Claus," he said, laying it on the coffin. "Nibsy knows." And he went out.

Santa Claus had come to Nibsy, after all, in his alley. And Nibsy knew.

IN THE CHILDREN'S HOSPITAL

The fact was printed the other day that the half-hundred children or more who are in the hospitals on North Brother Island had no playthings, not even a rattle, to make the long days skip by, which, set in smallpox, scarlet fever, and measles, must be longer there than anywhere else in the world. The toys that were brought over there with a consignment of nursery tots who had the typhus fever had been worn clean out, except some fish horns which the doctor frowned on, and which were therefore not allowed at large. Not as much as a red monkey on a yellow stick was there left on the island to make the youngsters happy.

That afternoon a big, hearty-looking man came into the office with the paper in his hand, and demanded to see the editor. He had come, he said, to see to it that those sick youngsters got the playthings they were entitled to; and a regular Santa Claus he proved to the friendless little colony on the lonely island; for he left a crisp fifty-dollar note behind when he went away without giving his name. The single condition was attached to the gift that it should be spent buying toys for the children on North Brother Island.

Accordingly, a strange invading army took the island by storm three or four nights ago. Under cover of the darkness it had itself ferried over from One Hundred and Thirty-eighth Street in the department yawl, and before morning it was in undisputed possession. It has come to stay. Not a doll or a sheep will ever leave the island again. They may riot upon it as they please, within certain well-defined limits, but none of them can ever cross the channel to the mainland again, unless it be the rubber dolls who can swim, so it is said. Here is the muster-roll:—

Six sheep (four with lambs), six fairies (big dolls in street dress), twelve rubber dolls (in woollen jackets), four railroad trains, twenty-eight base-balls, twenty rubber balls, six big painted (Scotch plaid) rubber balls, six still bigger ditto, seven boxes of blocks, half a dozen music-boxes, twenty-four rattles, six bubble (soap) toys, twelve small engines, six games of dominos, twelve rubber toys (old woman who lived in a shoe, etc.), five wooden toys (bad bear, etc.), thirty-six horse reins.

As there is only one horse on the island, and that one a very steady-going steed in no urgent need of restraint, this last item might seem superfluous, but only to the uninstructed mind. Within a brief week half the boys and girls on the island that are out of bed long enough to stand on their feet will be transformed into ponies and the other half into drivers, and flying teams will go cavorting around to the tune of "Johnny, Get your Gun," and the "Jolly Brothers Gallop," as they are ground out of the music-boxes by little fingers that but just now toyed feebly with the balusters on the golden stair.

That music! When I went over to the island it fell upon my ears in little drops of sweet melody, as soon as I came in sight of the nurses' quarters. I listened, but couldn't make out the tune. The drops seemed mixed. When I opened the door upon one of the nurses, Dr. Dixon, and the hospital matron, each grinding his or her music for all there was in it, and looking perfectly happy withal, I understood why.

They were all playing different tunes at the same time, the nurse "When the Robins Nest Again," Dr. Dixon "Nancy Lee," and the matron "Sweet Violets." A little child stood by in open-mouthed admiration, that became ecstasy when I joined in with "The Babies on our Block." It was all for the little one's benefit, and she thought it beautiful without a doubt.

The storekeeper, knowing that music hath charms to soothe the breast of even a typhus-fever patient, had thrown in a dozen boxes as his own gift. Thus one good deed brings on another, and a good deal more than fifty dollars' worth of happiness will be ground out on the island before there is an end of the music.

There is one little girl in the measles ward already who will eat only when her nurse sits by grinding out "Nancy Lee." She cannot be made to swallow one mouthful on any other condition. No other nurse and no other tune but "Nancy Lee" will do—neither the "Star-Spangled Banner" nor "The Babies on our Block." Whether it is Nancy all by her melodious self, or the beautiful picture of her in a sailor's suit on the lid of the box, or the two and the nurse and the dinner together, that serve to soothe her, is a question of some concern to the island, since Nancy and the nurse have shown signs of giving out together.

Three of the six sheep that were bought for the ridiculously low price of eighty-nine cents apiece, the lambs being thrown in as makeweight, were grazing on the mixed-measles lawn over on the east shore of the island, with a fairy in evening dress eying them rather disdainfully in the grasp of tearful Annie Cullum. Annie is a foundling from the asylum temporarily sojourning here. The measles and the scarlet fever were the only things that ever took kindly to her in her little life. They tackled her both at once, and poor Annie, after a six or eight weeks' tussle with them, has just about enough spunk left to cry when anybody looks at her.

Three woolly sheep and a fairy all at once have robbed her of all hope, and in the midst of it all she weeps as if her heart would break. Even when the nurse pulls one of the unresisting muttonheads, and it emits a loud "Baa-a," she stops only just for a second or two and then wails again. The sheep look rather surprised, as they have a right to. They have come to be little Annie's steady company, hers and her fellow-sufferers' in the mixed-measles ward. The triangular lawn upon which they are browsing is theirs to gambol on when the sun shines, but cross the walk that borders it they never can, any more than the babies with whom they play. Sumptuary law rules the island they are on. Habeas corpus and the constitution stop short of the ferry. Even Comstock's authority does not cross it: the one exception to the rule that dolls and sheep and babies shall not visit from ward to ward is in favor of the rubber dolls, and the etiquette of the island requires that they shall lay off their woollen jackets and go calling just as the factory turned them out, without a stitch or shred of any kind on.

As for the rest, they are assigned, babies, nurses, sheep, rattles, and railroad trains, to their separate measles, scarlet fever, and diphtheria lawns or wards, and there must be content to stay. A sheep may be transferred from the scarlet-fever ward with its patron to the mixed-measles or diphtheria, when symptoms of either of these diseases appear, as they often do; but it cannot then go back again, lest it carry the seeds of the new contagion to its old friends.

Even the fairies are put under the ban of suspicion by such evil associations, and, once they have crossed the line, are not allowed to go back to corrupt the good manners of the babies with only one complaint.

Pauline Meyer, the bigger of the two girls on the mixed-measles stoop,—the other is friendless Annie,—has just enough strength to laugh when her sheep's head is pulled. She has been on the limits of one ward after another these four months, and has had everything, short of typhus fever and smallpox, that the island affords.

It is a marvel that there is one laugh left in her whole little shrunken body after it all; but there is, and the grin on her face reaches almost from ear to ear, as she clasps the biggest fairy in an arm very little stouter than a boy's bean blower, and hears the lamb bleat. Why, that one smile on that ghastly face would be thought worth his fifty dollars by the children's friend, could he see it. Pauline is the child of Swedish emigrants. She and Annie will not fight over their lambs and their dolls, not for many weeks. They can't. They can't even stand up.

One of the railroad trains, drawn by a glorious tin engine, with the name "Union" painted on the cab, is making across the stoop for the little boy with the whooping-cough in the next building. But it won't get there; it is quarantined. But it will have plenty of exercise. Little hands are itching to get hold of it in one of the cribs inside. There are thirty-six sick children on the island just now, about half of them boys, who will find plenty of use for the balls and things as soon as they get about. How those base-balls are to be kept within bounds is a hopeless mystery the doctors are puzzling over.

Even if nines are organized in every ward, as has been suggested, it is hard to see how they can be allowed to play each other, as they would want to, of course, as soon as they could toddle about. It would be something, though, a smallpox nine pitted against the scarlets or the measles, with an umpire from the mixed ward!

The old woman that lived in a shoe, being of rubber, is a privileged character, and is away on a call in the female scarlet, says the nurse. It is a good thing that she was made that way, for she is very popular. So are Mother Goose and her ten companion rubber toys. The bear and the man that strike alternately a wooden anvil with a ditto hammer are scarcely less exciting to the infantile mind; but, being of wood, they are steady boarders permanently attached each to his ward. The dominos fell to the lot of the male scarlets.

That ward has half a dozen grown men in it at present, and they have never once lost sight of the little black blocks since they first saw them.

The doctor reports that they are getting better just as fast as they can since they took to playing dominos. If there is any hint in this to the profession at large, they are welcome to it, along with humanity.

A little girl with a rubber doll in a red woollen jacket—a combination to make the perspiration run right off one with the humidity at 98—looks wistfully down from the second-story balcony of the smallpox pavilion, as the doctor goes past with the last sheep tucked under his arm.

But though it baa-a ever so loudly, it is not for her. It is bound for the white tent on the shore, shunned even here, where sits a solitary watcher gazing wistfully all day toward the city that has passed out of his life. Perchance it may bring to him a message from the far-away home where the birds sang for him, and the waves and the flowers spoke to him, and "Unclean" had not been written against his name. Of all on the Pest Island he alone is hopeless. He is a leper, and his sentence is that of a living death in a strange land.

NIGGER MARTHA'S WAKE

A woman with face all seared and blotched by something that had burned through the skin sat propped up in the doorway of a Bowery restaurant at four o'clock in the morning, senseless, apparently dying. A policeman stood by, looking anxiously up the street and consulting his watch. At intervals he shook her to make sure she was not dead. The drift of the Bowery that was borne that way eddied about, intent upon what was going on. A dumpy little man edged through the crowd and peered into the woman's face.

"Phew!" he said, "it's Nigger Martha! What is gettin' into the girls on the Bowery I don't know. Remember my Maggie? She was her chum."

This to the watchman on the block. The watchman remembered. He knows everything that goes on in the Bowery. Maggie was the wayward daughter of a decent laundress, and killed herself by drinking carbolic acid less than a month before. She had wearied of the Bowery. Nigger Martha was her one friend. And now she had followed her example.

She was drunk when she did it. It is in their cups that a glimpse of the life they traded away for the street comes sometimes to these wretches, with remorse not to be borne.

It came so to Nigger Martha. Ten minutes before, she had been sitting with two boon companions in the oyster saloon next door, discussing their night's catch. Elsie "Specs" was one of the two; the other was known to the street simply as Mame. Elsie wore glasses, a thing unusual enough in the Bowery to deserve recognition. From their presence Martha rose suddenly, to pull a vial from her pocket. Mame saw it, and, knowing what it meant in the heavy humor that was upon Nigger Martha, she struck it from her hand with a pepper-box. It fell, but was not broken. The woman picked it up, and staggering out, swallowed its contents upon the sidewalk—that is, as much as went into her mouth. Much went over her face, burning it. She fell shrieking.

Then came the crowd. The Bowery never sleeps. The policeman on the beat set her in the doorway and sent a hurry call for an ambulance. It came at last, and Nigger Martha was taken to the hospital.

As Mame told it, so it was recorded on the police blotter, with the addition that she was anywhere from forty to fifty years old. That was the strange part of it. It is not often that any one lasts out a generation in the Bowery. Nigger Martha did. Her beginning was way back in the palmy days of Billy McGlory and Owney Geoghegan. Her first remembered appearance was on the occasion of the mock wake they got up at Geoghegan's for Police

Captain Foley when he was broken. That was in the days when dive-keepers made and broke police captains, and made no secret of it. Billy McGlory did not. Ever since, Martha was on the street.

In time she picked up Maggie Mooney, and they got to be chummy. The friendships of the Bowery by night may not be of a very exalted type, but when death breaks them it leaves nothing to the survivor. That is the reason suicides there happen in pairs. The story of Tilly Lorrison and Tricksy came from the Tenderloin not long ago. This one of Maggie Mooney and Nigger Martha was theirs over again.

In each case it was the younger, the one nearest the life that was forever past, who took the step first, in despair. The other followed. To her it was the last link with something that had long ceased to be anything but a dream, which was broken. But without the dream life was unbearable, in the Tenderloin and on the Bowery.

The newsboys were crying their night extras when Undertaker Reardon's wagon jogged across the Bowery with Nigger Martha's body in it. She had given the doctors the slip, as she had the policeman many a time. A friend of hers, an Italian in The Bend, had hired the undertaker to "do it proper," and Nigger Martha was to have a funeral.

All the Bowery came to the wake. The all-nighters from Chatham Square to Bleecker Street trooped up to the top-floor flat in the Forsyth Street tenement where Nigger Martha was laid out. There they sat around, saying little and drinking much. It was not a cheery crowd.

The Bowery by night is not cheerful in the presence of The Mystery. Its one effort is to get away from it, to forget—the thing it can never do. When out of its sight it carouses boisterously, as children sing and shout in the dark to persuade themselves that they are not afraid. And some who hear think it happy.

Sheeny Rose was the master of ceremonies and kept the door. This for a purpose. In life Nigger Martha had one enemy whom she hated—cock-eyed Grace. Like all of her kind, Nigger Martha was superstitious. Grace's evil eye ever brought her bad luck when she crossed her path, and she shunned her as the pestilence. When inadvertently she came upon her, she turned as she passed and spat twice over her left shoulder. And Grace, with white malice in her wicked face, spurned her.

"I don't want," Nigger Martha had said one night in the hearing of Sheeny Rose—"I don't want that cock-eyed thing to look at my body when I am dead. She'll give me hard luck in the grave yet."

And Sheeny Rose was there to see that cock-eyed Grace didn't come to the wake.

She did come. She labored up the long stairs, and knocked, with no one will ever know what purpose in her heart. If it was a last glimmer of good, of forgiveness, it was promptly squelched. It was Sheeny Rose who opened the door.

"You can't come in here," she said curtly. "You know she hated you. She didn't want you to look at her stiff."

Cock-eyed Grace's face grew set with anger. Her curses were heard within. She threatened fight, but dropped it.

"All right," she said as she went down. "I'll fix you, Sheeny Rose!"

It was in the exact spot where Nigger Martha had sat and died that Grace met her enemy the night after the funeral. Lizzie La Blanche, the Marine's girl, was there; Elsie Specs, Little Mame, and Jack the Dog, toughest of all the girls, who for that reason had earned the name of "Mayor of the Bowery." She brooked no rivals. They were all within reach when the two enemies met under the arc light.

Cock-eyed Grace sounded the challenge.

"Now, you little Sheeny Rose," she said, "I'm goin' to do ye fer shuttin' of me out o' Nigger Martha's wake."

With that out came her hatpin, and she made a lunge at Sheeny Rose. The other was on her guard. Hatpin in hand, she parried the thrust and lunged back. In a moment the girls had made a ring about the two, shutting them out of sight. Within it the desperate women thrust and parried, backed and squared off, leaping like tigers when they saw an opening. Their hats had fallen off, their hair was down, and eager hate glittered in their eyes. It was a battle for life; for there is no dagger more deadly than the hatpin these women carry, chiefly as a weapon of defence in the hour of need.

They were evenly matched. Sheeny Rose made up in superior suppleness of limb for the pent-up malice of the other. Grace aimed her thrusts at her opponent's face. She tried to reach her eye. Once the sharp steel just pricked Sheeny Rose's cheek and drew blood. In the next turn Rose's hatpin passed within a quarter-inch of Grace's jugular.

But the blow nearly threw her off her feet, and she was at her enemy's mercy. With an evil oath the fiend thrust full at her face just as the policeman, who had come through the crowd unobserved, so intent was it upon the fight, knocked the steel from her hand.

At midnight two dishevelled hags with faces flattened against the bars of adjoining cells in the police station were hurling sidelong curses at each other and at the maddened doorman. Nigger Martha's wake had received its appropriate and foreordained ending.

WHAT THE CHRISTMAS SUN SAW IN THE TENEMENTS

The December sun shone clear and cold upon the city. It shone upon rich and poor alike. It shone into the homes of the wealthy on the avenues and in the up-town streets, and into courts and alleys hedged in by towering tenements down town. It shone upon throngs of busy holiday shoppers that went out and in at the big stores, carrying bundles big and small, all alike filled with Christmas cheer and kindly messages from Santa Claus.

It shone down so gayly and altogether cheerily there, that wraps and overcoats were unbuttoned for the north wind to toy with. "My, isn't it a nice day?" said one young lady in a fur shoulder cape to a friend, pausing to kiss and compare lists of Christmas gifts.

"Most too hot," was the reply, and the friends passed on. There was warmth within and without. Life was very pleasant under the Christmas sun up on the avenue.

Down in Cherry Street the rays of the sun climbed over a row of tall tenements with an effort that seemed to exhaust all the life that was in them, and fell into a dirty block, half choked with trucks, with ash barrels and rubbish of all sorts, among which the dust was whirled in clouds upon fitful, shivering blasts that searched every nook and cranny of the big barracks. They fell upon a little girl, barefooted and in rags, who struggled out of an alley with a broken pitcher in her grimy fist, against the wind that set down the narrow slit like the draught through a big factory chimney. Just at the mouth of the alley it took her with a sudden whirl, a cyclone of dust and drifting ashes, tossed her fairly off her feet, tore from her grip the threadbare shawl she clutched at her throat, and set her down at the saloon door breathless and half smothered. She had just time to dodge through the storm-doors before another whirlwind swept whistling down the street.

"My, but isn't it cold?" she said, as she shook the dust out of her shawl and set the pitcher down on the bar. "Gimme a pint," laying down a few pennies that had been wrapped in a corner of the shawl, "and mamma says make it good and full."

"All'us the way with youse kids—want a barrel when yees pays fer a pint," growled the bartender. "There, run along, and don't ye hang around that stove no more. We ain't a steam-heatin' the block fer nothin'."

The little girl clutched her shawl and the pitcher, and slipped out into the street where the wind lay in ambush and promptly bore down on her in pillars of whirling dust as soon as she appeared. But the sun that pitied her bare feet and little frozen hands played a trick on old Boreas—it showed her a way between the pillars, and only just her skirt was caught by one and whirled over her head as she dodged into her alley. It peeped after her halfway down its dark depths, where it seemed colder even than in the bleak street, but there it had to leave her.

It did not see her dive through the doorless opening into a hall where no sun-ray had ever entered. It could not have found its way in there had it tried. But up the narrow, squeaking stairs the girl with the pitcher was climbing. Up one flight of stairs, over a knot of children, half babies, pitching pennies on the landing, over wash-tubs and bedsteads that encumbered the next—house-cleaning going on in that "flat"; that is to say, the surplus of bugs was being turned out with petroleum and a feather—up still another, past a half-open door through which came the noise of brawling and curses. She dodged and quickened her step a little until she stood panting before a door on the fourth landing that opened readily as she pushed it with her bare foot.

A room almost devoid of stick or rag one might dignify with the name of furniture. Two chairs, one with a broken back, the other on three legs, beside a rickety table that stood upright only by leaning against the wall. On the unwashed floor a heap of straw covered with dirty bedtick for a bed; a foul-smelling slop-pail in the middle of the room; a crazy stove, and back of it a door or gap opening upon darkness. There was something in there, but what it was could only be surmised from a heavy snore that rose and fell regularly. It was the bedroom of the apartment, windowless, airless, and sunless, but rented at a price a millionnaire would denounce as robbery.

"That you, Liza?" said a voice that discovered a woman bending over the stove. "Run 'n' get the childer. Dinner's ready."

The winter sun glancing down the wall of the opposite tenement, with a hopeless effort to cheer the back yard, might have peeped through the one window of the room in Mrs. McGroarty's "flat," had that window not been coated with the dust of ages, and discovered that dinner party in action. It might have found a score like it in the alley. Four unkempt children, copies each in his or her way of Liza and their mother, Mrs. McGroarty, who "did washing" for a living. A meat bone, a "cut" from the butcher's at four cents a pound, green pickles, stale bread and beer. Beer for the four, a sup all round, the baby included. Why not? It was the one relish the searching ray would have found there. Potatoes were there, too—potatoes and meat! Say not the poor in the tenements are starving. In New York only those starve who cannot get work and have not the courage to beg. Fifty thousand always out of a job, say those who pretend to know. A round half-million asking and getting charity in eight years, say the statisticians of the Charity Organization. Any one can go round and see for himself that no one need starve in New York.

From across the yard the sunbeam, as it crept up the wall, fell slantingly through the attic window whence issued the sound of hammer-blows. A man with a hard face stood in its light, driving nails into the lid of a soap box that was partly filled with straw. Something else was there; as he shifted the lid that didn't fit, the glimpse of sunshine fell across it; it was a dead child, a little baby in a white slip, bedded in straw in a soap box for a coffin. The man was hammering down the lid to take it to the Potter's Field. At the bed knelt the mother, dry-eyed, delirious from starvation that had killed her child. Five hungry, frightened children cowered in the corner, hardly daring to whisper as they looked from the father to the mother in terror.

There was a knock on the door that was drowned once, twice, in the noise of the hammer on the little coffin. Then it was opened gently, and a young woman came in with a basket. A little silver cross shone upon her breast. She went to the poor mother, and, putting her hand soothingly on her head, knelt by her with gentle and loving words. The half-crazed woman listened with averted face, then suddenly burst into tears and hid her throbbing head in the other's lap.

The man stopped hammering and stared fixedly upon the two; the children gathered around with devouring looks as the visitor took from her basket bread, meat, and tea. Just then, with a parting wistful look into the bare attic room, the sun-ray slipped away, lingered for a moment about the coping outside, and fled over the housetops.

As it sped on its winter-day journey, did it shine into any cabin in an Irish bog more desolate than these Cherry Street "homes"? An army of thousands, whose one bright and wholesome memory, only tradition of home, is that poverty-stricken cabin in the desolate bog, are herded in such barracks to-day in New York. Potatoes they have; yes, and meat at four cents—even seven. Beer for a relish—never without beer. But home? The home that was home, even in a bog, with the love of it that has made Ireland immortal and a tower of strength in the midst of her suffering—what of that? There are no homes in New York's poor tenements.

Down the crooked path of the Mulberry Street Bend the sunlight slanted into the heart of New York's Italy. It shone upon bandannas and yellow neckerchiefs; upon swarthy faces and corduroy breeches; upon black-haired girls—mothers at thirteen; upon hosts of bow-legged children rolling in the dirt; upon pedlers' carts and rag-pickers staggering under burdens that threatened to crush them at every step. Shone upon unnumbered Pasquales dwelling, working, idling, and gambling there. Shone upon the filthiest and foulest of New York's tenements, upon Bandit's Roost, upon Bottle Alley, upon the hidden byways that lead to the tramps' burrows. Shone upon the scene of annual infant slaughter. Shone into the foul core of New York's slums that was at last to go to the realm of bad memories because civilized man might not look upon it and live without blushing.

It glanced past the rag-shop in the cellar, whence welled up stenches to poison the town, into an apartment three flights up that held two women, one young, the other old and bent. The young one had a baby at her breast. She was rocking it tenderly in her arms, singing in the soft Italian tongue a lullaby, while the old granny listened eagerly, her elbows on her knees, and a stumpy clay pipe, blackened with age, between her teeth. Her eyes were set on the wall, on which the musty paper hung in tatters, fit frame for the wretched, poverty-stricken room, but they saw neither poverty nor want; her aged limbs felt not the cold draught from without, in which they shivered; she looked far over the seas to sunny Italy, whose music was in her ears.

"O dolce Napoli," she mumbled between her toothless jaws, "O suol beato—"

The song ended in a burst of passionate grief. The old granny and the baby woke up at once. They were not in sunny Italy; not under southern, cloudless skies. They were in "The Bend," in Mulberry Street, and the wintry wind rattled the door as if it would say, in the language of their new home, the land of the free: "Less music! More work! Root, hog, or die!"

Around the corner the sunbeam danced with the wind into Mott Street, lifted the blouse of a Chinaman and made it play tag with his pigtail. It used him so roughly that he was glad to skip from it down a cellar-way that gave out fumes of opium strong enough to scare even the north wind from its purpose. The soles of his felt shoes showed as he disappeared down the ladder that passed for cellar steps. Down there, where daylight never came, a group of yellow, almond-eyed men were bending over a table playing fan-tan. Their very souls were in the game, every faculty of the mind bent on the issue and the stake. The one blouse that was indifferent to what went on was stretched on a mat in a corner. One end of a clumsy pipe was in his mouth, the other held over a little spirit-lamp on the divan on which he lay. Something fluttered in the flame with a pungent, unpleasant smell. The smoker took a long draught, inhaling the white smoke, then sank back on his couch in senseless content.

Upstairs tiptoed the noiseless felt shoes, bent on some house errand, to the "household" floors above, where young white girls from the tenements of The Bend and the East Side live in slavery worse, if not more galling, than any of the galley with ball and chain—the slavery of the pipe. Four, eight, sixteen, twenty odd such "homes" in this tenement, disgracing the very name of home and family, for marriage and troth are not in the bargain.

In one room, between the half-drawn curtains of which the sunbeam works its way in, three girls are lying on as many bunks, smoking all. They are very young, "under age," though each and every one would glibly swear in court to the satisfaction of the police that she is sixteen, and therefore free to make her own bad choice. Of these, one was brought up among the rugged hills of Maine; the other two are from the tenement crowds, hardly missed there. But their companion? She is twirling the sticky brown pill over the lamp, preparing to fill the bowl of her pipe with it. As she does so, the sunbeam dances across the bed, kisses the red spot on her cheek that betrays the secret her tyrant long has known,—though to her it is hidden yet,—that the pipe has claimed its victim and soon will pass it on to the Potter's Field.

"Nell," says one of her chums in the other bunk, something stirred within her by the flash, "Nell, did you hear from the old farm to home since you come here?"

Nell turns half around, with the toasting-stick in her hand, an ugly look on her wasted features, a vile oath on her lips.

"To hell with the old farm," she says, and putting the pipe to her mouth inhales it all, every bit, in one long breath, then falls back on her pillow in drunken stupor.

That is what the sun of a winter day saw and heard in Mott Street.

It had travelled far toward the west, searching many dark corners and vainly seeking entry to others; had gilded with equal impartiality the spires of five hundred churches and the tin cornices of thirty thousand tenements, with their million tenants and more; had smiled courage and cheer to patient mothers trying to make the most of life in the teeming crowds, that had too little sunshine by far; hope to toiling fathers striving early and late for bread to fill the many mouths clamoring to be fed.

The brief December day was far spent. Now its rays fell across the North River and lighted up the windows of the tenements in Hell's Kitchen and Poverty Gap. In the Gap especially they made a brave show; the windows of the crazy old frame-house under the big tree that sat back from the street looked as if they were made of beaten gold. But the glory did not cross the threshold. Within it was dark and dreary and cold. The room at the foot of the rickety, patched stairs was empty. The last tenant was beaten to death by her husband in his drunken fury. The sun's rays shunned the spot ever after, though it was long since it could have made out the red daub from the mould on the rotten floor.

Upstairs, in the cold attic, where the wind wailed mournfully through every open crack, a little girl sat sobbing as if her heart would break. She hugged an old doll to her breast. The paint was gone from its face; the yellow hair was in a tangle; its clothes hung in rags. But she only hugged it closer. It was her doll. They had been friends so long, shared hunger and hardship together, and now—

Her tears fell faster. One drop trembled upon the wan cheek of the doll. The last sunbeam shot athwart it and made it glisten like a priceless jewel. Its glory grew and filled the room. Gone were the black walls, the darkness, and the cold. There was warmth and light and joy. Merry voices and glad faces were all about. A flock of children danced with gleeful shouts about a great Christmas tree in the middle of the floor. Upon its branches hung drums and trumpets and toys, and countless candles gleamed like beautiful stars. Farthest up, at the very top, her doll, her very own, with arms outstretched, as if appealing to be taken down and hugged. She knew it, knew the mission-school that had seen her first and only real Christmas, knew the gentle face of her teacher, and the writing on the wall she had taught her to spell out: "In His name." His name, who, she had said, was all little children's friend. Was He also her dolly's friend, and would He know it among the strange people?

The light went out; the glory faded. The bare room, only colder and more cheerless than before, was left. The child shivered. Only that morning the doctor had told her mother that she must have medicine and food and warmth, or she must go to the great hospital where papa had gone before, when their money was all spent. Sorrow and want had laid the mother upon the bed he had barely left. Every stick of furniture, every stitch of clothing on which money could be borrowed, had gone to the pawnbroker. Last of all, she had carried mamma's wedding-ring to pay the druggist. Now there was no more left, and they had nothing to eat. In a little while mamma would wake up, hungry.

The little girl smothered a last sob and rose quickly. She wrapped the doll in a threadbare shawl as well as she could, tiptoed to the door, and listened a moment to the feeble breathing of the sick mother within. Then she went out, shutting the door softly behind her, lest she wake her.

Up the street she went, the way she knew so well, one block and a turn round the saloon corner, the sunset glow kissing the track of her bare feet in the snow as she went, to a door that rang a noisy bell as she opened it and went in. A musty smell filled the close room. Packages, great and small, lay piled high on shelves behind the worn counter. A slovenly woman was haggling with the pawnbroker about the money for a skirt she had brought to pledge.

"Not a cent more than a quarter," he said, contemptuously, tossing the garment aside. "It's half worn out it is, dragging it back and forth over the counter these six months. Take it or leave it. Hallo! What have we here? Little Finnegan, eh? Your mother not dead yet? It's in the poorhouse ye will be if she lasts much longer. What the—"

He had taken the package from the trembling child's hand—the precious doll—and unrolled the shawl. A moment he stood staring in dumb amazement at its contents. Then he caught it up and flung it with an angry oath upon the floor, where it was shivered against the coal-box.

"Get out o' here, ye Finnegan brat," he shouted; "I'll tache ye to come a-guyin' o' me. I'll—"

The door closed with a bang upon the frightened child, alone in the cold night. The sun saw not its home-coming. It had hidden behind the night clouds, weary of the sight of man and his cruelty.

Evening had worn into night. The busy city slept. Down by the wharves, now deserted, a poor boy sat on the bulwark, hungry, foot-sore, and shivering with cold. He sat thinking of friends and home, thousands of miles away over the sea, whom he had left six months before to go among strangers. He had been alone ever since, but never more so than that night. His money gone, no work to be found, he had slept in the streets for nights. That day he had eaten nothing; he would rather die than beg, and one of the two he must do soon.

There was the dark river rushing at his feet; the swirl of the unseen waters whispered to him of rest and peace he had not known since—it was so cold—and who was there to care, he thought bitterly. No one would ever know. He moved a little nearer the edge, and listened more intently.

A low whine fell on his ear, and a cold, wet face was pressed against his. A little crippled dog that had been crouching silently beside him nestled in his lap. He had picked it up in the street, as forlorn and friendless as himself, and it had stayed by him. Its touch recalled him to himself. He got up hastily, and, taking the dog in his arms, went to the police station near by, and asked for shelter. It was the first time he had accepted even such charity, and as he lay down on his rough plank he hugged a little gold locket he wore around his neck, the last link with better days, and thought with a hard sob of home. In the middle of the night he awoke with a start. The locket was gone. One of the tramps who slept with him had stolen it. With bitter tears he went up and complained to the Sergeant at the desk, and the Sergeant ordered him to be kicked out into the street as a liar, if not a thief. How should a tramp boy have come honestly by a gold locket? The doorman put him out as he was bidden, and when the little dog showed its teeth, a policeman seized it and clubbed it to death on the step.

*** **

Far from the slumbering city the rising moon shines over a wide expanse of glistening water. It silvers the snow upon a barren heath between two shores, and shortens with each passing minute the shadows of countless headstones that bear no names, only numbers. The breakers that beat against the bluff wake not those who sleep there. In the deep trenches they lie, shoulder to shoulder, an army of brothers, homeless in life, but here at rest and at peace. A great cross stands upon the lonely shore. The moon sheds its rays upon it in silent benediction and floods the garden of the unknown, unmourned dead with its soft light. Out on the Sound the fishermen see it flashing white against the starlit sky, and bare their heads reverently as their boats speed by, borne upon the wings of the west wind.

MIDWINTER IN NEW YORK

The very earliest impression I received of America's metropolis was through a print in my child's picture-book that was entitled "Winter in New York." It showed a sleighing party, or half a dozen such, muffled to the ears in furs, and racing with grim determination for some place or another that lay beyond the page, wrapped in the mystery which so tickles the childish fancy. For it was clear to me that it was not accident that they were all going the same way. There was evidently some prize away off there in the waste of snow that beckoned them on. The text gave me no clew to what it was. It only confirmed the impression, which was strengthened by the introduction of a half-naked savage who shivered most wofully in the foreground, that New York was somewhere within the arctic circle and a perfect paradise for a healthy boy, who takes to snow as naturally as a duck takes to water. I do not know how the discovery that they were probably making for Gabe Case's and his bottle of champagne, which always awaited the first sleigh on the road, would have struck me in those days. Most likely as a grievous disappointment; for my fancy, busy ever with Uncas and Chingachgook and Natty Bumppo, had certainly a buffalo hunt, or an ambush, or, at the very least, a big fire, ready at the end of the road. But such is life. Its most cherished hopes have to be surrendered one by one to the prosy facts of every-day existence. I recall distinctly how it cut me to the heart when I first walked up Broadway, with an immense navy pistol strapped around my waist, to find it a paved street, actually paved, with no buffaloes in sight and not a red man or a beaver hut.

However, life has its compensations also. At fifty I am as willing to surrender the arctic circle as I was hopeful of it at ten, with the price of coal in the chronic plight of my little boy when he has a troublesome hitch in his trousers: "O dear me! my pants hang up and don't hang down." And Gabe Case's is a most welcome exchange to me for the ambush, since I have left out the pistol and the rest of the armament. I listen to the stories of the oldest inhabitant, of the winters when "the snow lay to the second-story windows in the Bowery," with the fervent wish that they may never come back, and secretly gloat over his wail that the seasons have changed and are not what they were. The man who exuberantly proclaims that New York is getting to have the finest winter-resort climate in the world is my friend, and I do not care if I never see another snowball. Alas, yes! though Deerslayer and I are still on the old terms, I fear the evidence is that I am growing old.

In the midst of the rejoicing comes old Boreas, as last winter, for instance, and blows down my house of cards. Just when we thought ourselves safe in referring to the great blizzard as a monstrous, unheard-of thing, and were dwelling securely in the memory of how we gathered violets in the woods out in Queens and killed mosquitoes in the house in Christmas week, comes grim winter and locks the rivers and buries us up to the neck in snow, before the Thanksgiving dinner is cold. Then the seasons when Gabe's much-coveted bottle stood unclaimed on the shelf in its bravery of fine ribbons till far into the New Year, and was won then literally "by a scratch" on a road hardly downy with white, seem like a tale that is told, and we realize that latitude does not unaided make temperature. It is only in exceptional winters, after all, that we class for a brief spell with Naples. Greenland and the polar stream are never long in asserting their claim and Santa Claus's to unchecked progress to our hearths.

And now, when one comes to think of it, who would say them nay for the sake of a ton of coal, or twenty? If one grows old, he is still young in his children. There is the smallest tot at this very moment sliding under my window with shrieks of delight, in the first fall of the season, though the November election is barely a week gone, and snowballing the hired girl in quite the fashion of the good old days, with the grocer's clerk stamping his feet at the back gate and roaring out his enjoyment at her plight in a key only Jack Frost has in keeping. A hundred thousand pairs of boys' eyes are stealing anxious glances toward school windows to-day, lest the storm cease before they are let out, and scant attention is paid to the morning's lessons, I will warrant. Who would exchange the bob-sled and the slide and the hurricane delights of coasting for eternal summer and magnolias in January? Not I, for one—not yet. Human nature is, after all, more robust than it seems at the study fire. I never declared in the board of deacons why I stood up so stoutly for the minister we called that winter to our little church,—with deacons discretion is sometimes quite the best part of valor,—but I am not ashamed of it. It was the night when we were going home, and neighbor Connery gave us a ride on his new bob down that splendid hill,—the whole board, men and women,—that I judged him for what he really was—that resolute leg out behind that kept us on our course as straight as a die, rounding every log and reef with the skill of a river pilot, never flinching once. It was the leg that did it; but it was, as I thought, an index to the whole man.

Discomfort and suffering are usually the ideas associated with deep winter in a great city like New York, and there is a deal of it—discomfort to us all and suffering among the poor. The mere statement that the Street-Cleaning Department last winter carted away and dumped into the river 1,679,087 cubic yards of snow at thirty cents a yard, and was then hotly blamed for leaving us in the slush, fairly measures the one and is enough to set the taxpayer to thinking. The suffering in the tenements of the poor is as real, but even their black cloud is not without its silver lining. It calls out among those who have much as tender a charity as is ever alive among those who have little or nothing and who know one another for brothers without needing the reminder of a severe cold snap or a big storm to tell them of it. More money was poured into the coffers of the charitable societies in the last big cold snap than they could use for emergency relief; and the reckless advertising in sensational newspapers of the starvation that was said to be abroad called forth an emphatic protest from representatives of the social settlements and of the Charity Organization Society, who were in immediate touch with the poor. The old question whether a heavy fall of snow does not more than make up to the poor man the suffering it causes received a wide discussion at the time, but in the end was left open as always. The simple truth is that it brings its own relief to those who are always just on the verge. It sets them to work, and the charity visitor sees the effect in wages coming in, even if only for a brief season. The far greater loss which it causes, and which the visitor does not see, is to those who are regularly employed, and with whom she has therefore no concern, in suspending all other kinds of outdoor work than snow-shovelling.

Take it all together, and I do not believe even an unusual spell of winter carries in its trail in New York such hopeless martyrdom to the poor as in Old World cities, London for instance. There is something in the clear skies and bracing air of our city that keeps the spirits up to the successful defiance of anything short of actual hunger. There abides with me from days and nights of poking about in dark London alleys an impression of black and sooty rooms, and discouraged, red-eyed women blowing ever upon smouldering fires, that is disheartening beyond anything I ever encountered in the dreariest tenements here. Outside, the streets lay buried in fog and slush that brought no relief to the feelings.

Misery enough I have seen in New York's tenements; but deep as the shadows are in the winter picture of it, it has no such darkness as that. The newsboys and the sandwich-men warming themselves upon the cellar gratings in Twenty-third Street and elsewhere have oftener than not a ready joke to crack with the passer-by, or a little jig step to relieve their feelings and restore the circulation. The very tramp who hangs by his arms on the window-bars of the power-house at Houston Street and Broadway indulges in safe repartee with the engineer down in the depths, and chuckles at being more than a match for him. Down there it is always July, rage the storm king ever so boisterously up on the level. The windows on the Mercer Street corner of the building are always open—or else there are no windows. The spaces between the bars admit a man's arm very handily, and as a result there are always on cold nights as many hands pointing downward at the engineer and his boilers as there are openings in the iron fence. The tramps sleep, so suspended the night long, toasting themselves alternately on front and back.

The good humor under untoward circumstances that is one of the traits of our people never comes out so strongly as when winter blocks river and harbor with ice and causes no end of trouble and inconvenience to the vast army of workers which daily invades New York in the morning and departs again with the gathering twilight. The five-minute trip across sometimes takes hours then, and there is never any telling where one is likely to land, once the boat is in the stream. I have, on one occasion, spent nearly six hours on an East River ferry-boat, trying to cross to Fulton Street in Brooklyn, during which time we circumnavigated Governor's Island and made an involuntary excursion down the bay. It was during the Beecher trial, and we had a number of the lawyers on both sides on board, so that the court had to adjourn that day while we tried the case among the ice-floes. But though the loss of time was very great, yet I saw no sign of annoyance among the passengers through all that trip. Everybody made the best of a bad bargain.

Many a time since, have I stood jammed in a hungry and tired crowd on the Thirty-fourth Street ferry for an hour at a time, watching the vain efforts of the pilot to make a landing, while train after train went out with no passengers, and have listened to the laughter and groans that heralded each failure. Then, when at last the boat touched the end of the slip and one man after another climbed upon the swaying piles and groped his perilous way toward the shore, the cheers that arose and followed them on their way, with everybody offering advice and encouragement, and accepting it in the same good-humored way!

In the two big snow-storms of a recent winter, when traffic was for a season interrupted, and in the great blizzard of 1888, when it was completely suspended, even on the elevated road, and news reached us from Boston only by cable via London, it was laughing and snowballing crowds one encountered plodding through the drifts. It was as if real relief had come with the lifting of the strain of our modern life and the momentary relapse into the slow-going way of our fathers. Out in Queens, where we were snow-bound for days, we went about digging one another out and behaving like a lot of boys, once we had made sure that the office would have to mind itself for a season.

It is, however, not to the outlying boroughs one has to go if he wishes to catch the real human spirit that is abroad in the city in a snow-storm, or to the avenues where the rich live, though the snow to them might well be a real luxury; or even to the rivers, attractive as they are in the wild grandeur of arctic festooning from mastheads and rigging; with incoming steamers, armored in shining white, picking their way as circumspectly among the floes as if they were navigating Baffin's Bay instead of the Hudson River; and with their swarms of swift sea-gulls, some of them spotless white, others as rusty and dusty as the scavengers whom for the time being they replace ineffectually, all of them greedily intent upon wresting from the stream the food which they no longer find outside the Hook. I should like you well enough to linger with me on the river till the storm is over, and watch the marvellous sunsets that flood the western sky with colors of green and gold which no painter's brush ever matched; and when night has dropped the curtain, to see the lights flashing forth from the tall buildings in story after story until it is as if the fairyland of our childhood's dreams lay there upon the brooding waters within grasp of mortal hands.

Beautiful as these are, it is to none of them I should take you, nevertheless, to show you the spirit of winter in New York. Not to "the road," where the traditional strife for the magnum of champagne is waged still; or to that other road farther east upon which the young—and the old, too, for that matter—take straw-rides to City Island, there to eat clam chowder, the like of which is not to be found, it is said, in or out of Manhattan. I should lead you, instead, down among the tenements, where, mayhap, you thought to find only misery and gloom, and bid you observe what goes on there.

All night the snow fell steadily and silently, sifting into each nook and corner and searching out every dark spot, until when the day came it dawned upon a city mantled in spotless white, all the dirt and the squalor and the ugliness gone out of it, and all the harsh sounds of mean streets hushed. The storekeeper opened his door and shivered as he thought of the job of shovelling, with the policeman and his "notice" to hurry it up; shivered more as he heard the small boy on the stairs with the premonitory note of trouble in his exultant yell, and took a firmer grip on his broom. But his alarm was needless. The boy had other feuds on hand. His gang had been feeding fat an ancient grudge against the boys in the next block or the block beyond, waiting for the first storm to wipe it out in snow, and the day opened with a brisk skirmish between the opposing hosts. In the school the plans for the campaign were perfected, and when it was out they met in the White Garden, known to the directory as Tompkins Square, the traditional duelling-ground of the lower East Side; and there ensued such a battle as Homer would have loved to sing.

Full many a lad fell on the battlements that were thrown up in haste, only to rise again and fight until a "soaker," wrung out in the gutter and laid away to harden in the frost, caught him in the eye and sent him to the rear, a reeling, bawling invalid, but prouder of his hurt than any veteran of his scars, just as his gang carried the band stand by storm and drove the Seventh-streeters from the Garden in ignominious flight. That night the gang celebrated the victory with a mighty bonfire, while the beaten one, viewing the celebration from afar, nursed its bruises and its wrath, and recruited its hosts for the morrow. And on the next night, behold! the bonfire burned in Seventh Street and not in Eleventh. The fortunes of war are proverbially fickle. The band stand in the Garden has been taken many a time since the police took it by storm in battle with the mob in the seventies, but no mob has succeeded that one to clamor for "bread or blood." It may be that the snow-fights have been a kind of safety-valve for the young blood to keep it from worse mischief later on. There are worse things in the world than to let the boys have a fling where no greater harm can befall than a bruised eye or a strained thumb.

In the corner where the fight did not rage, and in a hundred back yards, smaller bands of boys and girls were busy rolling huge balls into a mighty snow man with a broom for a gun and bits of purloined coal for eyes and nose, and making mock assaults upon it and upon one another, just as the dainty little darlings in curls and leggings were doing in the up-town streets, but with ever so much more zest in their play. Their screams of delight rose to the many windows in the tenements, from which the mothers were exchanging views with next-door neighbors as to the probable duration of the "spell o' weather," and John's or Pat's chance of getting or losing a job in consequence. The snow man stood there till long after all doubts were settled on these mooted points, falling slowly into helpless decrepitude in spite of occasional patching. But long before that time the frost succeeding the snow had paved the way for coasting in the hilly streets, and discovered countless "slides" in those that were flat, to the huge delight of the small boy and the discomfiture of his unsuspecting elders. With all the sedateness of my fifty years, I confess that I cannot to this day resist a "slide" in a tenement street, with its unending string of boys and girls going down it with mighty whoops. I am bound to join in, spectacles, umbrella, and all, at the risk of literally going down in a heap with the lot.

There is one over on First Avenue, on the way I usually take when I go home. It begins at a hydrant, which I suspect has had something to do in more than one way with its beginning, and runs down fully half a block. If some of my dignified associates on various committees of sobriety beyond reproach could see me "take it" not once, but two or three times, with a ragged urchin clinging to each of the skirts of my coat, I am afraid—I am afraid I might lose caste, to put it mildly. But the children enjoy it, and so do I, nearly as much as the little fellows in the next block enjoy their "skating on one" in the gutter, with little skids of wood twisted in the straps to hold the skate on tight.

In sight of my slide I pass after a big storm between towering walls of snow in front of a public school which for years was the only one in the city that had an outdoor playground. It was wrested from the dead for the benefit of the living, by the condemnation of an old burying-ground, after years of effort. The school has ever since been one of the brightest, most successful in town. The snowbanks exhibit the handiwork of the boys, all of them from the surrounding tenements. They are shaped into regular walls with parapets cunningly wrought and sometimes with no little artistic effect. One winter the walls were much higher than a man's head, and the passageways between them so narrow that a curious accident happened, which came near being fatal. A closed wagon with a cargo of ginger-beer was caught between them and upset. The beer popped, and the driver's boy, who was inside and unable to get out, was rescued only with much trouble from the double peril of being smothered and drowned in the sudden flood.

But the coasting! Let any one who wishes to see real democratic New York at play take a trip on such a night through the up-town streets that dip east and west into the great arteries of traffic, and watch the sights there when young America is in its glory. Only where there is danger from railroad crossings do the police interfere to stop the fun. In all other blocks they discreetly close an eye, or look the other way. New York is full of the most magnificent coasting-slides, and there is not one of them that is not worked overtime when the snow is on the ground. There are possibilities in the slopes of the "Acropolis" and the Cathedral Parkway as yet undeveloped to their full extent; but wherever the population crowds, it turns out without stint to enjoy the fun whenever and as soon as occasion offers.

There is a hill over on Avenue A, near by the East River Park, that is typical in more ways than one. To it come the children of the tenements with their bob-sleds and "belly-whoppers" made up of bits of board, sometimes without runners, and the girls from the fine houses facing the park and up along Eighty-sixth Street, in their toboggan togs with caps and tassels, and chaperoned by their young fellows, just a little disposed to turn up their noses at the motley show. But they soon forget about that in the fun of the game. Down they go, rich and poor, boys and girls, men and women, with yells of delight as the snow seems to fly from under them, and the twinkling lights far up the avenue come nearer and nearer with lightning speed. The slide is lined on both sides with a joyous throng of their elders, who laugh and applaud equally the poor sled and the flexible flyer of prouder pedigree, urging on the returning horde that toils panting up the steep to take its place in the line once more. Till far into the young day does the avenue resound with the merriment of the people's winter carnival.

On the railroad streets the storekeeper is still battling "between calls" with the last of the day's fall, fervently wishing it may be the last of the season's, when whir! comes the big sweeper along the track, raising a whirlwind of snow and dirt that bespatters him and his newly cleaned flags with stray clods from its brooms, until, out of patience, and seized at last, in spite of himself, by the spirit of the thing, he drops broom and shovel and joins the children in pelting the sweeper in turn. The motorman ducks his head, humps his shoulders, and grins. The whirlwind sweeps on, followed by a shower of snowballs, and vanishes in the dim distance.

One of the most impressive sights of winter in New York has gone with so much else that was picturesque, in this age of results, and will never be seen in our streets again. The old horse-plough that used to come with rattle and bang and clangor of bells, drawn by five spans of big horses, the pick of the stables, wrapped in a cloud of steam, and that never failed to draw a crowd where it went, is no more. The rush and the swing of the long line, the crack of the driver's mighty whip and his warning shouts to "Jack" or "Pete" to pull and keep step, the steady chop-chop thud of the sand-shaker, will be seen and heard no more. In the place of the horse-plough has come the electric sweeper, a less showy but a good deal more effective device.

The plough itself is gone. It has been retired by the railroads as useless in practice except to remove great masses of snow, which are not allowed to accumulate nowadays, if it can be helped. The share could be lowered only to within four or five inches of the ground, while the wheel-brooms of the sweeper "sweep between every stone," making a clean job of it. Lacking the life of the horse-plough, it is suggestive of concentrated force far beyond anything in the elaborate show of its predecessor.

The change suggests, not inaptly, the evolution of the old ship of the line under full canvas into the modern man-of-war, sailless and grim, and the conceit is strengthened by the warlike build of the electric sweeper. It is easy to imagine the iron flanges that sweep the snow from the track to be rammers for a combat at close quarters, and the canvas hangers that shield the brushes, torpedo-nets for defence against a hidden enemy. The motorman on the working end of the sweeper looks like nothing so much as the captain on the bridge of a man-of-war, and he conducts himself with the same imperturbable calm under the petty assaults of the guerillas of the street.

From the moment a storm breaks till the last flake has fallen, the sweepers are run unceasingly over the tracks of the railroads, each in its own division, which it is its business to keep clear. The track is all the companies have to mind. There was a law, or a rule, or an understanding, nobody seems to know exactly which, that they were to sweep also between the tracks, and two feet on each side, in return for their franchises; but in effect this proved impracticable. It was never done. Under the late Colonel Waring the Street-Cleaning Department came to an understanding with the railroad companies under which they clear certain streets, not on their routes, that are computed to have a surface space equal to that which they would have had to clean had they lived up to the old rule. The department in its turn removes the accumulations piled up by their sweepers, unless a providential thaw gets ahead of it.

Removing the snow after a big storm from the streets of New York, or even from an appreciable number of them, is a task beside which the cleaning of the Augean stables was a mean and petty affair. In dealing with the dirt, Hercules's expedient has sometimes been attempted, with more or less success; but not even turning the East River into our streets would rid them of the snow. Though in the last severe winter the department employed at times as many as four thousand extra men and all the carts that were to be drummed up in the city, carting away, as I have said, the enormous total of more than a million and a half cubic yards of snow, every citizen knows, and testified loudly at the time, that it all hardly scratched the ground. The problem is one of the many great ones of modern city life which our age of invention must bequeath unsolved to the dawning century.

In the Street-Cleaning Department's service the snow-plough holds yet its ancient place of usefulness. Eleven of them are kept for use in Manhattan and the Bronx alone. The service to which they are put is to clear at the shortest notice, not the travelled avenues where the railroad sweepers run, but the side streets that lead from these to the fire-engine and truck-houses, to break a way for the apparatus for the emergency that is sure to come. Upon the paths so made the engines make straight for the railroad tracks when called out, and follow these to the fire.

A cold snap inevitably brings a "run" of fires in its train. Stoves are urged to do their utmost all day, and heaped full of coal to keep overnight. The fire finds at last the weak point in the flue, and mischief is abroad. Then it is that the firemen are put upon their mettle, and then it is, too, that they show of what stuff they are made. In none of the three big blizzards within the memory of us all did any fire "get away" from them. During the storm of 1888, when the streets were nearly impassable for three whole days, they were called out to fight forty-five fires, any one of which might have threatened the city had it been allowed to get beyond control; but they smothered them all within the walls where they started. It was the same in the bad winter I spoke of. In one blizzard the men of Truck 7 got only four hours' sleep in four days. When they were not putting out fires they were compelled to turn in and shovel snow to help the paralyzed Street-Cleaning Department clear the way for their trucks. Their plight was virtually that of all the rest.

What Colonel Roosevelt said of his Rough Riders after the fight in the trenches before Santiago, that it is the test of men's nerve to have them roused up at three o'clock in the morning, hungry and cold, to fight an enemy attacking in the dark, and then have them all run the same way,—forward,—is true of the firemen as well, and, like the Rough Riders, they never failed when the test came. The firemen going to the front at the tap of the bell, no less surely to grapple with lurking death than the men who faced Mauser bullets, but with none of the incidents of glorious war, the flag, the hurrah, and all the things that fire a soldier's heart, to urge them on,—clinging, half naked, with numb fingers to the ladders as best they can while trying to put on their stiff and frozen garments,—is one of the sights that make one proud of being a man. To see them in action, dripping icicles from helmet and coat, high upon the ladder, perhaps incased in solid ice and frozen to the rungs, yet holding the stream as steady to its work as if the spray from the nozzle did not fall upon them in showers of stinging hail, is very apt to make a man devoutly thankful that it is not his lot to fight fires in winter. It is only a few winters since, at the burning of a South Street warehouse, two pipemen had to be chopped from their ladder with axes, so thick was the armor of ice that had formed about and upon them while they worked.

The terrible beauty of such a sight is very vivid in my memory. It was on the morning when Chief Bresnan and Foreman Rooney went down with half a dozen of their men in the collapse of the roof in a burning factory. The men of the rank and file hewed their way through to the open with their axes. The chief and the foreman were caught under the big water-tank, the wooden supports of which had been burned away, and were killed. They were still lying under the wreck when I came. The fire was out. The water running over the edge of the tank had frozen into huge icicles that hung like a great white shroud over the bier of the two dead heroes. It was a gas-fixture factory, and the hundreds of pipes, twisted into all manner of fantastic shapes of glittering ice, lent a most weird effect to the sorrowful scene. I can still see Chief Gicquel, all smoke-begrimed, and with the tears streaming down his big, manly face,—poor Gicquel! he went to join his brothers in so many a hard fight only a little while after,—pointing back toward the wreck with the choking words, "They are in there!" They had fought their last fight and won, as they ever did, even if they did give their lives for the victory. Greater end no fireman could crave.

Winter in New York has its hardships and toil, and it has its joys as well, among rich and poor. Grim and relentless, it is beautiful at all times until man puts his befouling hand upon the landscape it paints in street and alley, where poetry is never at home in summer. The great city lying silent under its soft white blanket at night, with its myriad of lights twinkling and rivalling the stars, is beautiful beyond compare. Go watch the moonlight on forest and lake in the park, when the last straggler has gone and the tramp of the lonely policeman's horse has died away under the hill; listen to the whisper of the trees, all shining with dew of Boreas's breath: of the dreams they dream in their long sleep, of the dawn that is coming, the warm sunlight of spring, and say that life is not worth living in America's metropolis, even in winter, whatever the price of coal, and I shall tell you that you are fit for nothing but treason, stratagem, and spoils; for you have no music in your soul.

A CHIP FROM THE MAELSTROM

"The cop just sceert her to death, that's what he done. For Gawd's sake, boss, don't let on I tole you."

The negro, stopping suddenly in his game of craps in the Pell Street back yard, glanced up with a look of agonized entreaty. Discovering no such fell purpose in his questioner's face, he added quickly, reassured:—

"And if he asks if you seed me a-playing craps, say no, not on yer life, boss, will yer?" And he resumed the game where he left off.

An hour before he had seen Maggie Lynch die in that hallway, and it was of her he spoke. She belonged to the tenement and to Pell Street, as he did himself. They were part of it while they lived, with all that that implied; when they died, to make part of it again, reorganized and closing ranks in the trench on Hart's Island. It is only the Celestials in Pell Street who escape the trench. The others are booked for it from the day they are pushed out from the rapids of the Bowery into this maelstrom that sucks under all it seizes. Thenceforward they come to the surface only at intervals in the police courts, each time more forlorn, but not more hopeless, until at last they disappear and are heard of no more.

When Maggie Lynch turned the corner no one there knows. The street keeps no reckoning, and it doesn't matter. She took her place unchallenged, and her "character" was registered in due time. It was good. Even Pell Street has its degrees and its standard of perfection. The standard's strong point is contempt of the Chinese, who are hosts in Pell Street. Maggie Lynch came to be known as homeless, without a man, though with the prospects of motherhood approaching, yet she "had never lived with a Chink." To Pell Street that was heroic. It would have forgiven all the rest, had there been anything to forgive. But there was not. Whatever else may be, cant is not among the vices of Pell Street.

And it is well. Maggie Lynch lived with the Cuffs on the top floor of No. 21 until the Cuffs moved. They left an old lounge they didn't want, and Maggie. Maggie was sick, and the housekeeper had no heart to put her out. Heart sometimes survives in the slums, even in Pell Street, long after respectability has been hopelessly smothered. It provided shelter and a bed for Maggie when her only friends deserted her. In return she did what she could, helping about the hall and stairs. Queer that gratitude should be another of the virtues the slum has no power to smother, though dive and brothel and the scorn of the good do their best, working together.

There was an old mattress that had to be burned, and Maggie dragged it down with an effort. She took it out in the street, and there set it on fire. It burned and blazed high in the narrow street. The policeman saw the sheen in the windows on the opposite side of the way, and saw the danger of it as he came around the corner. Maggie did not notice him till he was right behind her. She gave a great start when he spoke to her.

"I've a good mind to lock you up for this," he said as he stamped out the fire. "Don't you know it's against the law?"

The negro heard it and saw Maggie stagger toward the door, with her hand pressed upon her heart, as the policeman went away down the street. On the threshold she stopped, panting.

"My Gawd, that cop frightened me!" she said, and sat down on the door-step.

A tenant who came out saw that she was ill, and helped her into the hall. She gasped once or twice, and then lay back, dead.

Word went around to the Elizabeth Street station, and was sent on from there with an order for the dead-wagon. Maggie's turn had come for the ride up the Sound. She was as good as checked for the Potter's Field, but Pell Street made an effort and came up almost to Maggie's standard.

Even while the dead-wagon was rattling down the Bowery, one of the tenants ran all the way to Henry Street, where he had heard that Maggie's father lived, and brought him to the police station. The old man wiped his eyes as he gazed upon his child, dead in her sins.

"She had a good home," he said to Captain Young, "but she didn't know it, and she wouldn't stay. Send her home, and I will bury her with her mother."

The Potter's Field was cheated out of a victim, and by Pell Street. But the maelstrom grinds on and on.

SARAH JOYCE'S HUSBANDS

Policeman Muller had run against a boisterous crowd surrounding a drunken woman at Prince Street and the Bowery. When he joined the crowd it scattered, but got together again before it had run half a block, and slunk after him and his prisoner to the Mulberry Street station. There Sergeant Woodruff learned by questioning the woman that she was Mary Donovan and had come down from Westchester to have a holiday. She had had it without a doubt. The Sergeant ordered her to be locked up for safe-keeping, when, unexpectedly, objection was made.

A small lot of the crowd had picked up courage to come into the station to see what became of the prisoner. From out of this, one spoke up: "Don't lock that woman up; she is my wife."

"Eh," said the Sergeant, "and who are you?"

The man said he was George Reilly and a salesman. The prisoner had given her name as Mary Donovan and said she was single. The Sergeant drew Mr. Reilly's attention to the street door, which was there for his accommodation, but he did not take the hint. He became so abusive that he, too, was locked up, still protesting that the woman was his wife.

She had gone on her way to Elizabeth Street, where there is a matron, to be locked up there; and the objections of Mr. Reilly having been silenced at last, peace was descending once more upon the station-house, when the door was opened, and a man with a swagger entered.

"Got that woman locked up here?" he demanded.

"What woman?" asked the Sergeant, looking up.

"Her what Muller took in."

"Well," said the Sergeant, looking over the desk, "what of her?"

"I want her out; she is my wife. She—"

The Sergeant rang his bell. "Here, lock this man up with that woman's other husband," he said, pointing to the stranger.

The fellow ran out just in time, as the doorman made a grab for him. The Sergeant drew a tired breath and picked up the ruler to make a red line in his blotter. There was a brisk step, a rap, and a young fellow stood in the open door.

"Say, Serg," he began.

The Sergeant reached with his left hand for the inkstand, while his right clutched the ruler. He never took his eyes off the stranger.

"Say," wheedled he, glancing around and seeing no trap, "Serg, I say: that woman w'at's locked up, she's—"

"She's what?" asked the Sergeant, getting the range as well as he could.

"My wife," said the fellow.

There was a bang, the slamming of a door, and the room was empty. The doorman came running in, looked out, and up and down the street. But nothing was to be seen. There is no record of what became of the third husband of Mary Donovan.

The first slept serenely in the jail. The woman herself, when she saw the iron bars in the Elizabeth Street station, fell into hysterics and was taken to the Hudson Street Hospital.

Reilly was arraigned in the Tombs Police Court in the morning. He paid his fine and left, protesting that he was her only husband.

He had not been gone ten minutes when Claimant No. 4 entered.

"Was Sarah Joyce brought here?" he asked Clerk Betts.

The clerk couldn't find the name.

"Look for Mary Donovan," said No. 4.

"Who are you?" asked the clerk.

"I am Sarah's husband," was the answer.

Clerk Betts smiled, and told the man the story of the other three.

"Well, I am blamed," he said.

MERRY CHRISTMAS IN THE TENEMENTS

It was just a sprig of holly, with scarlet berries showing against the green, stuck in, by one of the office boys probably, behind the sign that pointed the way up to the editorial rooms. There was no reason why it should have made me start when I came suddenly upon it at the turn of the stairs; but it did. Perhaps it was because that dingy hall, given over to dust and draughts all the days of the year, was the last place in which I expected to meet with any sign of Christmas; perhaps it was because I myself had nearly forgotten the holiday. Whatever the cause, it gave me quite a turn.

I stood, and stared at it. It looked dry, almost withered. Probably it had come a long way. Not much holly grows about Printing-House Square, except in the colored supplements, and that is scarcely of a kind to stir tender memories. Withered and dry, this did. I thought, with a twinge of conscience, of secret little conclaves of my children, of private views of things hidden from mamma at the bottom of drawers, of wild flights when papa appeared unbidden in the door, which I had allowed for once to pass unheeded. Absorbed in the business of the office, I had hardly thought of Christmas coming on, until now it was here. And this sprig of holly on the wall that had come to remind me,—come nobody knew how far,—did it grow yet in the beech-wood clearings, as it did when I gathered it as a boy, tracking through the snow? "Christ-thorn" we called it in our Danish tongue. The red berries, to our simple faith, were the drops of blood that fell from the Saviour's brow as it drooped under its cruel crown upon the cross.

Back to the long ago wandered my thoughts: to the moss-grown beech in which I cut my name and that of a little girl with yellow curls, of blessed memory, with the first jack-knife I ever owned; to the story-book with the little fir tree that pined because it was small, and because the hare jumped over it, and would not be content though the wind and the sun kissed it, and the dews wept over it and told it to rejoice in its young life; and that was so proud when, in the second year, the hare had to go round it, because then it knew it was getting big,—Hans Christian Andersen's story that we loved above all the rest; for we knew the tree right well, and the hare; even the tracks it left in the snow we had seen. Ah, those were the Yule-tide seasons, when the old Domkirke shone with a thousand wax candles on Christmas eve; when all business was laid aside to let the world make merry one whole week; when big red apples were roasted on the stove, and bigger doughnuts were baked within it for the long feast! Never such had been known since. Christmas to-day is but a name, a memory.

A door slammed below, and let in the noises of the street. The holly rustled in the draught. Some one going out said, "A Merry Christmas to you all!" in a big, hearty voice. I awoke from my revery to find myself back in New York with a glad glow at the heart. It was not true. I had only forgotten. It was myself that had changed, not Christmas. That was here, with the old cheer, the old message of good-will, the old royal road to the heart of mankind. How often had I seen its blessed charity, that never corrupts, make light in the hovels of darkness and despair! how often watched its spirit of self-sacrifice and devotion in those who had, besides themselves, nothing to give! and as often the sight had made whole my faith in human nature. No! Christmas was not of the past, its spirit not dead. The lad who fixed the sprig of holly on the stairs knew it; my reporter's note-book bore witness to it. Witness of my contrition for the wrong I did the gentle spirit of the holiday, here let the book tell the story of one Christmas in the tenements of the poor:—

It is evening in Grand Street. The shops east and west are pouring forth their swarms of workers. Street and sidewalk are filled with an eager throng of young men and women, chatting gayly, and elbowing the jam of holiday shoppers that linger about the big stores. The street-cars labor along, loaded down to the steps with passengers carrying bundles of every size and odd shape. Along the curb a string of pedlers hawk penny toys in push-carts with noisy clamor, fearless for once of being moved on by the police. Christmas brings a two weeks' respite from persecution even to the friendless street-fakir. From the window of one brilliantly lighted store a bevy of mature dolls in dishabille stretch forth their arms appealingly to a troop of factory-hands passing by. The young men chaff the girls, who shriek with laughter and run. The policeman on the corner stops beating his hands together to keep warm, and makes a mock attempt to catch them, whereat their shrieks rise shriller than ever. "Them stockin's o' yourn 'll be the death o' Santa Claus!" he shouts after them, as they dodge. And they, looking back, snap saucily, "Mind yer business, freshy!" But their laughter belies their words. "They giv' it to ye straight that time," grins the grocer's clerk, come out to snatch a look at the crowds; and the two swap holiday greetings.

At the corner, where two opposing tides of travel form an eddy, the line of push-carts debouches down the darker side street. In its gloom their torches burn with a fitful glare that wakes black shadows among the trusses of the railroad structure overhead. A woman, with worn shawl drawn tightly about head and shoulders, bargains with a pedler for a monkey on a stick and two cents' worth of flitter-gold. Five ill-clad youngsters flatten their noses against the frozen pane of the toy-shop, in ecstasy at something there, which proves to be a milk wagon, with driver, horses, and cans that can be unloaded. It is something their minds can grasp. One comes forth with a penny goldfish of pasteboard clutched tightly in his hand, and, casting cautious glances right and left, speeds across the way to the door of a tenement, where a little girl stands waiting. "It's yer Chris'mas, Kate," he says, and thrusts it into her eager fist. The black doorway swallows them up.

Across the narrow yard, in the basement of the rear house, the lights of a Christmas tree show against the grimy window pane. The hare would never have gone around it, it is so very small. The two children are busily engaged fixing the goldfish upon one of its branches. Three little candles that burn there shed light upon a scene of utmost desolation. The room is black with smoke and dirt. In the middle of the floor oozes an oil-stove that serves at once to take the raw edge off the cold and to cook the meals by. Half the window panes are broken, and the holes stuffed with rags. The sleeve of an old coat hangs out of one, and beats drearily upon the sash when the wind sweeps over the fence and rattles the rotten shutters. The family wash, clammy and gray, hangs on a clothes-line stretched across the room. Under it, at a table set with cracked and empty plates, a discouraged woman sits eying the children's show gloomily. It is evident that she has been drinking. The peaked faces of the little ones wear a famished look. There are three—the third an infant, put to bed in what was once a baby carriage. The two from the street are pulling it around to get the tree in range. The baby sees it, and crows with delight. The boy shakes a branch, and the goldfish leaps and sparkles in the candle-light.

"See, sister!" he pipes; "see Santa Claus!" And they clap their hands in glee. The woman at the table wakes out of her stupor, gazes around her, and bursts into a fit of maudlin weeping.

The door falls to. Five flights up, another opens upon a bare attic room which a patient little woman is setting to rights. There are only three chairs, a box, and a bedstead in the room, but they take a deal of careful arranging. The bed hides the broken plaster in the wall through which the wind came in; each chair-leg stands over a rat-hole, at once to hide it and to keep the rats out. One is left; the box is for that. The plaster of the ceiling is held up with pasteboard patches. I know the story of that attic. It is one of cruel desertion. The woman's husband is even now living in plenty with the creature for whom he forsook her, not a dozen blocks away, while she "keeps the home together for the childer." She sought justice, but the lawyer demanded a retainer; so she gave it up, and went back to her little ones. For this room that barely keeps the winter wind out she pays four dollars a month, and is behind with the rent. There is scarce bread in the house; but the spirit of Christmas has found her attic. Against a broken wall is tacked a hemlock branch, the leavings of the corner grocer's fitting-block; pink string from the packing-counter hangs on it in festoons. A tallow dip on the box furnishes the illumination. The children sit up in bed, and watch it with shining eyes.

"We're having Christmas!" they say.

The lights of the Bowery glow like a myriad twinkling stars upon the ceaseless flood of humanity that surges ever through the great highway of the homeless. They shine upon long rows of lodging-houses, in which hundreds of young men, cast helpless upon the reef of the strange city, are learning their first lessons of utter loneliness; for what desolation is there like that of the careless crowd when all the world rejoices? They shine upon the tempter setting his snares there, and upon the missionary and the Salvation Army lass, disputing his catch with him; upon the police detective going his rounds with coldly observant eye intent upon the outcome of the contest; upon the wreck that is past hope, and upon the youth pausing on the verge of the pit in which the other has long ceased to struggle. Sights and sounds of Christmas there are in plenty in the Bowery. Balsam and hemlock and fir stand in groves along the busy thoroughfare, and garlands of green embower mission and dive impartially. Once a year the old street recalls its youth with an effort. It is true that it is largely a commercial effort; that the evergreen, with an instinct that is not of its native hills, haunts saloon-corners by preference; but the smell of the pine woods is in the air, and—Christmas is not too critical—one is grateful for the effort. It varies with the opportunity. At "Beefsteak John's" it is content with artistically embalming crullers and mince-pies in green cabbage under the window lamp. Over yonder, where the mile-post of the old lane still stands,—in its unhonored old age become the vehicle of publishing the latest "sure cure" to the world,—a florist, whose undenominational zeal for the holiday and trade outstrips alike distinction of creed and property, has transformed the sidewalk and the ugly railroad structure into a veritable bower, spanning it with a canopy of green, under which dwell with him, in neighborly good-will, the Young Men's Christian Association and the Jewish tailor next door.

In the next block a "turkey-shoot" is in progress. Crowds are trying their luck at breaking the glass balls that dance upon tiny jets of water in front of a marine view with the moon rising, yellow and big, out of a silver sea. A man-of-war, with lights burning aloft, labors under a rocky coast. Groggy sailormen, on shore leave, make unsteady attempts upon the dancing balls. One mistakes the moon for the target, but is discovered in season. "Don't shoot that," says the man who loads the guns; "there's a lamp behind it." Three scared birds in the window recess try vainly to snatch a moment's sleep between shots and the trains that go roaring overhead on the elevated road. Roused by the sharp crack of the rifles, they blink at the lights in the street, and peck moodily at a crust in their bed of shavings.

The dime museum gong clatters out its noisy warning that "the lecture" is about to begin. From the concert hall, where men sit drinking beer in clouds of smoke, comes the thin voice of a short-skirted singer, warbling, "Do they think of me at home?" The young fellow who sits near the door, abstractedly making figures in the wet track of the "schooners," buries something there with a sudden restless turn, and calls for another beer. Out in the street a band strikes up. A host with banners advances, chanting an unfamiliar hymn. In the ranks marches a cripple on crutches. Newsboys follow, gaping. Under the illuminated clock of the Cooper Institute the procession halts, and the leader, turning his face to the sky, offers a prayer. The passing crowds stop to listen. A few bare their heads. The devoted group, the flapping banners, and the changing torch-light on upturned faces, make a strange, weird picture. Then the drum-beat, and the band files into its barracks across the street. A few of the listeners follow, among them the lad from the concert hall, who slinks shamefacedly in when he thinks no one is looking.

Down at the foot of the Bowery is the "pan-handlers' beat," where the saloons elbow one another at every step, crowding out all other business than that of keeping lodgers to support them. Within call of it, across the square, stands a church which, in the memory of men yet living, was built to shelter the fashionable Baptist audiences of a day when Madison Square was out in the fields, and Harlem had a foreign sound. The fashionable audiences are gone long since. To-day the church, fallen into premature decay, but still handsome in its strong and noble lines, stands as a missionary outpost in the land of the enemy, its builders would have said, doing a greater work than they planned. To-night is the Christmas festival of its English-speaking Sunday-school, and the pews are filled. The banners of United Italy, of modern Hellas, of France and Germany and England, hang side by side with the Chinese dragon and the starry flag—signs of the cosmopolitan character of the congregation. Greek and Roman Catholics, Jews and joss-worshippers, go there; few Protestants, and no Baptists. It is easy to pick out the children in their seats by nationality, and as easy to read the story of poverty and suffering that stands written in more than one mother's haggard face, now beaming with pleasure at the little ones' glee. A gayly decorated Christmas tree has taken the place of the pulpit. At its foot is stacked a mountain of bundles, Santa Claus's gifts to the school. A self-conscious young man with soap-locks has just been allowed to retire, amid tumultuous applause, after blowing "Nearer, my God, to Thee" on his horn until his cheeks swelled almost to bursting. A trumpet ever takes the Fourth Ward by storm. A class of little girls is climbing upon the platform. Each wears a capital letter on her breast, and has a piece to speak that begins with the letter; together they spell its lesson. There is momentary consternation: one is missing. As the discovery is made, a child pushes past the doorkeeper, hot and breathless. "I am in 'Boundless Love,'" she says, and makes for the platform, where her arrival restores confidence and the language.

In the audience the befrocked visitor from up-town sits cheek by jowl with the pigtailed Chinaman and the dark-browed Italian. Up in the gallery, farthest from the preacher's desk and the tree, sits a Jewish mother with three boys, almost in rags. A dingy and threadbare shawl partly hides her poor calico wrap and patched apron. The woman shrinks in the pew, fearful of being seen; her boys stand upon the benches, and applaud with the rest. She endeavors vainly to restrain them. "Tick, tick!" goes the old clock over the door through which wealth and fashion went out long years ago, and poverty came in.

Tick, tick! the world moves, with us—without; without or with. She is the yesterday, they the to-morrow. What shall the harvest be?

Loudly ticked the old clock in time with the doxology, the other day, when they cleared the tenants out of Gotham Court down here in Cherry Street, and shut the iron doors of Single and Double Alley against them. Never did the world move faster or surer toward a better day than when the wretched slum was seized by the health officers as a nuisance unfit longer to disgrace a Christian city. The snow lies deep in the deserted passageways, and the vacant floors are given over to evil smells, and to the rats that forage in squads, burrowing in the neglected sewers. The "wall of wrath" still towers above the buildings in the adjoining Alderman's Court, but its wrath at last is wasted.

It was built by a vengeful Quaker, whom the alderman had knocked down in a quarrel over the boundary line, and transmitted its legacy of hate to generations yet unborn; for where it stood it shut out sunlight and air from the tenements of Alderman's Court. And at last it is to go, Gotham Court and all; and to the going the wall of wrath has contributed its share, thus in the end atoning for some of the harm it wrought. Tick! old clock; the world moves. Never yet did Christmas seem less dark on Cherry Hill than since the lights were put out in Gotham Court forever.

In "The Bend" the philanthropist undertaker who "buries for what he can catch on the plate" hails the Yule-tide season with a pyramid of green made of two coffins set on end. It has been a good day, he says cheerfully, putting up the shutters; and his mind is easy. But the "good days" of The Bend are over, too. The Bend itself is all but gone. Where the old pigsty stood, children dance and sing to the strumming of a cracked piano-organ propelled on wheels by an Italian and his wife. The park that has come to take the place of the slum will curtail the undertaker's profits, as it has lessened the work of the police. Murder was the fashion of the day that is past. Scarce a knife has been drawn since the sunlight shone into that evil spot, and grass and green shrubs took the place of the old rookeries. The Christmas gospel of peace and good-will moves in where the slum moves out. It never had a chance before.

The children follow the organ, stepping in the slush to the music, bareheaded and with torn shoes, but happy; across the Five Points and through "the Bay,"—known to the directory as Baxter Street,—to "the Divide," still Chatham Street to its denizens, though the aldermen have rechristened it Park Row. There other delegations of Greek and Italian children meet and escort the music on its homeward trip. In one of the crooked streets near the river its journey comes to an end. A battered door opens to let it in. A tallow dip burns sleepily on the creaking stairs. The water runs with a loud clatter in the sink: it is to keep it from freezing. There is not a whole window pane in the hall. Time was when this was a fine house harboring wealth and refinement. It has neither now. In the old parlor downstairs a knot of hard-faced men and women sit on benches about a deal table, playing cards. They have a jug between them, from which they drink by turns. On the stump of a mantel-shelf a lamp burns before a rude print of the Mother of God. No one pays any heed to the hand-organ man and his wife as they climb to their attic. There is a colony of them up there—three families in four rooms.

"Come in, Antonio," says the tenant of the double flat,—the one with two rooms,—"come and keep Christmas." Antonio enters, cap in hand. In the corner by the dormer-window a "crib" has been fitted up in commemoration of the Nativity. A soap-box and two hemlock branches are the elements. Six tallow candles and a night-light illuminate a singular collection of rarities, set out with much ceremonial show. A doll tightly wrapped in swaddling-clothes represents "the Child." Over it stands a ferocious-looking beast, easily recognized as a survival of the last political campaign,—the Tammany tiger,—threatening to swallow it at a gulp if one as much as takes one's eyes off it. A miniature Santa Claus, a pasteboard monkey, and several other articles of bric-a-brac of the kind the tenement affords, complete the outfit. The background is a picture of St. Donato, their village saint, with the Madonna "whom they worship most." But the incongruity harbors no suggestion of disrespect. The children view the strange show with genuine reverence, bowing and crossing themselves before it. There are five, the oldest a girl of seventeen, who works for a sweater, making three dollars a week. It is all the money that comes in, for the father has been sick and unable to work eight months and the mother has her hands full: the youngest is a baby in arms. Three of the children go to a charity school, where they are fed, a great help, now the holidays have come to make work slack for sister. The rent is six dollars—two weeks' pay out of the four. The mention of a possible chance of light work for the man brings the daughter with her sewing from the adjoining room, eager to hear. That would be Christmas indeed! "Pietro!" She runs to the neighbors to communicate the joyful tidings. Pietro comes, with his new-born baby, which he is tending while his wife lies ill, to look at the maestro, so powerful and good. He also has been out of work for months, with a family of mouths to fill, and nothing coming in. His children are all small yet, but they speak English.

"What," I say, holding a silver dime up before the oldest, a smart little chap of seven—"what would you do if I gave you this?"

"Get change," he replies promptly. When he is told that it is his own, to buy toys with, his eyes open wide with wondering incredulity. By degrees he understands. The father does not. He looks questioningly from one to the other. When told, his respect increases visibly for "the rich gentleman."

They were villagers of the same community in southern Italy, these people and others in the tenements thereabouts, and they moved their patron saint with them. They cluster about his worship here, but the worship is more than an empty form. He typifies to them the old neighborliness of home, the spirit of mutual help, of charity, and of the common cause against the common enemy. The community life survives through their saint in the far city to an unsuspected extent. The sick are cared for; the dreaded hospital is fenced out. There are no Italian evictions. The saint has paid the rent of this attic through two hard months; and here at his shrine the Calabrian village gathers, in the persons of these three, to do him honor on Christmas eve.

Where the old Africa has been made over into a modern Italy, since King Humbert's cohorts struck the up-town trail, three hundred of the little foreigners are having an uproarious time over their Christmas tree in the Children's Aid Society's school. And well they may, for the like has not been seen in Sullivan Street in this generation. Christmas trees are rather rarer over here than on the East Side, where the German leavens the lump with his loyalty to home traditions. This is loaded with silver and gold and toys without end, until there is little left of the original green. Santa Claus's sleigh must have been upset in a snow-drift over here, and righted by throwing the cargo overboard, for there is at least a wagon-load of things that can find no room on the tree. The appearance of "teacher" with a double armful of curly-headed dolls in red, yellow, and green Mother-Hubbards, doubtful how to dispose of them, provokes a shout of approval, which is presently quieted by the principal's bell. School is "in" for the preliminary exercises. Afterward there are to be the tree and ice-cream for the good children. In their anxiety to prove their title clear, they sit so straight, with arms folded, that the whole row bends over backward. The lesson is brief, the answers to the point.

"What do we receive at Christmas?" the teacher wants to know. The whole school responds with a shout, "Dolls and toys!" To the question, "Why do we receive them at Christmas?" the answer is not so prompt. But one youngster from Thompson Street holds up his hand. He knows. "Because we always get 'em," he says; and the class is convinced: it is a fact. A baby wails because it cannot get the whole tree at once. The "little mother"—herself a child of less than a dozen winters—who has it in charge, cooes over it, and soothes its grief with the aid of a surreptitious sponge-cake evolved from the depths of teacher's pocket. Babies are encouraged in these schools, though not originally included in their plan, as often the one condition upon which the older children can be reached. Some one has to mind the baby, with all hands out at work.

The school sings "Santa Lucia" and "Children of the Heavenly King," and baby is lulled to sleep.

"Who is this King?" asks the teacher, suddenly, at the end of a verse. Momentary stupefaction. The little minds are on ice-cream just then; the lad nearest the door has telegraphed that it is being carried up in pails. A little fellow on the back seat saves the day. Up goes his brown fist.

"Well, Vito, who is he?"

"McKinley!" pipes the lad, who remembers the election just past; and the school adjourns for ice-cream.

It is a sight to see them eat it. In a score of such schools, from the Hook to Harlem, the sight is enjoyed in Christmas week by the men and women who, out of their own pockets, reimburse Santa Claus for his outlay, and count it a joy, as well they may; for their beneficence sometimes makes the one bright spot in lives that have suffered of all wrongs the most cruel,—that of being despoiled of their childhood. Sometimes they are little Bohemians; sometimes the children of refugee Jews; and again, Italians, or the descendants of the Irish stock of Hell's Kitchen and Poverty Row; always the poorest, the shabbiest, the hungriest—the children Santa Claus loves best to find, if any one will show him the way. Having so much on hand, he has no time, you see, to look them up himself. That must be done for him; and it is done. To the teacher in the Sullivan Street school came one little girl, this last Christmas, with anxious inquiry if it was true that he came around with toys.

"I hanged my stocking last time," she said, "and he didn't come at all." In the front house indeed, he left a drum and a doll, but no message from him reached the rear house in the alley. "Maybe he couldn't find it," she said soberly. Did the teacher think he would come if she wrote to him? She had learned to write.

Together they composed a note to Santa Claus, speaking for a doll and a bell—the bell to play "go to school" with when she was kept home minding the baby. Lest he should by any chance miss the alley in spite of directions, little Rosa was invited to hang her stocking, and her sister's, with the janitor's children's in the school. And lo! on Christmas morning there was a gorgeous doll, and a bell that was a whole curriculum in itself, as good as a year's schooling any day! Faith in Santa Claus is established in that Thompson Street alley for this generation at least; and Santa Claus, got by hook or by crook into an Eighth Ward alley, is as good as the whole Supreme Court bench, with the Court of Appeals thrown in, for backing the Board of Health against the slum.

But the ice-cream! They eat it off the seats, half of them kneeling or squatting on the floor; they blow on it, and put it in their pockets to carry home to baby. Two little shavers discovered to be feeding each other, each watching the smack develop on the other's lips as the acme of his own bliss, are "cousins"; that is why. Of cake there is a double supply. It is a dozen years since "Fighting Mary," the wildest child in the Seventh Avenue school, taught them a lesson there which they have never forgotten. She was perfectly untamable, fighting everybody in school, the despair of her teacher, till on Thanksgiving, reluctantly included in the general amnesty and mince-pie, she was caught cramming the pie into her pocket, after eying it with a look of pure ecstasy, but refusing to touch it. "For mother" was her explanation, delivered with a defiant look before which the class quailed. It is recorded, but not in the minutes, that the board of managers wept over Fighting Mary, who, all unconscious of having caused such an astonishing "break," was at that moment engaged in maintaining her prestige and reputation by fighting the gang in the next block. The minutes contain merely a formal resolution to the effect that occasions of mince-pie shall carry double rations thenceforth. And the rule has been kept—not only in Seventh Avenue, but in every industrial school—since. Fighting Mary won the biggest fight of her troubled life that day, without striking a blow.

It was in the Seventh Avenue school last Christmas that I offered the truant class a four-bladed penknife as a prize for whittling out the truest Maltese cross. It was a class of black sheep, and it was the blackest sheep of the flock that won the prize. "That awful Savarese," said the principal in despair. I thought of Fighting Mary, and bade her take heart. I regret to say that within a week the hapless Savarese was black-listed for banking up the school door with snow, so that not even the janitor could get out and at him.

Within hail of the Sullivan Street school camps a scattered little band, the Christmas customs of which I had been trying for years to surprise. They are Indians, a handful of Mohawks and Iroquois, whom some ill wind has blown down from their Canadian reservation, and left in these West Side tenements to eke out such a living as they can, weaving mats and baskets, and threading glass pearls on slippers and pin-cushions, until, one after another, they have died off and gone to happier hunting-grounds than Thompson Street. There were as many families as one could count on the fingers of both hands when I first came upon them, at the death of old Tamenund, the basket maker. Last Christmas there were seven. I had about made up my mind that the only real Americans in New York did not keep the holiday at all, when, one Christmas eve, they showed me how. Just as dark was setting in, old Mrs. Benoit came from her Hudson Street attic—where she was known among the neighbors, as old and poor as she, as Mrs. Ben Wah, and was believed to be the relict of a warrior of the name of Benjamin Wah—to the office of the Charity Organization Society, with a bundle for a friend who had helped her over a rough spot—the rent, I suppose. The bundle was done up elaborately in blue cheese-cloth, and contained a lot of little garments which she had made out of the remnants of blankets and cloth of her own from a younger and better day. "For those," she said, in her French patois, "who are poorer than myself;" and hobbled away. I found out, a few days later, when I took her picture weaving mats in her attic room, that she had scarcely food in the house that Christmas day and not the car fare to take her to church! Walking was bad, and her old limbs were stiff. She sat by the window through the winter evening, and watched the sun go down behind the western hills, comforted by her pipe. Mrs. Ben Wah, to give her her local name, is not really an Indian; but her husband was one, and she lived all her life with the tribe till she came here. She is a philosopher in her own quaint way. "It is no disgrace to be poor," said she to me, regarding her empty tobacco-pouch; "but it is sometimes a great inconvenience." Not even the recollection of the vote of censure that was passed upon me once by the ladies of the Charitable Ten for surreptitiously supplying an aged couple, the special object of their charity, with army plug, could have deterred me from taking the hint.

Very likely, my old friend Miss Sherman, in her Broome Street cellar,—it is always the attic or the cellar,—would object to Mrs. Ben Wah's claim to being the only real American in my note-book. She is from Down East, and says "stun" for stone. In her youth she was lady's-maid to a general's wife, the recollection of which military career equally condones the cellar and prevents her holding any sort of communication with her common neighbors, who add to the offence of being foreigners the unpardonable one of being mostly men. Eight cats bear her steady company, and keep alive her starved affections. I found them on last Christmas eve behind barricaded doors; for the cold that had locked the water-pipes had brought the neighbors down to the cellar, where Miss Sherman's cunning had kept them from freezing. Their tin pans and buckets were even then banging against her door. "They're a miserable lot," said the old maid, fondling her cats defiantly; "but let 'em. It's Christmas. Ah!" she added, as one of the eight stood up in her lap and rubbed its cheek against hers, "they're innocent. It isn't poor little animals that does the harm. It's men and women that does it to each other." I don't know whether it was just philosophy, like Mrs. Ben Wah's, or a glimpse of her story. If she had one, she kept it for her cats.

In a hundred places all over the city, when Christmas comes, as many open-air fairs spring suddenly into life. A kind of Gentile Feast of Tabernacles possesses the tenement districts especially. Green-embowered booths stand in rows at the curb, and the voice of the tin trumpet is heard in the land. The common source of all the show is down by the North River, in the district known as "the Farm." Down there Santa Claus establishes headquarters early in December and until past New Year. The broad quay looks then more like a clearing in a pine forest than a busy section of the metropolis. The steamers discharge their loads of fir trees at the piers until they stand stacked mountain-high, with foot-hills of holly and ground-ivy trailing off toward the land side. An army train of wagons is engaged in carting them away from early morning till late at night; but the green forest grows, in spite of it all, until in places it shuts the shipping out of sight altogether. The air is redolent with the smell of balsam and pine. After nightfall, when the lights are burning in the busy market, and the homeward-bound crowds with baskets and heavy burdens of Christmas greens jostle one another with good-natured banter,—nobody is ever cross down here in the holiday season,—it is good to take a stroll through the Farm, if one has a spot in his heart faithful yet to the hills and the woods in spite of the latter-day city. But it is when the moonlight is upon the water and upon the dark phantom forest, when the heavy breathing of some passing steamer is the only sound that breaks the stillness of the night, and the watchman smokes his only pipe on the bulwark, that the Farm has a mood and an atmosphere all its own, full of poetry which some day a painter's brush will catch and hold.

Into the ugliest tenement street Christmas brings something of picturesqueness, of cheer. Its message was ever to the poor and the heavy-laden, and by them it is understood with an instinctive yearning to do it honor. In the stiff dignity of the brownstone streets up-town there may be scarce a hint of it. In the homes of the poor it blossoms on stoop and fire-escape, looks out of the front window, and makes the unsightly barber-pole to sprout overnight like an Aaron's-rod. Poor indeed is the home that has not its sign of peace over the hearth, be it but a single sprig of green. A little color creeps with it even into rabbinical Hester Street, and shows in the shop-windows and in the children's faces. The very feather dusters in the pedler's stock take on brighter hues for the occasion, and the big knives in the cutler's shop gleam with a lively anticipation of the impending goose "with fixin's"—a concession, perhaps, to the commercial rather than the religious holiday: business comes then, if ever. A crowd of ragamuffins camp out at a window where Santa Claus and his wife stand in state, embodiment of the domestic ideal that has not yet gone out of fashion in these tenements, gazing hungrily at the announcement that "A silver present will be given to every purchaser by a real Santa Claus.—M. Levitsky." Across the way, in a hole in the wall, two cobblers are pegging away under an oozy lamp that makes a yellow splurge on the inky blackness about them, revealing to the passer-by their bearded faces, but nothing of the environment save a single sprig of holly suspended from the lamp. From what forgotten brake it came with a message of cheer, a thought of wife and children across the sea waiting their summons, God knows. The shop is their house and home. It was once the hall of the tenement; but to save space, enough has been walled in to make room for their bench and bed; the tenants go through the next house. No matter if they are cramped; by and by they will have room. By and by comes the spring, and with it the steamer. Does not the green branch speak of spring and of hope? The policeman on the beat hears their hammers beat a joyous tattoo past midnight, far into Christmas morning. Who shall say its message has not reached even them in their slum?

Where the noisy trains speed over the iron highway past the second-story windows of Allen Street, a cellar door yawns darkly in the shadow of one of the pillars that half block the narrow sidewalk. A dull gleam behind the cobweb-shrouded window pane supplements the sign over the door, in Yiddish and English: "Old Brasses." Four crooked and mouldy steps lead to utter darkness, with no friendly voice to guide the hapless customer. Fumbling along the dank wall, he is left to find the door of the shop as best he can. Not a likely place to encounter the fastidious from the Avenue! Yet ladies in furs and silk find this door and the grim old smith within it. Now and then an artist stumbles upon them, and exults exceedingly in his find. Two holiday shoppers are even now haggling with the coppersmith over the price of a pair of curiously wrought brass candlesticks. The old man has turned from the forge, at which he was working, unmindful of his callers roving among the dusty shelves. Standing there, erect and sturdy, in his shiny leather apron, hammer in hand, with the firelight upon his venerable head, strong arms bared to the elbow, and the square paper cap pushed back from a thoughtful, knotty brow, he stirs strange fancies. One half expects to see him fashioning a gorget or a sword on his anvil. But his is a more peaceful craft. Nothing more warlike is in sight than a row of brass shields, destined for ornament, not for battle. Dark shadows chase one another by the flickering light among copper kettles of ruddy glow, old-fashioned samovars, and massive andirons of tarnished brass. The bargaining goes on. Overhead the nineteenth century speeds by with rattle and roar; in here linger the shadows of the centuries long dead. The boy at the anvil listens open-mouthed, clutching the bellows-rope.

In Liberty Hall a Jewish wedding is in progress. Liberty! Strange how the word echoes through these sweaters' tenements, where starvation is at home half the time. It is as an all-consuming passion with these people, whose spirit a thousand years of bondage have not availed to daunt. It breaks out in strikes, when to strike is to hunger and die. Not until I stood by a striking cloak-maker whose last cent was gone, with not a crust in the house to feed seven hungry mouths, yet who had voted vehemently in the meeting that day to keep up the strike to the bitter end,—bitter indeed, nor far distant,—and heard him at sunset recite the prayer of his fathers: "Blessed art thou, O Lord our God, King of the world, that thou hast redeemed us as thou didst redeem our fathers, hast delivered us from bondage to liberty, and from servile dependence to redemption!"—not until then did I know what of sacrifice the word might mean, and how utterly we of another day had forgotten. But for once shop and tenement are left behind. Whatever other days may have in store, this is their day of play, when all may rejoice.

The bridegroom, a cloak-presser in a hired dress suit, sits alone and ill at ease at one end of the hall, sipping whiskey with a fine air of indifference, but glancing apprehensively toward the crowd of women in the opposite corner that surround the bride, a pale little shop-girl with a pleading, winsome face. From somewhere unexpectedly appears a big man in an ill-fitting coat and skullcap, flanked on either side by a fiddler, who scrapes away and away, accompanying the improvisator in a plaintive minor key as he halts before the bride and intones his lay. With many a shrug of stooping shoulders and queer excited gesture, he drones, in the harsh, guttural Yiddish of Hester Street, his story of life's joys and sorrows, its struggles and victories in the land of promise. The women listen, nodding and swaying their bodies sympathetically. He works himself into a frenzy, in which the fiddlers vainly try to keep up with him. He turns and digs the laggard angrily in the side without losing the metre. The climax comes. The bride bursts into hysterical sobs, while the women wipe their eyes. A plate, heretofore concealed under his coat, is whisked out. He has conquered; the inevitable collection is taken up.

The tuneful procession moves upon the bridegroom. An Essex Street girl in the crowd, watching them go, says disdainfully: "None of this humbug when I get married." It is the straining of young America at the fetters of tradition. Ten minutes later, when, between double files of women holding candles, the couple pass to the canopy where the rabbi waits, she has already forgotten; and when the crunching of a glass under the bridegroom's heel announces that they are one, and that until the broken pieces be reunited he is hers and hers alone, she joins with all the company in the exulting shout of "Mozzel tov!" ("Good luck!"). Then the *dupka*, men and women joining in, forgetting all but the moment, hands on hips, stepping in time, forward, backward, and across. And then the feast.

They sit at the long tables by squads and tribes. Those who belong together sit together. There is no attempt at pairing off for conversation or mutual entertainment, at speech-making or toasting. The business in hand is to eat, and it is attended to. The bridegroom, at the head of the table, with his shiny silk hat on, sets the example; and the guests emulate it with zeal, the men smoking big, strong cigars between mouthfuls. "Gosh! ain't it fine?" is the grateful comment of one curly-headed youngster, bravely attacking his third plate of chicken-stew. "Fine as silk," nods his neighbor in knickerbockers. Christmas, for once, means something to them that they can understand. The crowd of hurrying waiters make room for one bearing aloft a small turkey adorned with much tinsel and many paper flowers. It is for the bride, the one thing not to be touched until the next day—one day off from the drudgery of housekeeping; she, too, can keep Christmas.

A group of bearded, dark-browed men sit apart, the rabbi among them. They are the orthodox, who cannot break bread with the rest, for fear, though the food be kosher, the plates have been defiled. They brought their own to the feast, and sit at their own table, stern and justified. Did they but know what depravity is harbored in the impish mind of the girl yonder, who plans to hang her stocking overnight by the window! There is no fireplace in the tenement. Queer things happen over here, in the strife between the old and the new. The girls of the College Settlement, last summer, felt compelled to explain that the holiday in the country which they offered some of these children was to be spent in an Episcopal clergyman's house, where they had prayers every morning. "Oh," was the mother's indulgent answer, "they know it isn't true, so it won't hurt them."

The bell of a neighboring church tower strikes the vesper hour. A man in working-clothes uncovers his head reverently, and passes on. Through the vista of green bowers formed of the grocer's stock of Christmas trees a passing glimpse of flaring torches in the distant square is caught. They touch with flame the gilt cross towering high above the "White Garden," as the German residents call Tompkins Square. On the sidewalk the holy-eve fair is in its busiest hour. In the pine-board booths stand rows of staring toy dogs alternately with plaster saints. Red apples and candy are hawked from carts. Pedlers offer colored candles with shrill outcry. A huckster feeding his horse by the curb scatters, unseen, a share for the sparrows. The cross flashes white against the dark sky.

In one of the side streets near the East River has stood for thirty years a little mission church, called Hope Chapel by its founders, in the brave spirit in which they built it. It has had plenty of use for the spirit since. Of the kind of problems that beset its pastor I caught a glimpse the other day, when, as I entered his room, a rough-looking man went out.

"One of my cares," said Mr. Devins, looking after him with contracted brow. "He has spent two Christmas days of twenty-three out of jail. He is a burglar, or was. His daughter has brought him round. She is a seamstress. For three months, now, she has been keeping him and the home, working nights. If I could only get him a job! He won't stay honest long without it; but who wants a burglar for a watchman? And how can I recommend him?"

A few doors from the chapel an alley sets into the block. We halted at the mouth of it.

"Come in," said Mr. Devins, "and wish Blind Jennie a Merry Christmas."

We went in, in single file; there was not room for two. As we climbed the creaking stairs of the rear tenement, a chorus of children's shrill voices burst into song somewhere above.

"It is her class," said the pastor of Hope Chapel, as he stopped on the landing. "They are all kinds. We never could hope to reach them; Jennie can. They fetch her the papers given out in the Sunday-school, and read to her what is printed under the pictures; and she tells them the story of it. There is nothing Jennie doesn't know about the Bible."

The door opened upon a low-ceiled room, where the evening shades lay deep. The red glow from the kitchen stove discovered a jam of children, young girls mostly, perched on the table, the chairs, in one another's laps, or squatting on the floor; in the midst of them, a little old woman with heavily veiled face, and wan, wrinkled hands folded in her lap. The singing ceased as we stepped across the threshold.

"Be welcome," piped a harsh voice with a singular note of cheerfulness in it. "Whose step is that with you, pastor? I don't know it. He is welcome in Jennie's house, whoever he be. Girls, make him to home." The girls moved up to make room.

"Jennie has not seen since she was a child," said the clergyman, gently; "but she knows a friend without it. Some day she shall see the great Friend in his glory, and then she shall be Blind Jennie no more."

The little woman raised the veil from a face shockingly disfigured, and touched the eyeless sockets. "Some day," she repeated, "Jennie shall see. Not long now—not long!" Her pastor patted her hand. The silence of the dark room was broken by Blind Jennie's voice, rising cracked and quavering: "Alas! and did my Saviour bleed?" The shrill chorus burst in:—

It was there by faith I received my sight,
And now I am happy all the day.

The light that falls from the windows of the Neighborhood Guild, in Delancey Street, makes a white path across the asphalt pavement. Within, there is mirth and laughter. The Tenth Ward Social Reform Club is having its Christmas festival. Its members, poor mothers, scrubwomen,—the president is the janitress of a tenement near by,—have brought their little ones, a few their husbands, to share in the fun. One little girl has to be dragged up to the grab-bag. She cries at the sight of Santa Claus. The baby has drawn a woolly horse. He kisses the toy with a look of ecstatic bliss, and toddles away. At the far end of the hall a game of blindman's-buff is starting up. The aged grandmother, who has watched it with growing excitement, bids one of the settlement workers hold her grandchild, that she may join in; and she does join in, with all the pent-up hunger of fifty joyless years. The worker, looking on, smiles; one has been reached. Thus is the battle against the slum waged and won with the child's play.

Tramp! tramp! comes the to-morrow upon the stage. Two hundred and fifty pairs of little feet, keeping step, are marching to dinner in the Newsboys' Lodging-house. Five hundred pairs more are restlessly awaiting their turn upstairs. In prison, hospital, and almshouse to-night the city is host, and gives of her plenty. Here an unknown friend has spread a generous repast for the waifs who all the rest of the days shift for themselves as best they can. Turkey, coffee, and pie, with "vegetubles" to fill in. As the file of eagle-eyed youngsters passes down the long tables, there are swift movements of grimy hands, and shirt-waists bulge, ragged coats sag at the pockets. Hardly is the file seated when the plaint rises: "I ain't got no pie! It got swiped on me." Seven despoiled ones hold up their hands.

The superintendent laughs—it is Christmas eve. He taps one tentatively on the bulging shirt. "What have you here, my lad?"

"Me pie," responds he, with an innocent look; "I wuz scart it would get stole."

A little fellow who has been eying one of the visitors attentively takes his knife out of his mouth, and points it at him with conviction.

"I know you," he pipes. "You're a p'lice commissioner. I seen yer picter in the papers. You're Teddy Roosevelt!"

The clatter of knives and forks ceases suddenly. Seven pies creep stealthily over the edge of the table, and are replaced on as many plates. The visitors laugh. It was a case of mistaken identity.

Farthest down town, where the island narrows toward the Battery, and warehouses crowd the few remaining tenements, the sombre-hued colony of Syrians is astir with preparation for the holiday. How comes it that in the only settlement of the real Christmas people in New York the corner saloon appropriates to itself all the outward signs of it? Even the floral cross that is nailed over the door of the Orthodox church is long withered and dead; it has been there since Easter, and it is yet twelve days to Christmas by the belated reckoning of the Greek Church. But if the houses show no sign of the holiday, within there is nothing lacking. The whole colony is gone a-visiting. There are enough of the unorthodox to set the fashion, and the rest follow the custom of the country. The men go from house to house, laugh, shake hands, and kiss one another on both cheeks, with the salutation, "Kol am va antom Salimoon." "Every year and you are safe," the Syrian guide renders it into English; and a non-professional interpreter amends it: "May you grow happier year by year." Arrack made from grapes and flavored with anise seed, and candy baked in little white balls like marbles, are served with the indispensable cigarette; for long callers, the pipe.

In a top-floor room of one of the darkest of the dilapidated tenements, the dusty window panes of which the last glow in the winter sky is tinging faintly with red, a dance is in progress. The guests, most of them fresh from the hillsides of Mount Lebanon, squat about the room. A reed-pipe and a tambourine furnish the music. One has the centre of the floor. With a beer jug filled to the brim on his head, he skips and sways, bending, twisting, kneeling, gesturing, and keeping time, while the men clap their hands. He lies down and turns over, but not a drop is spilled. Another succeeds him, stepping proudly, gracefully, furling and unfurling a handkerchief like a banner. As he sits down, and the beer goes around, one in the corner, who looks like a shepherd fresh from his pasture, strikes up a song—a far-off, lonesome, plaintive lay. "'Far as the hills,'" says the guide; "a song of the old days and the old people, now seldom heard." All together croon the refrain. The host delivers himself of an epic about his love across the seas, with the most agonizing expression, and in a shockingly bad voice. He is the worst singer I ever heard; but his companions greet his effort with approving shouts of "Yi! yi!" They look so fierce, and yet are so childishly happy, that at the thought of their exile and of the dark tenement the question arises, "Why all this joy?" The guide answers it with a look of surprise. "They sing," he says, "because they are glad they are free. Did you not know?"

The bells in old Trinity chime the midnight hour. From dark hallways men and women pour forth and hasten to the Maronite church. In the loft of the dingy old warehouse wax candles burn before an altar of brass. The priest, in a white robe with a huge gold cross worked on the back, chants the ritual. The people respond. The women kneel in the aisles, shrouding their heads in their shawls; a surpliced acolyte swings his censer; the heavy perfume of burning incense fills the hall.

The band at the anarchists' ball is tuning up for the last dance. Young and old float to the happy strains, forgetting injustice, oppression, hatred. Children slide upon the waxed floor, weaving fearlessly in and out between the couples—between fierce, bearded men and short-haired women with crimson-bordered kerchiefs. A Punch-and-Judy show in the corner evokes shouts of laughter.

Outside the snow is falling. It sifts silently into each nook and corner, softens all the hard and ugly lines, and throws the spotless mantle of charity over the blemishes, the shortcomings. Christmas morning will dawn pure and white.

ABE'S GAME OF JACKS

Time hung heavily on Abe Seelig's hands, alone, or as good as alone, in the flat on the "stoop" of the Allen Street tenement. His mother had gone to the butcher's. Chajim, the father,—"Chajim" is the Yiddish of "Herman,"—was long at the shop. To Abe was committed the care of his two young brothers, Isaac and Jacob. Abraham was nine, and past time for fooling. Play is "fooling" in the sweaters' tenements, and the muddling of ideas makes trouble, later on, to which the police returns have the index.

"Don't let 'em on the stairs," the mother had said, on going, with a warning nod toward the bed where Jake and Ikey slept. He didn't intend to. Besides, they were fast asleep. Abe cast about him for fun of some kind, and bethought himself of a game of jacks. That he had no jackstones was of small moment to him. East Side tenements, where pennies are infrequent, have resources. One penny was Abe's hoard. With that, and an accidental match, he began the game.

It went on well enough, albeit slightly lopsided by reason of the penny being so much the weightier, until the match, in one unlucky throw, fell close to a chair by the bed, and, in falling, caught fire.

Something hung down from the chair, and while Abe gazed, open-mouthed, at the match, at the chair, and at the bed right alongside, with his sleeping brothers on it, the little blaze caught it. The flame climbed up, up, up, and a great smoke curled under the ceiling. The children still slept, locked in each other's arms, and Abe—Abe ran.

He ran, frightened half out of his senses, out of the room, out of the house, into the street, to the nearest friendly place he knew, a grocery store five doors away, where his mother traded; but she was not there. Abe merely saw that she was not there, then he hid himself, trembling.

In all the block, where three thousand tenants live, no one knew what cruel thing was happening on the stoop of No. 19.

A train passed on the elevated road, slowing up for the station near by. The engineer saw one wild whirl of fire within the room, and opening the throttle of his whistle wide, let out a screech so long and so loud that in ten seconds the street was black with men and women rushing out to see what dreadful thing had happened.

No need of asking. From the door of the Seelig flat, burned through, fierce flames reached across the hall, barring the way. The tenement was shut in.

Promptly it poured itself forth upon fire-escape ladders, front and rear, with shrieks and wailing. In the street the crowd became a deadly crush. Police and firemen battered their way through, ran down and over men, women, and children, with a desperate effort.

The firemen from Hook and Ladder Six, around the corner, had heard the shrieks, and, knowing what they portended, ran with haste. But they were too late with their extinguishers; could not even approach the burning flat. They could only throw up their ladders to those above. For the rest they must needs wait until the engines came.

One tore up the street, coupled on a hose, and ran it into the house. Then died out the fire in the flat as speedily as it had come. The burning room was pumped full of water, and the firemen entered.

Just within the room they came upon little Jacob, still alive, but half roasted. He had struggled from the bed nearly to the door. On the bed lay the body of Isaac, the youngest, burned to a crisp.

They carried Jacob to the police station. As they brought him out, a frantic woman burst through the throng and threw herself upon him. It was the children's mother come back. When they took her to the blackened corpse of little Ike, she went stark mad. A dozen neighbors held her down, shrieking, while others went in search of the father.

In the street the excitement grew until it became almost uncontrollable when the dead boy was carried out.

In the midst of it little Abe returned, pale, silent, and frightened, to stand by his raving mother.

A LITTLE PICTURE

The fire-bells rang on the Bowery in the small hours of the morning. One of the old dwelling-houses that remain from the day when the "Bouwerie" was yet remembered as an avenue of beer-gardens and pleasure resorts was burning. Down in the street stormed the firemen, coupling hose and dragging it to the front. Upstairs in the peak of the roof, in the broken skylight, hung a man, old, feeble, and gasping for breath, struggling vainly to get out. He had piled chairs upon tables, and climbed up where he could grasp the edge, but his strength had given out when one more effort would have freed him. He felt himself sinking back. Over him was the sky, reddened now by the fire that raged below. Through the hole the pent-up smoke in the building found vent and rushed in a black and stifling cloud.

"Air, air!" gasped the old man. "O God, water!"

There was a swishing sound, a splash, and the copious spray of a stream sent over the house from the street fell upon his upturned face. It beat back the smoke. Strength and hope returned. He took another grip on the rafter just as he would have let go.

"Oh, that I might be reached yet and saved from this awful death!" he prayed. "Help, O God, help!"

An answering cry came over the adjoining roof. He had been heard, and the firemen, who did not dream that any one was in the burning building, had him in a minute. He had been asleep in the store when the fire aroused him and drove him, blinded and bewildered, to the attic, where he was trapped.

Safe in the street, the old man fell upon his knees.

"I prayed for water, and it came; I prayed for freedom, and was saved. The God of my fathers be praised!" he said, and bowed his head in thanksgiving.

A DREAM OF THE WOODS

Something came over Police Headquarters in the middle of the summer night. It was like the sighing of the north wind in the branches of the tall firs and in the reeds along lonely river-banks where the otter dips from the brink for its prey. The doorman, who yawned in the hall, and to whom reed-grown river banks have been strangers so long that he has forgotten they ever were, shivered and thought of pneumonia.

The Sergeant behind the desk shouted for some one to close the door; it was getting as cold as January. The little messenger boy on the lowest step of the oaken stairs nodded and dreamed in his sleep of Uncas and Chingachgook and the great woods. The cunning old beaver was there in his hut, and he heard the crack of Deerslayer's rifle.

He knew all the time he was dreaming, sitting on the steps of Police Headquarters, and yet it was all as real to him as if he were there, with the Mingoes creeping up to him in ambush all about and reaching for his scalp.

While he slept, a light step had passed, and the moccasin of the woods left its trail in his dream. In with the gust through the Mulberry Street door had come a strange pair, an old woman and a bright-eyed child, led by a policeman, and had passed up to Matron Travers's quarters on the top floor.

Strangely different, they were yet alike, both children of the woods. The woman was a squaw typical in looks and bearing, with the straight, black hair, dark skin, and stolid look of her race. She climbed the steps wearily, holding the child by the hand. The little one skipped eagerly, two steps at a time. There was the faintest tinge of brown in her plump cheeks, and a roguish smile in the corner of her eyes that made it a hardship not to take her up in one's lap and hug her at sight. In her frock of red-and-white calico she was a fresh and charming picture, with all the grace of movement and the sweet shyness of a young fawn.

The policeman had found them sitting on a big trunk in the Grand Central Station, waiting patiently for something or somebody that didn't come. When he had let them sit until he thought the child ought to be in bed, he took them into the police station in the depot, and there an effort was made to find out who and what they were. It was not an easy matter. Neither could speak English. They knew a few words of French, however, and between that and a note the old woman had in her pocket the general outline of the trouble was gathered. They were of the Canaghwaga tribe of Iroquois, domiciled in the St. Regis reservation across the Canadian border, and had come down to sell a trunkful of beads, and things worked with beads. Some one was to meet them, but had failed to come, and these two, to whom the trackless wilderness was as an open book, were lost in the city of ten thousand homes.

The matron made them understand by signs that two of the nine white beds in the nursery were for them, and they turned right in, humbly and silently thankful. The little girl had carried up with her, hugged very close under her arm, a doll that was a real ethnological study. It was a faithful rendering of the Indian pappoose, whittled out of a chunk of wood, with two staring glass beads for eyes, and strapped to a board the way Indian babies are, under a coverlet of very gaudy blue. It was a marvellous doll baby, and its nurse was mighty proud of it. She didn't let it go when she went to bed. It slept with her, and got up to play with her as soon as the first ray of daylight peeped in over the tall roofs.

The morning brought visitors, who admired the doll, chirruped to the little girl, and tried to talk with her grandmother, for that they made her out to be. To most questions she simply answered by shaking her head and holding out her credentials. There were two letters: one to the conductor of the train from Montreal, asking him to see that they got through all right; the other, a memorandum, for her own benefit apparently, recounting the number of hearts, crosses, and other treasures she had in her trunk. It was from those she had left behind at the reservation.

"Little Angus," it ran, "sends what is over to sell for him. Sarah sends the hearts. As soon as you can, will you try and sell some hearts?" Then there was "love to mother," and lastly an account of what the mason had said about the chimney of the cabin. They had sent for him to fix it. It was very dangerous the way it was, ran the message, and if mother would get the bricks, he would fix it right away.

The old squaw looked on with an anxious expression while the note was being read, as if she expected some sense to come out of it that would find her folks; but none of that kind could be made out of it, so they sat and waited until General Parker should come in.

General Ely S. Parker was the "big Indian" of Mulberry Street in a very real sense. Though he was a clerk in the Police Department and never went on the war-path any more, he was the head of the ancient Indian Confederacy, chief of the Six Nations, once so powerful for mischief, and now a mere name that frightens no one. Donegahawa—one cannot help wishing that the picturesque old chief had kept his name of the council lodge—was not born to sit writing at an office desk. In youth he tracked the bear and the panther in the Northern woods. The scattered remnants of the tribes East and West owned his rightful authority as chief. The Canaghwagas were one of these. So these lost ones had come straight to the official and actual head of their people when they were stranded in the great city. They knew it when they heard the magic name of Donegahawa, and sat silently waiting and wondering till he should come. The child looked up admiringly at the gold-laced cap of Inspector Williams, when he took her on his knee, and the stern face of the big policeman relaxed and grew tender as a woman's as he took her face between his hands and kissed it.

When the general came in he spoke to them at once in their own tongue, and very sweet and musical it was. Then their troubles were soon over. The sachem, when he had heard their woes, said two words between puffs of his pipe that cleared all the shadows away. They sounded to the paleface ear like "Huh Hoo—ochsjawai," or something equally barbarous, but they meant that there were not so many Indians in town but that theirs could be found, and in that the sachem was right. The number of redskins in Thompson Street—they all live over there—is about seven.

The old squaw, when she was told that her friend would be found, got up promptly, and, bowing first to Inspector Williams and the other officials in the room, and next to the general, said very sweetly, "Njeawa," and Lightfoot—that was the child's name, it appeared—said it after her; which meant, the general explained, that they were very much obliged. Then they went out in charge of a policeman to begin their search, little Lightfoot hugging her doll and looking back over her shoulder at the many gold-laced policemen who had captured her little heart. And they kissed their hands after her.

Mulberry Street awoke from its dream of youth, of the fields and the deep woods, to the knowledge that it was a bad day. The old doorman, who had stood at the gate patiently answering questions for twenty years, told the first man who came looking for a lost child, with sudden resentment, that he ought to be locked up for losing her, and, pushing him out in the rain, slammed the door after him.

'TWAS 'LIZA'S DOINGS

Joe drove his old gray mare along the stony road in deep thought. They had been across the ferry to Newtown with a load of Christmas truck. It had been a hard pull uphill for them both, for Joe had found it necessary not a few times to get down and give old 'Liza a lift to help her over the roughest spots; and now, going home, with the twilight coming on and no other job a-waiting, he let her have her own way. It was slow, but steady, and it suited Joe; for his head was full of busy thoughts, and there were few enough of them that were pleasant.

Business had been bad at the big stores, never worse, and what trucking there was there were too many about. Storekeepers who never used to look at a dollar, so long as they knew they could trust the man who did their hauling, were counting the nickels these days. As for chance jobs like this one, that was all over with the holidays, and there had been little enough of it, too.

There would be less, a good deal, with the hard winter at the door, and with 'Liza to keep and the many mouths to fill. Still, he wouldn't have minded it so much but for mother fretting and worrying herself sick at home, and all along o' Jim, the eldest boy, who had gone away mad and never come back. Many were the dollars he had paid the doctor and the druggist to fix her up, but it was no use. She was worrying herself into a decline, it was clear to be seen.

Joe heaved a heavy sigh as he thought of the strapping lad who had brought such sorrow to his mother. So strong and so handy on the wagon. Old 'Liza loved him like a brother and minded him even better than she did himself. If he only had him now, they could face the winter and the bad times, and pull through. But things never had gone right since he left. He didn't know, Joe thought humbly as he jogged along over the rough road, but he had been a little hard on the lad. Boys wanted a chance once in a while. All work and no play was not for them. Likely he had forgotten he was a boy once himself. But Jim was such a big lad, 'most like a man. He took after his mother more than the rest. She had been proud, too, when she was a girl. He wished he hadn't been hasty that time they had words about those boxes at the store. Anyway, it turned out that it wasn't Jim's fault. But he was gone that night, and try as they might to find him, they never had word of him since. And Joe sighed again more heavily than before.

Old 'Liza shied at something in the road, and Joe took a firmer hold on the reins. It turned his thoughts to the horse. She was getting old, too, and not as handy as she was. He noticed that she was getting winded with a heavy load. It was well on to ten years she had been their capital and the breadwinner of the house. Sometimes he thought that she missed Jim. If she was to leave them now, he wouldn't know what to do, for he couldn't raise the money to buy another horse nohow, as things were. Poor old 'Liza! He stroked her gray coat musingly with the point of his whip as he thought of their old friendship. The horse pointed one ear back toward her master and neighed gently, as if to assure him that she was all right.

Suddenly she stumbled. Joe pulled her up in time, and throwing the reins over her back, got down to see what it was. An old horseshoe, and in the dust beside it a new silver quarter. He picked both up and put the shoe in the wagon.

"They say it is luck," he mused, "finding horse-iron and money. Maybe it's my Christmas. Get up, 'Liza!" And he drove off to the ferry.

The glare of a thousand gas lamps had chased the sunset out of the western sky, when Joe drove home through the city's streets. Between their straight, mile-long rows surged the busy life of the coming holiday. In front of every grocery store was a grove of fragrant Christmas trees waiting to be fitted into little green stands with fairy fences. Within, customers were bargaining, chatting, and bantering the busy clerks. Pedlers offering tinsel and colored candles waylaid them on the door-step. The rack under the butcher's awning fairly groaned with its weight of plucked geese, of turkeys, stout and skinny, of poultry of every kind. The saloon-keeper even had wreathed his door-posts in ground-ivy and hemlock, and hung a sprig of holly in the window, as if with a spurious promise of peace on earth and good-will toward men who entered there. It tempted not Joe. He drove past it to the corner, where he turned up a street darker and lonelier than the rest, toward a stretch of rocky, vacant lots fenced in by an old stone wall. 'Liza turned in at the rude gate without being told, and pulled up at the house.

A plain little one-story frame with a lean-to for a kitchen, and an adjoining stable-shed, overshadowed all by two great chestnuts of the days when there were country lanes where now are paved streets, and on Manhattan Island there was farm by farm. A light gleamed in the window looking toward the street. As 'Liza's hoofs were heard on the drive, a young girl with a shawl over her head ran out from some shelter where she had been watching, and took the reins from Joe.

"You're late," she said, stroking the mare's steaming flank. 'Liza reached around and rubbed her head against the girl's shoulder, nibbling playfully at the fringe of her shawl.

"Yes; we've come far, and it's been a hard pull. 'Liza is tired. Give her a good feed, and I'll bed her down. How's mother?"

"Sprier than she was," replied the girl, bending over the shaft to unbuckle the horse; "seems as if she'd kinder cheered up for Christmas." And she led 'Liza to the stable while her father backed the wagon into the shed.

It was warm and very comfortable in the little kitchen, where he joined the family after "washing up." The fire burned brightly in the range, on which a good-sized roast sizzled cheerily in its pot, sending up clouds of savory steam. The sand on the white-pine floor was swept in tongues, old-country fashion. Joe and his wife were both born across the sea, and liked to keep Christmas eve as they had kept it when they were children. Two little boys and a younger girl than the one who had met him at the gate received him with shouts of glee, and pulled him straight from the door to look at a hemlock branch stuck in the tub of sand in the corner. It was their Christmas tree, and they were to light it with candles, red and yellow and green, which mamma got them at the grocer's where the big Santa Claus stood on the shelf. They pranced about like so many little colts, and clung to Joe by turns, shouting all at once, each one anxious to tell the great news first and loudest.

Joe took them on his knee, all three, and when they had shouted until they had to stop for breath, he pulled from under his coat a paper bundle, at which the children's eyes bulged. He undid the wrapping slowly.

"Who do you think has come home with me?" he said, and he held up before them the veritable Santa Claus himself, done in plaster and all snow-covered. He had bought it at the corner toy-store with his lucky quarter. "I met him on the road over on Long Island, where 'Liza and I was to-day, and I gave him a ride to town. They say it's luck falling in with Santa Claus, partickler when there's a horseshoe along. I put hisn up in the barn, in 'Liza's stall. Maybe our luck will turn yet, eh! old woman?" And he put his arm around his wife, who was setting out the dinner with Jennie, and gave her a good hug, while the children danced off with their Santa Claus.

She was a comely little woman, and she tried hard to be cheerful. She gave him a brave look and a smile, but there were tears in her eyes, and Joe saw them, though he let on that he didn't. He patted her tenderly on the back and smoothed his Jennie's yellow braids, while he swallowed the lump in his throat and got it down and out of the way. He needed no doctor to tell him that Santa Claus would not come again and find her cooking their Christmas dinner, unless she mended soon and swiftly.

It may be it was the thought of that which made him keep hold of her hand in his lap as they sat down together, and he read from the good book the "tidings of great joy which shall be to all people," and said the simple grace of a plain and ignorant, but reverent, man. He held it tight, as though he needed its support, when he came to the petition for "those dear to us and far away from home," for his glance strayed to the empty place beside the mother's chair, and his voice would tremble in spite of himself. He met his wife's eyes there, but, strangely, he saw no faltering in them. They rested upon Jim's vacant seat with a new look of trust that almost frightened him. It was as if the Christmas peace, the tidings of great joy, had sunk into her heart with rest and hope which presently throbbed through his, with new light and promise, and echoed in the children's happy voices.

So they ate their dinner together, and sang and talked until it was time to go to bed. Joe went out to make all snug about 'Liza for the night and to give her an extra feed. He stopped in the door, coming back, to shake the snow out of his clothes. It was coming on with bad weather and a northerly storm, he reported. The snow was falling thick already and drifting badly. He saw to the kitchen fire and put the children to bed. Long before the clock in the neighboring church tower struck twelve, and its doors were opened for the throngs come to worship at the midnight mass, the lights in the cottage were out, and all within it fast asleep.

The murmur of the homeward-hurrying crowds had died out, and the last echoing shout of "Merry Christmas!" had been whirled away on the storm, now grown fierce with bitter cold, when a lonely wanderer came down the street. It was a lad, big and strong-limbed, and, judging from the manner in which he pushed his way through the gathering drifts, not unused to battle with the world, but evidently in hard luck. His jacket, white with the falling snow, was scant and worn nearly to rags, and there was that in his face which spoke of hunger and suffering silently endured. He stopped at the gate in the stone fence, and looked long and steadily at the cottage in the chestnuts. No life stirred within, and he walked through the gap with slow and hesitating step. Under the kitchen window he stood awhile, sheltered from the storm, as if undecided, then stepped to the horse shed and rapped gently on the door.

"'Liza!" he called, "'Liza, old girl! It's me—Jim!"

A low, delighted whinnying from the stall told the shivering boy that he was not forgotten there. The faithful beast was straining at her halter in a vain effort to get at her friend. Jim raised a bar that held the door closed by the aid of a lever within, of which he knew the trick, and went in. The horse made room for him in her stall, and laid her shaggy head against his cheek.

"Poor old 'Liza!" he said, patting her neck and smoothing her gray coat, "poor old girl! Jim has one friend that hasn't gone back on him. I've come to keep Christmas with you, 'Liza! Had your supper, eh? You're in luck. I haven't; I wasn't bid, 'Liza; but never mind. You shall feed for both of us. Here goes!" He dug into the oats-bin with the measure, and poured it full into 'Liza's crib.

"Fill up, old girl! and good night to you." With a departing pat he crept up the ladder to the loft above, and, scooping out a berth in the loose hay, snuggled down in it to sleep. Soon his regular breathing up there kept step with the steady munching of the horse in her stall. The two reunited friends were dreaming happy Christmas dreams.

The night wore into the small hours of Christmas morning. The fury of the storm was unabated. The old cottage shook under the fierce blasts, and the chestnuts waved their hoary branches wildly, beseechingly, above it, as if they wanted to warn those within of some threatened danger. But they slept and heard them not. From the kitchen chimney, after a blast more violent than any that had gone before, a red spark issued, was whirled upward and beaten against the shingle roof of the barn, swept clean of snow. Another followed it, and another. Still they slept in the cottage; the chestnuts moaned and brandished their arms in vain. The storm fanned one of the sparks into a flame. It flickered for a moment and then went out. So, at least, it seemed. But presently it reappeared, and with it a faint glow was reflected in the attic window over the door. Down in her stall 'Liza moved uneasily. Nobody responding, she plunged and reared, neighing loudly for help. The storm drowned her calls; her master slept, unheeding.

But one heard it, and in the nick of time. The door of the shed was thrown violently open, and out plunged Jim, his hair on fire and his clothes singed and smoking. He brushed the sparks off himself as if they were flakes of snow. Quick as thought, he tore 'Liza's halter from its fastening, pulling out staple and all, threw his smoking coat over her eyes, and backed her out of the shed. He reached in, and, pulling the harness off the hook, threw it as far into the snow as he could, yelling "Fire!" at the top of his voice. Then he jumped on the back of the horse, and beating her with heels and hands into a mad gallop, was off up the street before the bewildered inmates of the cottage had rubbed the sleep out of their eyes and come out to see the barn on fire and burning up.

Down street and avenue fire-engines raced with clanging bells, leaving tracks of glowing coals in the snow-drifts, to the cottage in the chestnut lots. They got there just in time to see the roof crash into the barn, burying, as Joe and his crying wife and children thought, 'Liza and their last hope in the fiery wreck. The door had blown shut, and the harness Jim threw out was snowed under. No one dreamed that the mare was not there. The flames burst through the wreck and lit up the cottage and swaying chestnuts. Joe and his family stood in the shelter of it, looking sadly on. For the second time that Christmas night tears came into the honest truckman's eyes. He wiped them away with his cap.

"Poor 'Liza!" he said.

A hand was laid with gentle touch upon his arm. He looked up. It was his wife. Her face beamed with a great happiness.

"Joe," she said, "you remember what you read: 'tidings of great joy.' Oh, Joe, Jim has come home!"

She stepped aside, and there was Jim, sister Jennie hanging on his neck, and 'Liza alive and neighing her pleasure. The lad looked at his father and hung his head.

"Jim saved her, father," said Jennie, patting the gray mare; "it was him fetched the engines."

Joe took a step toward his son and held out his hand to him.

"Jim," he said, "you're a better man nor yer father. From now on, you 'n' I run the truck on shares. But mind this, Jim: never leave mother no more."

And in the clasp of the two hands all the past was forgotten and forgiven. Father and son had found each other again.

"'Liza," said the truckman, with sudden vehemence, turning to the old mare and putting his arm around her neck, "'Liza! It was your doin's. I knew it was luck when I found them things. Merry Christmas!" And he kissed her smack on her hairy mouth, one, two, three times.

HEROES WHO FIGHT FIRE

Thirteen years have passed since,[2] but it is all to me as if it had happened yesterday—the clanging of the fire-bells, the hoarse shouts of the firemen, the wild rush and terror of the streets; then the great hush that fell upon the crowd; the sea of upturned faces, with the fire-glow upon it; and up there, against the background of black smoke that poured from roof and attic, the boy clinging to the narrow ledge, so far up that it seemed humanly impossible that help could ever come.

But even then it was coming. Up from the street, while the crew of the truck company were laboring with the heavy extension-ladder that at its longest stretch was many feet too short, crept four men upon long, slender poles with cross-bars, iron-hooked at the end. Standing in one window, they reached up and thrust the hook through the next one above, then mounted a story higher. Again the crash of glass, and again the dizzy ascent. Straight up the wall they crept, looking like human flies on the ceiling, and clinging as close, never resting, reaching one recess only to set out for the next; nearer and nearer in the race for life, until but a single span separated the foremost from the boy. And now the iron hook fell at his feet, and the fireman stood upon the step with the rescued lad in his arms, just as the pent-up flame burst lurid from the attic window, reaching with impotent fury for its prey. The next moment they were safe upon the great ladder waiting to receive them below.

Then such a shout went up! Men fell on each other's necks, and cried and laughed at once. Strangers slapped one another on the back, with glistening faces, shook hands, and behaved generally like men gone suddenly mad. Women wept in the street. The driver of a car stalled in the crowd, who had stood through it all speechless, clutching the reins, whipped his horses into a gallop, and drove away yelling like a Comanche, to relieve his feelings. The boy and his rescuer were carried across the street without any one knowing how. Policemen forgot their dignity, and shouted with the rest. Fire, peril, terror, and loss were alike forgotten in the one touch of nature that makes the whole world kin.

Fireman John Binns was made captain of his crew, and the Bennett medal was pinned on his coat on the next parade-day. The burning of the St. George Flats was the first opportunity New York had of witnessing a rescue with the scaling-ladders that form such an essential part of the equipment of the fire-fighters to-day. Since then there have been many such. In the company in which John Binns was a private of the second grade, two others to-day bear the medal for brave deeds: the foreman, Daniel J. Meagher, and Private Martin M. Coleman, whose name has been seven times inscribed on the roll of honor for twice that number of rescues, any one of which stamped him as a man among men, a real hero. And Hook-and-Ladder No. 3 is not especially distinguished among the fire-crews of the metropolis for daring and courage. New Yorkers are justly proud of their firemen. Take it all in all, there is not, I think, to be found anywhere a body of men as fearless, as brave, and as efficient as the Fire Brigade of New York. I have known it well for twenty years, and I speak from a personal acquaintance with very many of its men, and from a professional knowledge of more daring feats, more hairbreadth escapes, and more brilliant work, than could well be recorded between the covers of this book.

Indeed, it is hard, in recording any, to make a choice and to avoid giving the impression that recklessness is a chief quality in the fireman's make-up. That would not be true. His life is too full of real peril for him to expose it recklessly—that is to say, needlessly. From the time when he leaves his quarters in answer to an alarm until he returns, he takes a risk that may at any moment set him face to face with death in its most cruel form. He needs nothing so much as a clear head; and nothing is prized so highly, nothing puts him so surely in the line of promotion; for as he advances in rank and responsibility, the lives of others, as well as his own, come to depend on his judgment. The act of conspicuous daring which the world applauds is oftenest to the fireman a matter of simple duty that had to be done in that way because there was no other. Nor is it always, or even usually, the hardest duty, as he sees it. It came easy to him because he is an athlete, trained to do just such things, and because once for all it is easier to risk one's life in the open, in the sight of one's fellows, than to face death alone, caught like a rat in a trap. That is the real peril which he knows too well; but of that the public hears only when he has fought his last fight, and lost.

How literally our every-day security—of which we think, if we think of it at all, as a mere matter of course—is built upon the supreme sacrifice of these devoted men, we realize at long intervals, when a disaster occurs such as the one in which Chief Bresnan and Foreman Rooney[3] lost their lives three years ago. They were crushed to death under the great water-tank in a Twenty-fourth Street factory that was on fire. Its supports had been burned away. An examination that was then made of the water-tanks in the city discovered eight thousand that were either wholly unsupported, except by the roof-beams, or propped on timbers, and therefore a direct menace, not only to the firemen when they were called there, but daily to those living under them. It is not pleasant to add that the department's just demand for a law that should compel landlords either to build tanks on the wall or on iron supports has not been heeded yet; but that is, unhappily, an old story.

Seventeen years ago the collapse of a Broadway building during a fire convinced the community that stone pillars were unsafe as supports. The fire was in the basement, and the firemen had turned the hose on. When the water struck the hot granite columns, they cracked and fell, and the building fell with them. There were upon the roof at the time a dozen men of the crew of Truck Company No. 1, chopping holes for smoke-vents. The majority clung to the parapet, and hung there till rescued. Two went down into the furnace from which the flames shot up twenty feet when the roof broke. One, Fireman Thomas J. Dougherty, was a wearer of the Bennett medal, too. His foreman answers on parade-day, when his name is called, that he "died on the field of duty." These, at all events, did not die in vain. Stone columns are not now used as supports for buildings in New York.

So one might go on quoting the perils of the firemen as so many steps forward for the better protection of the rest of us. It was the burning of the St. George Flats, and more recently of the Manhattan Bank, in which a dozen men were disabled, that stamped the average fire-proof construction as faulty and largely delusive. One might even go further, and say that the fireman's risk increases in the ratio of our progress or convenience. The water-tanks came with the very high buildings, which in themselves offer problems to the fire-fighters that have not yet been solved. The very air-shafts that were hailed as the first advance in tenement-house building added enormously to the fireman's work and risk, as well as to the risk of every one dwelling under their roofs, by acting as so many huge chimneys that carried the fire to the windows opening upon them in every story. More than half of all the fires in New York occur in tenement houses. When the Tenement House Commission of 1894 sat in this city, considering means of making them safer and better, it received the most practical help and advice from the firemen, especially from Chief Bresnan, whose death occurred only a few days after he had testified as a witness. The recommendations upon which he insisted are now part of the general tenement-house law.

Chief Bresnan died leading his men against the enemy. In the Fire Department the battalion chief leads; he does not direct operations from a safe position in the rear. Perhaps this is one of the secrets of the indomitable spirit of his men. Whatever hardships they have to endure, his is the first and the biggest share. Next in line comes the captain, or foreman, as he is called. Of the six who were caught in the fatal trap of the water-tank, four hewed their way out with axes through an intervening partition. They were of the ranks. The two who were killed were the chief and Assistant Foreman John L. Rooney, who was that day in charge of his company, Foreman Shaw having just been promoted to Bresnan's rank. It was less than a year after that Chief Shaw was killed in a fire in Mercer Street. I think I could reckon up as many as five or six battalion chiefs who have died in that way, leading their men. The men would not deserve the name if they did not follow such leaders, no matter where the road led.

In the chief's quarters of the Fourteenth Battalion up in Wakefield there sits to-day a man, still young in years, who in his maimed body but unbroken spirit bears such testimony to the quality of New York's fire-fighters as the brave Bresnan and his comrade did in their death. Thomas J. Ahearn led his company as captain to a fire in the Consolidated Gas-Works on the East Side. He found one of the buildings ablaze. Far toward the rear, at the end of a narrow lane, around which the fire swirled and arched itself, white and wicked, lay the body of a man—dead, said the panic-stricken crowd. His sufferings had been brief. A worse fate threatened all unless the fire was quickly put out. There were underground reservoirs of naphtha—the ground was honeycombed with them—that might explode at any moment with the fire raging overhead. The peril was instant and great. Captain Ahearn looked at the body, and saw it stir. The watch-chain upon the man's vest rose and fell as if he were breathing.

"He is not dead," he said. "I am going to get that man out." And he crept down the lane of fire, unmindful of the hidden dangers, seeing only the man who was perishing. The flames scorched him; they blocked his way; but he came through alive, and brought out his man, so badly hurt, however, that he died in the hospital that day. The Board of Fire Commissioners gave Ahearn the medal for bravery, and made him chief. Within a year he all but lost his life in a gallant attempt to save the life of a child that was supposed to be penned in a burning Rivington Street tenement. Chief Ahearn's quarters were near by, and he was first on the ground. A desperate man confronted him in the hallway. "My child! my child!" he cried, and wrung his hands. "Save him! He is in there." He pointed to the back room. It was black with smoke. In the front room the fire was raging. Crawling on hands and feet, the chief made his way into the room the man had pointed out. He groped under the bed, and in it, but found no child there. Satisfied that it had escaped, he started to return. The smoke had grown so thick that breathing was no longer possible, even at the floor. The chief drew his coat over his head, and made a dash for the hall door. He reached it only to find that the spring-lock had snapped shut. The door-knob burned his hand. The fire burst through from the front room, and seared his face. With a last effort, he kicked the lower panel out of the door, and put his head through. And then he knew no more.

His men found him lying so when they came looking for him. The coat was burned off his back, and of his hat only the wire rim remained. He lay ten months in the hospital, and came out deaf and wrecked physically. At the age of forty-five the board retired him to the quiet of the country district, with this formal resolution, that did the board more credit than it could do him. It is the only one of its kind upon the department books:—

Resolved, That in assigning Battalion Chief Thomas J. Ahearn to command the Fourteenth Battalion, in the newly annexed district, the Board deems it proper to express the sense of obligation felt by the Board and all good citizens for the brilliant and meritorious services of Chief Ahearn in the discharge of duty which will always serve as an example and an inspiration to our uniformed force, and to express the hope that his future years of service at a less arduous post may be as comfortable and pleasant as his former years have been brilliant and honorable.

Firemen are athletes as a matter of course. They have to be, or they could not hold their places for a week, even if they could get into them at all. The mere handling of the scaling-ladders, which, light though they seem, weigh from sixteen to forty pounds, requires unusual strength. No particular skill is needed. A man need only have steady nerve, and the strength to raise the long pole by its narrow end, and jam the iron hook through a window which he cannot see but knows is there. Once through, the teeth in the hook and the man's weight upon the ladder hold it safe, and there is no real danger unless he loses his head. Against that possibility the severe drill in the school of instruction is the barrier. Any one to whom climbing at dizzy heights, or doing the hundred and one things of peril to ordinary men which firemen are constantly called upon to do, causes the least discomfort, is rejected as unfit. About five percent of all appointees are eliminated by the ladder test, and never get beyond their probation service. A certain smaller percentage takes itself out through loss of "nerve" generally. The first experience of a room full of smothering smoke, with the fire roaring overhead, is generally sufficient to convince the timid that the service is not for him. No cowards are dismissed from the department, for the reason that none get into it.

The notion that there is a life-saving corps apart from the general body of firemen rests upon a mistake. They are one. Every fireman nowadays must pass muster at life-saving drill, must climb to the top of any building on his scaling-ladder, slide down with a rescued comrade, or jump without hesitation from the third story into the life-net spread below. By such training the men are fitted for their work, and the occasion comes soon that puts them to the test. It came to Daniel J. Meagher, of whom I spoke as foreman of Hook-and-Ladder Company No. 3, when, in the midnight hour, a woman hung from the fifth-story window of a burning building, and the longest ladder at hand fell short ten or a dozen feet of reaching her. The boldest man in the crew had vainly attempted to get to her, and in the effort had sprained his foot. There were no scaling-ladders then. Meagher ordered the rest to plant the ladder on the stoop and hold it out from the building so that he might reach the very topmost step. Balanced thus where the slightest tremor might have caused ladder and all to crash to the ground, he bade the woman drop, and receiving her in his arms, carried her down safe.

No one but an athlete with muscles and nerves of steel could have performed such a feat, or that which made Dennis Ryer, of the crew of Engine No. 36, famous three years ago. That was on Seventh Avenue at One Hundred and Thirty-fourth Street. A flat was on fire, and the tenants had fled; but one, a woman, bethought herself of her parrot, and went back for it, to find escape by the stairs cut off when she again attempted to reach the street. With the parrot-cage, she appeared at the top-floor window, framed in smoke, calling for help. Again there was no ladder to reach. There were neighbors on the roof with a rope, but the woman was too frightened to use it herself. Dennis Ryer made it fast about his own waist, and bade the others let him down, and hold on for life. He drew the woman out, but she was heavy, and it was all they could do above to hold them. To pull them over the cornice was out of the question. Upon the highest step of the ladder, many feet below, stood Ryer's father, himself a fireman of another company, and saw his boy's peril.

"Hold fast, Dennis!" he shouted. "If you fall I will catch you." Had they let go, all three would have been killed. The young fireman saw the danger, and the one door of escape, with a glance. The window before which he swung, half smothered by the smoke that belched from it, was the last in the house. Just beyond, in the window of the adjoining house, was safety, if he could but reach it. Putting out a foot, he kicked the wall, and made himself swing toward it, once, twice, bending his body to add to the motion. The third time he all but passed it, and took a mighty grip on the affrighted woman, shouting into her ear to loose her own hold at the same time. As they passed the window on the fourth trip, he thrust her through sash and all with a supreme effort, and himself followed on the next rebound, while the street, that was black with a surging multitude, rang with a mighty cheer. Old Washington Ryer, on his ladder, threw his cap in the air, and cheered louder than all the rest. But the parrot was dead—frightened to death, very likely, or smothered.

I once asked Fireman Martin M. Coleman, after one of those exhibitions of coolness and courage that thrust him constantly upon the notice of the newspaper men, what he thought of when he stood upon the ladder, with this thing before him to do that might mean life or death the next moment. He looked at me in some perplexity.

"Think?" he said slowly. "Why, I don't think. There ain't any time to. If I'd stopped to think, them five people would 'a' been burnt. No; I don't think of danger. If it is anything, it is that—up there—I am boss. The rest are not in it. Only I wish," he added, rubbing his arm ruefully at the recollection, "that she hadn't fainted. It's hard when they faint. They're just so much dead-weight. We get no help at all from them heavy women."

And that was all I could get out of him. I never had much better luck with Chief Benjamin A. Gicquel, who is the oldest wearer of the Bennett medal, just as Coleman is the youngest, or the one who received it last. He was willing enough to talk about the science of putting out fires; of Department Chief Bonner, the "man of few words," who, he thinks, has mastered the art beyond any man living; of the back-draught, and almost anything else pertaining to the business: but when I insisted upon his telling me the story of the rescue of the Schaefer family of five from a burning tenement down in Cherry Street, in which he earned his rank and reward, he laughed a good-humored little laugh, and said that it was "the old man"—meaning Schaefer—who should have had the medal. "It was a grand thing in him to let the little ones come out first." I have sometimes wished that firemen were not so modest. It would be much easier, if not so satisfactory, to record their gallant deeds. But I am not sure that it is, after all, modesty so much as a wholly different point of view. It is business with them, the work of their lives. The one feeling that is allowed to rise beyond this is the feeling of exultation in the face of peril conquered by courage, which Coleman expressed. On the ladder he was boss! It was the fancy of a masterful man, and none but a masterful man would have got upon the ladder at all.

Doubtless there is something in the spectacular side of it that attracts. It would be strange if there were not. There is everything in a fireman's existence to encourage it. Day and night he leads a kind of hair-trigger life, that feeds naturally upon excitement, even if only as a relief from the irksome idling in quarters. Try as they may to give him enough to do there, the time hangs heavily upon his hands, keyed up as he is, and need be, to adventurous deeds at shortest notice. He falls to grumbling and quarrelling, and the necessity becomes imperative of holding him to the strictest discipline, under which he chafes impatiently. "They nag like a lot of old women," said Department Chief Bonner to me once; "and the best at a fire are often the worst in the house." In the midst of it all the gong strikes a familiar signal. The horses' hoofs thunder on the planks; with a leap the men go down the shining pole to the main floor, all else forgotten; and with crash and clatter and bang the heavy engine swings into the street, and races away on a wild gallop, leaving a trail of fire behind.

Presently the crowd sees rubber-coated, helmeted men with pipe and hose go through a window from which such dense smoke pours forth that it seems incredible that a human being could breathe it for a second and live. The hose is dragged squirming over the sill, where shortly a red-eyed face with dishevelled hair appears, to shout something hoarsely to those below, which they understand. Then, unless some emergency arise, the spectacular part is over. Could the citizen whose heart beat as he watched them enter see them now, he would see grimy shapes, very unlike the fine-looking men who but just now had roused his admiration, crawling on hands and knees, with their noses close to the floor if the smoke be very dense, ever pointing the "pipe" in the direction where the enemy is expected to appear. The fire is the enemy; but he can fight that, once he reaches it, with something of a chance. The smoke kills without giving him a show to fight back. Long practice toughens him against it, until he learns the trick of "eating the smoke." He can breathe where a candle goes out for want of oxygen. By holding his mouth close to the nozzle, he gets what little air the stream of water brings with it and sets free; and within a few inches of the floor there is nearly always a current of air. In the last emergency, there is the hose that he can follow out. The smoke always is his worst enemy. It lays ambushes for him which he can suspect, but not ward off. He tries to, by opening vents in the roof as soon as the pipemen are in place and ready; but in spite of all precautions, he is often surprised by the dreaded back-draught.

I remember standing in front of a burning Broadway store, one night, when the back-draught blew out the whole front without warning. It is simply an explosion of gases generated by the heat, which must have vent, and go upon the line of least resistance, up, or down, or in a circle—it does not much matter, so that they go. It swept shutters, windows, and all, across Broadway, in this instance, like so much chaff, littering the street with heavy rolls of cloth. The crash was like a fearful clap of thunder. Men were knocked down on the opposite sidewalk, and two teams of engine horses, used to almost any kind of happening at a fire, ran away in a wild panic. It was a blast of that kind that threw down and severely injured Battalion Chief M'Gill, one of the oldest and most experienced of firemen, at a fire on Broadway in March, 1890; and it has cost more brave men's lives than the fiercest fire that ever raged. The "puff," as the firemen call it, comes suddenly, and from the corner where it is least expected. It is dread of that, and of getting overcome by the smoke generally, which makes firemen go always in couples or more together. They never lose sight of one another for an instant, if they can help it. If they do, they go at once in search of the lost. The delay of a moment may prove fatal to him.

Lieutenant Samuel Banta of the Franklin Street company, discovering the pipe that had just been held by Fireman Quinn at a Park Place fire thrashing aimlessly about, looked about him, and saw Quinn floating on his face in the cellar, which was running full of water. He had been overcome, had tumbled in, and was then drowning, with the fire raging above and alongside. Banta jumped in after him, and endeavored to get his head above water. While thus occupied, he glanced up, and saw the preliminary puff of the back-draught bearing down upon him. The lieutenant dived at once, and tried to pull his unhappy pipe-man with him; but he struggled and worked himself loose. From under the water Banta held up a hand, and it was burnt. He held up the other, and knew that the puff had passed when it came back unsinged. Then he brought Quinn out with him; but it was too late. Caught between flood and fire, he had no chance. When I asked the lieutenant about it, he replied simply: "The man in charge of the hose fell into the cellar. I got him out; that was all." "But how?" I persisted. "Why, I went down through the cellar," said the lieutenant, smiling, as if it was the most ordinary thing in the world.

It was this same Banta who, when Fireman David H. Soden had been buried under the falling walls of a Pell Street house, crept through a gap in the basement wall, in among the fallen timbers, and, in imminent peril of his own life, worked there with a hand-saw two long hours to free his comrade, while the firemen held the severed timbers up with ropes to give him a chance. Repeatedly, while he was at work, his clothes caught fire, and it was necessary to keep playing the hose upon him. But he brought out his man safe and sound, and, for the twentieth time perhaps, had his name recorded on the roll of merit. His comrades tell how, at one of the twenty, the fall of a building in Hall Place had left a workman lying on a shaky piece of wall, helpless, with a broken leg. It could not bear the weight of a ladder, and it seemed certain death to attempt to reach him, when Banta, running up a slanting beam that still hung to its fastening with one end, leaped from perch to perch upon the wall, where hardly a goat could have found footing, reached his man, and brought him down slung over his shoulder, and swearing at him like a trooper lest the peril of the descent cause him to lose his nerve and with it the lives of both.

Firemen dread cellar fires more than any other kind, and with reason. It is difficult to make a vent for the smoke, and the danger of drowning is added to that of being smothered when they get fairly to work. If a man is lost to sight or touch of his fellows there for ever so brief a while, there are five chances to one that he will not again be seen alive. Then there ensues such a fight as the city witnessed only last May at the burning of a Chambers Street paper-warehouse. It was fought out deep underground, with fire and flood, freezing cold and poisonous gases, leagued against Chief Bonner's forces. Next door was a cold-storage house, whence the cold. Something that was burning—I do not know that it was ever found out just what—gave forth the smothering fumes before which the firemen went down in squads. File after file staggered out into the street, blackened and gasping, to drop there. The near engine-house was made into a hospital, where the senseless men were laid on straw hastily spread. Ambulance surgeons worked over them. As fast as they were brought to, they went back to bear a hand in the work of rescue. In delirium they fought to return. Down in the depths one of their number was lying helpless.

There is nothing finer in the records of glorious war than the story of the struggle these brave fellows kept up for hours against tremendous odds for the rescue of their comrade. Time after time they went down into the pit of deadly smoke, only to fail. Lieutenant Banta tried twice and failed. Fireman King was pulled up senseless, and having been brought round went down once more. Fireman Sheridan returned empty-handed, more dead than alive. John O'Connell, of Truck No. 1, at length succeeded in reaching his comrade and tying a rope about him, while from above they drenched both with water to keep them from roasting. They drew up a dying man; but John G. Reinhardt dead is more potent than a whole crew of firemen alive. The story of the fight for his life will long be told in the engine-houses of New York, and will nerve the Kings and the Sheridans and the O'Connells of another day to like deeds.

How firemen manage to hear in their sleep the right signal, while they sleep right through any number that concerns the next company, not them, is one of the mysteries that will probably always remain unsolved. "I don't know," said Department Chief Bonner, when I asked him once. "I guess it is the same way with everybody. You hear what you have to hear. There is a gong right over my bed at home, and I hear every stroke of it, but I don't hear the baby. My wife hears the baby if it as much as stirs in its crib, but not the gong." Very likely he is right. The fact that the fireman can hear and count correctly the strokes of the gong in his sleep has meant life to many hundreds, and no end of properly saved; for it is in the early moments of a fire that it can be dealt with summarily. I recall one instance in which the failure to interpret a signal properly, or the accident of taking a wrong road to the fire, cost a life, and, singularly enough, that of the wife of one of the firemen who answered the alarm. It was all so pitiful, so tragic, that it has left an indelible impression on my mind. It was the fire at which Patrick F. Lucas earned the medal for that year by snatching five persons out of the very jaws of death in a Dominick Street tenement. The alarm-signal rang in the hook-and-ladder company's quarters in North Moore Street, but was either misunderstood or they made a wrong start. Instead of turning east to West Broadway, the truck turned west, and went galloping toward Greenwich Street. It was only a few seconds, the time that was lost, but it was enough. Fireman Murphy's heart went up in his throat when, from his seat on the truck as it flew toward the fire, he saw that it was his own home that was burning. Up on the fifth floor he found his wife penned in. She died in his arms as he carried her to the fire-escape. The fire, for once, had won in the race for a life.

While I am writing this, the morning paper that is left at my door tells the story of a fireman who, laid up with a broken ankle in an up-town hospital, jumped out of bed, forgetting his injury, when the alarm-gong rang his signal, and tried to go to the fire. The fire-alarms are rung in the hospitals for the information of the ambulance corps. The crippled fireman heard the signal at the dead of night, and, only half awake, jumped out of bed, groped about for the sliding-pole, and, getting hold of the bedpost, tried to slide down that. The plaster cast about his ankle was broken, the old injury reopened, and he was seriously hurt.

New York firemen have a proud saying that they "fight fire from the inside." It means unhesitating courage, prompt sacrifice, and victory gained, all in one. The saving of life that gets into the newspapers and wins applause is done, of necessity, largely from the outside, but is none the less perilous for that. Sometimes, though rarely, it has in its intense gravity almost a comic tinge, as at one of the infrequent fires in the Mulberry Bend some years ago. The Italians believe, with reason, that there is bad luck in fire, therefore do not insure, and have few fires. Of this one the Romolo family shrine was the cause. The lamp upon it exploded, and the tenement was ablaze when the firemen came. The policeman on the beat had tried to save Mrs. Romolo; but she clung to the bedpost, and refused to go without the rest of the family. So he seized the baby, and rolled down the burning stairs with it, his beard and coat afire. The only way out was shut off when the engines arrived. The Romolos shrieked at the top-floor window, threatening to throw themselves out. There was not a moment to be lost. Lying flat on the roof, with their heads over the cornice, the firemen fished the two children out of the window with their hooks. The ladders were run up in time for the father and mother.

The readiness of resource no less than the intrepid courage and athletic skill of the rescuers evoke enthusiastic admiration. Two instances stand out in my recollection among many. Of one Fireman Howe, who had on more than one occasion signally distinguished himself, was the hero. It happened on the morning of January 2, 1896, when the Geneva Club on Lexington Avenue was burnt out. Fireman Howe drove Hook-and-Ladder No. 7 to the fire that morning, to find two boarders at the third-story window, hemmed in by flames which already showed behind them. Followed by Fireman Pearl, he ran up in the adjoining building, and presently appeared at a window on the third floor, separated from the one occupied by the two men by a blank wall-space of perhaps four or five feet. It offered no other footing than a rusty hook, but it was enough. Astride of the window-sill, with one foot upon the hook, the other anchored inside by his comrade, his body stretched at full length along the wall, Howe was able to reach the two, and to swing them, one after the other, through his own window to safety. As the second went through, the crew in the street below set up a cheer that raised the sleeping echoes of the street. Howe looked down, nodded, and took a firmer grip; and that instant came his great peril.

A third face had appeared at the window just as the fire swept through. Howe shut his eyes to shield them, and braced himself on the hook for a last effort. It broke; and the man, frightened out of his wits, threw himself headlong from the window upon Howe's neck.

The fireman's form bent and swayed. His comrade within felt the strain, and dug his heels into the boards. He was almost dragged out of the window, but held on with a supreme effort. Just as he thought the end had come, he felt the strain ease up. The ladder had reached Howe in the very nick of time, and given him support, but in his desperate effort to save himself and the other, he slammed his burden back over his shoulder with such force that he went crashing through, carrying sash and all, and fell, cut and bruised, but safe, upon Fireman Pearl, who grovelled upon the door, prostrate and panting.

The other case New York remembers yet with a shudder. It was known long in the department for the bravest act ever done by a fireman—an act that earned for Foreman William Quirk the medal for 1888. He was next in command of Engine No. 22 when, on a March morning, the Elberon Flats in East Eighty-fifth street were burned. The Westlake family, mother, daughter, and two sons, were in the fifth story, helpless and hopeless. Quirk ran up on the scaling-ladder to the fourth floor, hung it on the sill above, and got the boys and their sister down. But the flames burst from the floor below, cutting off their retreat. Quirk's captain had seen the danger, and shouted to him to turn back while it was yet time. But Quirk had no intention of turning back. He measured the distance and the risk with a look, saw the crowd tugging frantically at the life-net under the window, and bade them jump, one by one. They jumped, and were saved. Last of all, he jumped himself, after a vain effort to save the mother. She was already dead. He caught her gown, but the body slipped from his grasp and fell crashing to the street fifty feet below. He himself was hurt in his jump. The volunteers who held the net looked up, and were frightened; they let go their grip, and the plucky fireman broke a leg and hurt his back in the fall.

"Like a cry of fire in the night" appeals to the dullest imagination with a sense of sudden fear. There have been nights in this city when the cry swelled into such a clamor of terror and despair as to make the stoutest heart quake—when it seemed to those who had to do with putting out fires as if the end of all things was at hand. Such a night was that of the burning of "Cohnfeld's Folly," in Bleecker Street, March 17, 1891. The burning of the big store involved the destruction, wholly or in part, of ten surrounding buildings, and called out nearly one-third of the city's Fire Department. While the fire raged as yet unchecked,—while walls were falling with shock and crash of thunder, the streets full of galloping engines and ambulances carrying injured firemen, with clangor of urgent gongs; while insurance patrolmen were being smothered in buildings a block away by the smoke that hung like a pall over the city,—another disastrous fire broke out in the dry-goods district, and three alarm-calls came from West Seventeenth Street. Nine other fires were signalled, and before morning all the crews that were left were summoned to Allen Street, where four persons were burned to death in a tenement. Those are the wild nights that try firemen's souls, and never yet found them wanting. During the great blizzard, when the streets were impassable and the system crippled, the fires in the city averaged nine a day,—forty-five for the five days from March 12 to 16,—and not one of them got beyond control. The fire commissioners put on record their pride in the achievement, as well they might. It was something to be proud of, indeed.

Such a night promised to be the one when the Manhattan Bank and the State Bank across the street on the other Broadway corner, with three or four other buildings, were burned, and when the ominous "two nines" were rung, calling nine-tenths of the whole force below Central Park to the threatened quarter. But, happily, the promise was not fully kept. The supposed fire-proof bank crumbled in the withering blast like so much paper; the cry went up that whole companies of firemen were perishing within it; and the alarm had reached Police Headquarters in the next block, where they were counting the election returns. Thirteen firemen, including the deputy department chief, a battalion chief, and two captains, limped or were carried from the burning bank, more or less injured. The stone steps of the fire-proof stairs had fallen with them or upon them. Their imperilled comrades, whose escape was cut off, slid down hose and scaling-ladders. The last, the crew of Engine Company No. 3, had reached the street, and all were thought to be out, when the assistant foreman, Daniel Fitzmaurice, appeared at the fifth-story window. The fire beating against it drove him away, but he found footing at another, next adjoining the building on the north. To reach him from below, with the whole building ablaze, was impossible. Other escape there was none, save a cornice ledge extending halfway to his window; but it was too narrow to afford foothold.

Then an extraordinary scene was enacted in the sight of thousands. In the other building were a number of fire-insurance patrolmen, covering goods to protect them against water damage. One of these—Patrolman John Rush—stepped out on the ledge, and edged his way toward a spur of stone that projected from the bank building. Behind followed Patrolman Barnett, steadying him and pressing him close against the wall. Behind him was another, with still another holding on within the room, where the living chain was anchored by all the rest. Rush, at the end of the ledge, leaned over and gave Fitzmaurice his hand. The fireman grasped it, and edged out upon the spur. Barnett, holding the rescuer fast, gave him what he needed—something to cling to. Once he was on the ledge, the chain wound itself up as it had unwound itself. Slowly, inch by inch, it crept back, each man pushing the next flat against the wall with might and main, while the multitudes in the street held their breath, and the very engines stopped panting, until all were safe.

John Rush is a fireman to-day, a member of "Thirty-three's" crew in Great Jones Street. He was an insurance patrolman then. The organization is unofficial. Its main purpose is to save property; but in the face of the emergency firemen and patrolmen become one body, obeying one head.

That the spirit which has made New York's Fire Department great equally animates its commercial brother has been shown more than once, but never better than at the memorable fire in the Hotel Royal, which cost so many lives. No account of heroic life-saving at fires, even as fragmentary as this, could pass by the marvellous feat, or feats, of Sergeant (now Captain) John R. Vaughan on that February morning six years ago. The alarm rang in patrol station No. 3 at 3.20 o'clock on Sunday morning. Sergeant Vaughan, hastening to the fire with his men, found the whole five-story hotel ablaze from roof to cellar. The fire had shot up the elevator shaft, round which the stairs ran, and from the first had made escape impossible. Men and women were jumping and hanging from windows. One, falling from a great height, came within an inch of killing the sergeant as he tried to enter the building. Darting up into the next house, and leaning out of the window with his whole body, while one of the crew hung on to one leg,—as Fireman Pearl did to Howe's in the splendid rescue at the Geneva Club,—he took a half-hitch with the other in some electric-light wires that ran up the wall, trusting to his rubber boots to protect him from the current, and made of his body a living bridge for the safe passage from the last window of the burning hotel of three men and a woman whom death stared in the face, steadying them as they went with his free hand. As the last passed over, ladders were being thrown up against the wall, and what could be done there was done.

Sergeant Vaughan went up on the roof. The smoke was so dense there that he could see little, but through it he heard a cry for help, and made out the shape of a man standing upon a window-sill in the fifth story, overlooking the courtyard of the hotel. The yard was between them. Bidding his men follow,—they were five, all told,—he ran down and around in the next street to the roof of the house that formed an angle with the hotel wing. There stood the man below him, only a jump away, but a jump which no mortal might take and live. His face and hands were black with smoke. Vaughan, looking down, thought him a negro. He was perfectly calm.

"It is no use," he said, glancing up. "Don't try. You can't do it."

The sergeant looked wistfully about him. Not a stick or a piece of rope was in sight. Every shred was used below. There was absolutely nothing. "But I couldn't let him," he said to me, months after, when he had come out of the hospital, a whole man again, and was back at work,—"I just couldn't, standing there so quiet and brave." To the man he said sharply:—

"I want you to do exactly as I tell you, now. Don't grab me, but let me get the first grab." He had noticed that the man wore a heavy overcoat, and had already laid his plan.

"Don't try," urged the man. "You cannot save me. I will stay here till it gets too hot; then I will jump."

"No, you won't," from the sergeant, as he lay at full length on the roof, looking over. "It is a pretty hard yard down there. I will get you, or go dead myself."

The four sat on the sergeant's legs as he swung free down to the waist; so he was almost able to reach the man on the window with outstretched hands.

"Now jump—quick!" he commanded; and the man jumped. He caught him by both wrists as directed, and the sergeant got a grip on the collar of his coat.

"Hoist!" he shouted to the four on the roof; and they tugged with their might. The sergeant's body did not move. Bending over till the back creaked, it hung over the edge, a weight of two hundred and three pounds suspended from and holding it down. The cold sweat started upon his men's foreheads as they tried and tried again, without gaining an inch. Blood dripped from Sergeant Vaughan's nostrils and ears. Sixty feet below was the paved courtyard; over against him the window, behind which he saw the back-draught coming, gathering headway with lurid, swirling smoke. Now it burst through, burning the hair and the coats of the two. For an instant he thought all hope was gone.

But in a flash it came back to him. To relieve the terrible dead-weight that wrenched and tore at his muscles, he was swinging the man to and fro like a pendulum, head touching head. He could *swing him up*! A smothered shout warned his men. They crept nearer the edge without letting go their grip on him, and watched with staring eyes the human pendulum swing wider and wider, farther and farther, until now, with a mighty effort, it swung within their reach. They caught the skirt of the coat, held on, pulled in, and in a moment lifted him over the edge.

They lay upon the roof, all six, breathless, sightless, their faces turned to the winter sky. The tumult on the street came up as a faint echo; the spray of a score of engines pumping below fell upon them, froze, and covered them with ice. The very roar of the fire seemed far off. The sergeant was the first to recover. He carried down the man he had saved, and saw him sent off to the hospital. Then first he noticed that he was not a negro; the smut had been rubbed from his face. Monday had dawned before he came to, and days passed before he knew his rescuer. Sergeant Vaughan was laid up himself then. He had returned to his work, and finished it; but what he had gone through was too much for human strength. It was spring before he returned to his quarters, to find himself promoted, petted, and made much of.

From the sublime to the ridiculous is but a little step. Among the many who journeyed to the insurance patrol station to see the hero of the great fire, there came, one day, a woman. She was young and pretty, the sweetheart of the man on the window-sill. He was a lawyer, since a state senator of Pennsylvania. She wished the sergeant to repeat exactly the words he spoke to him in that awful moment when he bade him jump—to life or death. She had heard them, and she wanted the sergeant to repeat them to her, that she might know for sure he was the man who did it. He stammered and hitched—tried subterfuges. She waited, inexorable. Finally, in desperation, blushing fiery red, he blurted out "a lot of cuss-words." "You know," he said apologetically, in telling of it, "when I am in a place like that I can't help it."

When she heard the words which her fiance had already told her, straightway she fell upon the fireman's neck. The sergeant stood dumfounded. "Women are queer," he said.

Thus a fireman's life. That the very horses that are their friends in quarters, their comrades at the fire, sharing with them what comes of good and evil, catch the spirit of it, is not strange. It would be strange if they did not. With human intelligence and more than human affection, the splendid animals follow the fortunes of their masters, doing their share in whatever is demanded of them. In the final showing that in thirty years, while with the growing population the number of fires has steadily increased, the average loss per fire has as steadily decreased, they have their full share, also, of the credit. In 1866 there were 796 fires in New York, with an average loss of $8075.38 per fire. In 1876, with 1382 fires, the loss was but $2786.70 at each. In 1896, 3890 fires averaged only $878.81. It means that every year more fires are headed off than run down—smothered at the start, as a fire should be. When to the verdict of "faithful unto death" that record is added, nothing remains to be said. The firemen know how much of that is the doing of their four-legged comrades. It is the one blot on the fair picture that the city which owes these horses so much has not seen fit, in gratitude, to provide comfort for their worn old age. When a fireman grows old, he is retired on half-pay for the rest of his days. When a horse that has run with the heavy engines to fires by night and by day for perhaps ten or fifteen years is worn out, it is—sold, to a huckster, perhaps, or a contractor, to slave for him until it is fit only for the bone-yard! The city receives a paltry two or three thousand dollars a year for this rank treachery, and pockets the blood-money without a protest. There is room next, in New York, for a movement that shall secure to the fireman's faithful friend the grateful reward of a quiet farm, a full crib, and a green pasture to the end of its days, when it is no longer young enough and strong enough to "run with the machine."

JOHN GAVIN, MISFIT

John Gavin was to blame—there is no doubt of that. To be sure, he was out of a job, with never a cent in his pockets, his babies starving, and notice served by the landlord that day. He had travelled the streets till midnight looking for work, and had found none. And so he gave up. Gave up, with the Employment Bureau in the next street registering applicants; with the Wayfarers' Lodge over in Poverty Gap, where he might have earned fifty cents, anyway, chopping wood; with charities without end, organized and unorganized, that would have sat upon and registered his case, and numbered it properly. With all these things and a hundred like them to meet their wants, the Gavins of our day have been told often enough that they have no business to lose hope. That they will persist is strange. But perhaps this one had never heard of them.

Anyway, Gavin is dead. But yesterday he was the father of six children, running from May, the eldest, who was thirteen and at school, to the baby, just old enough to poke its little fingers into its father's eyes and crow and jump when he came in from his long and dreary tramps. They were as happy a little family as a family of eight could be with the wolf scratching at the door, its nose already poking through. There had been no work and no wages in the house for months, and the landlord had given notice that at the end of the week, out they must go, unless the back rent was paid. And there was about as much likelihood of its being paid as of a slice of the February sun dropping down through the ceiling into the room to warm the shivering Gavin family.

It began when Gavin's health gave way. He was a lather and had a steady job till sickness came. It was the old story: nothing laid away—how could there be, with a houseful of children—and nothing coming in. They talk of death-rates to measure the misery of the slum by, but death does not touch the bottom. It ends the misery. Sickness only begins it. It began Gavin's. When he had to drop hammer and nails, he got a job in a saloon as a barkeeper; but the saloon didn't prosper, and when it was shut up, there was an end. Gavin didn't know it then. He looked at the babies and kept up spirits as well as he could, though it wrung his heart.

He tried everything under the sun to get a job. He travelled early and travelled late, but wherever he went they had men and to spare. And besides, he was ill. As they told him bluntly, sometimes, they didn't have any use for sick men. Men to work and earn wages must be strong. And he had to own that it was true.

Gavin was not strong. As he denied himself secretly the nourishment he needed that his little ones might have enough, he felt it more and more. It was harder work for him to get around, and each refusal left him more downcast. He was yet a young man, only thirty-four, but he felt as if he was old and tired—tired out; that was it.

The feeling grew on him while he went his last errand, offering his services at saloons and wherever, as he thought, an opening offered. In fact, he thought but little about it any more. The whole thing had become an empty, hopeless formality with him. He knew at last that he was looking for the thing he would never find; that in a cityful where every man had his place he was a misfit with none. With his dull brain dimly conscious of that one idea, he plodded homeward in the midnight hour. He had been on the go since early morning, and excepting some lunch from the saloon counters, had eaten nothing.

The lamp burned dimly in the room where May sat poring yet over her books, waiting for papa. When he came in she looked up and smiled, but saw by his look, as he hung up his hat, that there was no good news, and returned with a sigh to her book. The tired mother was asleep on the bed, dressed, with the baby in her arms. She had lain down to quiet it and had been lulled to sleep with it herself.

Gavin did not wake them. He went to the bed where the four little ones slept, and kissed them, each in his turn, then came back and kissed his wife and baby.

May nestled close to him as he bent over her and gave her, too, a little hug.

"Where are you going, papa?" she asked.

He turned around at the door and cast a look back at the quiet room, irresolute. Then he went back once more to kiss his sleeping wife and baby softly.

But however softly, it woke the mother. She saw him making for the door, and asked him where he meant to go so late.

"Out, just a little while," he said, and his voice was husky. He turned his head away.

A woman's instinct made her arise hastily and go to him.

"Don't go," she said; "please don't go away."

As he still moved toward the door, she put her arm about his neck and drew his head toward her.

She strove with him anxiously, frightened, she hardly knew herself by what. The lamplight fell upon something shining which he held behind his back. The room rang with the shot, and the baby awoke crying, to see its father slip from mamma's arms to the floor, dead.

For John Gavin, alive, there was no place. At least he did not find it; for which, let it be said and done with, he was to blame. Dead, society will find one for him. And for the one misfit got off the list there are seven whom not employment bureau nor woodyard nor charity register can be made to reach. Social economy the thing is called; which makes the eighth misfit.

A HEATHEN BABY

A stack of mail comes to Police Headquarters every morning from the precincts by special department carrier. It includes the reports for the last twenty-four hours of stolen and recovered goods, complaints, and the thousand and one things the official mail-bag contains from day to day. It is all routine, and everything has its own pigeonhole into which it drops and is forgotten until some raking up in the department turns up the old blotters and the old things once more. But at last the mail-bag contained something that was altogether out of the usual run, to wit, a Chinese baby.

Pickaninnies have come in it before this, lots of them, black and shiny, and one pappoose from a West Side wigwam; but a Chinese baby never.

Sergeant Jack was so astonished that it took his breath away. When he recovered he spoke learnedly about its clothes as evidence of its heathen origin. Never saw such a thing before, he said. They were like they were sewn on; it was impossible to disentangle that child by any way short of rolling it on the floor.

Sergeant Jack is an old bachelor, and that is all he knows about babies. The child was not sewn up at all. It was just swaddled, and no Chinese had done that, but the Italian woman who found it. Sergeant Jack sees such babies every night in Mulberry Street, but that is the way with old bachelors. They don't know much, anyhow.

It was clear that the baby thought so. She was a little girl, very little, only one night old; and she regarded him through her almond eyes with a supercilious look, as who should say, "Now, if he was only a bottle, instead of a big, useless policeman, why, one might put up with him;" which reflection opened the flood-gates of grief and set the little Chinee squalling: "Yow! Yow! Yap!" until the Sergeant held his ears, and a policeman carried it upstairs in a hurry.

Downstairs first, in the Sergeant's big blotter, and upstairs in the matron's nursery next, the baby's brief official history was recorded. There was very little of it, indeed, and what there was was not marked by much ceremony. The stork hadn't brought it, as it does in far-off Denmark; nor had the doctor found it and brought it in, on the American plan.

An Italian woman had just scratched it out of an ash barrel. Perhaps that's the way they find babies in China, in which case the sympathy of all American mothers and fathers will be with the present despoilers of the heathen Chinee, who is entitled to no consideration whatever until he introduces a new way.

The Italian woman was Mrs. Maria Lepanto. She lives in Thompson Street, but she had come all the way down to the corner of Elizabeth and Canal streets with her little girl to look at a procession passing by. That, as everybody knows, is next door to Chinatown. It was ten o'clock, and the end of the procession was in sight, when she noticed something stirring in an ash barrel that stood against the wall. She thought first it was a rat, and was going to run, when a noise that was certainly not a rat's squeal came from the barrel. The child clung to her hand and dragged her toward the sound.

"Oh, mamma!" she cried, in wild excitement, "hear it! It isn't a rat! I know! Hear!"

It was a wail, a very tiny wail, ever so sorry, as well it might be, coming from a baby that was cradled in an ash barrel. It was little Susie's eager hands that snatched it out. Then they saw that it was indeed a child, a poor, helpless, grieving little baby.

It had nothing on at all, not even a rag. Perhaps they had not had time to dress it.

"Oh, it will fit my dolly's jacket!" cried Susie, dancing around and hugging it in glee. "It will, mamma! A real live baby! Now Tilde needn't brag of theirs. We will take it home, won't we, mamma?"

The bands brayed, and the flickering light of many torches filled the night. The procession had gone down the street, and the crowd with it. The poor woman wrapped the baby in her worn shawl and gave it to the girl to carry. And Susie carried it, prouder and happier than any of the men that marched to the music. So they arrived home. The little stranger had found friends and a resting-place.

But not for long. In the morning Mrs. Lepanto took counsel with the neighbors, and was told that the child must be given to the police. That was the law, they said, and though little Susie cried bitterly at having to part with her splendid new toy, Mrs. Lepanto, being a law-abiding woman, wrapped up her find and took it to the Macdougal Street station.

That was the way it got to Headquarters with the morning mail, and how Sergeant Jack got a chance to tell all he didn't know about babies. Matron Travers knew more, a good deal. She tucked the little heathen away in a trundle-bed with a big bottle, and blessed silence fell at once on Headquarters. In five minutes the child was asleep.

While it slept, Matron Travers entered it in her book as "No. 103" of that year's crop of the gutter, and before it woke up she was on the way with it, snuggled safely in a big gray shawl, up to the Charities. There Mr. Bauer registered it under yet another number, chucked it under the chin, and chirped at it in what he probably thought might pass for baby Chinese. Then it got another big bottle and went to sleep once more.

At ten o'clock there came a big ship on purpose to give the little Mott Street waif a ride up the river, and by dinner-time it was on a green island with four hundred other babies of all kinds and shades, but not one just like it in the whole lot. For it was New York's first and only Chinese foundling. As to that Superintendent Bauer, Matron Travers, and Mrs. Lepanto agreed. Sergeant Jack's evidence doesn't count, except as backed by his superiors. He doesn't know a heathen baby when he sees one.

The island where the waif from Mott Street cast anchor is called Randall's Island, and there its stay ends, or begins. The chances are that it ends, for with an ash barrel filling its past and a foundling asylum its future, a baby hasn't much of a show. Babies were made to be hugged each by one pair of mother's arms, and neither white-capped nurses nor sleek milch cows fed on the fattest of meadow-grass can take their place, try as they may. The babies know that they are cheated, and they will not stay.

THE CHRISTENING IN BOTTLE ALLEY

All Bottle Alley was bidden to the christening. It being Sunday, when Mulberry Street was wont to adjust its differences over the cards and the wine-cup, it came "heeled," ready for what might befall. From Tomaso, the ragpicker in the farthest rear cellar, to the Signor Undertaker, mainstay and umpire in the varying affairs of life, which had a habit in The Bend of lapsing suddenly upon his professional domain, they were all there, the men of Malpete's village. The baby was named for the village saint, so that it was a kind of communal feast as well. Carmen was there with her man, and Francisco Cessari.

If Carmen had any other name, neither Mulberry Street nor the Alley knew it. She was Carmen to them when, seven years before, she had taken up with Francisco, then a young mountaineer straight as the cedar of his native hills, the breath of which was yet in the songs with which he wooed her. Whether the priest had blessed their bonds no one knew or asked. The Bend only knew that one day, after three years during which the Francisco tenement had been the scene of more than one jealous quarrel, not, it was whispered, without cause, the mountaineer was missing. He did not come back. From over the sea The Bend heard, after a while, that he had reappeared in the old village to claim the sweetheart he had left behind. In the course of time new arrivals brought the news that Francisco was married and that they were living happily, as a young couple should. At the news Mulberry Street looked askance at Carmen; but she gave no sign. By tacit consent, she was the Widow Carmen after that.

The summers passed. The fourth brought Francisco Cessari, come back to seek his fortune, with his wife and baby. He greeted old friends effusively and made cautious inquiries about Carmen. When told that she had consoled herself with his old rival, Luigi, with whom she was then living in Bottle Alley, he laughed with a light heart, and took up his abode within half a dozen doors of the alley. That was but a short time before the christening at Malpete's. There their paths crossed each other for the first time since his flight.

She met him with a smile on her lips, but with hate in her heart. He, manlike, saw only the smile. The men smoking and drinking in the court watched them speak apart, saw him, with the laugh that sat so lightly upon his lips, turn to his wife, sitting by the hydrant with the child, and heard him say, "Look, Carmen! our baby!"

The woman bent over it, and, as she did, the little one woke suddenly out of its sleep and cried out in affright. It was noticed that Carmen smiled again then, and that the young mother shivered, why she herself could not have told. Francisco, joining the group at the farther end of the yard, said carelessly that Carmen had forgotten. They poked fun at him and spoke her name loudly, with laughter.

From the tenement, as they did, came Luigi and asked threateningly who insulted his wife. They only laughed the more, said he had drunk too much wine, and shouldering him out, bade him go look to his woman. He went. Carmen had witnessed it all from the house. She called him a coward and goaded him with bitter taunts until mad with anger and drink he went out in the court once more and shook his fist in the face of Francisco. They hailed his return with bantering words. Luigi was spoiling for a fight they laughed, and would find one before the day was much older. But suddenly silence fell upon the group. Carmen stood on the step, pale and cold. She hid something under her apron.

"Luigi!" she called, and he came to her. She drew from under the apron a cocked pistol, and, pointing to Francisco, pushed it into his hand. At the sight the alley was cleared as suddenly as if a tornado had swept through it. Malpete's guests leaped over fences, dived into cellar-ways anywhere for shelter. The door of the woodshed slammed behind

Francisco just as his old rival reached it. The maddened man tore it open and dragged him out by the throat. He pinned him against the fence, and levelled the pistol with frenzied curses. They died on his lips. The face that was turning livid in his grasp was the face of his boyhood's friend. They had gone to school together, danced together at the fairs in the old days. They had been friends—till Carmen came. The muzzle of the weapon fell.

"Shoot!" said a hard voice behind him. Carmen stood there with face of stone. She stamped her foot. "Shoot!" she commanded, pointing, relentless, at the struggling man. "Coward, shoot!"

Her lover's finger crooked itself upon the trigger. A shriek, wild and despairing, rang through the alley. A woman ran madly from the house, flew across the pavement, and fell panting at Carmen's feet.

"Mother of God! mercy!" she cried, thrusting her babe before the assassin's weapon. "Jesus Maria! Carmen, the child! He is my husband!"

No gleam of pity came into the cold eyes. Only hatred, fierce and bitter, was there. In one swift, sweeping glance she saw it all: the woman fawning at her feet, the man she hated limp and helpless in the grasp of her lover.

"He was mine once," she said, "and he had no mercy." She pushed the baby aside. "Coward, shoot!"

The shot was drowned in the shriek, hopeless, despairing, of the widow who fell upon the body of Francisco as it slipped lifeless from the grasp of the assassin. The christening party saw Carmen standing over the three with the same pale smile on her cruel lips.

For once The Bend did not shield a murderer. The door of the tenement was shut against him. The women spurned him. The very children spat upon him as he fled to the street. The police took him there. With him they seized Carmen. She made no attempt to escape. She had bided her time, and it had come. She had her revenge. To the end of its lurid life Bottle Alley remembered it as the murder accursed of God.

IN THE MULBERRY STREET COURT

"Conduct unbecoming an officer," read the charge, "in this, to wit, that the said defendants brought into the station-house, by means to deponent unknown, on the said Fourth of July, a keg of beer, and, when apprehended, were consuming the contents of the same." Twenty policemen, comprising the whole off platoon of the East One Hundred and Fourth Street squad, answered the charge as defendants. They had been caught grouped about a pot of chowder and the fatal keg in the top-floor dormitory, singing, "Beer, beer, glorious beer!" Sergeant McNally and Roundsman Stevenson interrupted the proceedings.

The Commissioner's eyes bulged as, at the call of the complaint clerk, the twenty marched up and ranged themselves in rows, three deep, before him.

They took the oath collectively, with a toss and a smack, as if to say, "I don't care if I do," and told separately and identically the same story, while the Sergeant stared and the Commissioner's eyes grew bigger and rounder.

Missing his reserves, Sergeant McNally had sent the Roundsman in search of them. He was slow in returning, and the Sergeant went on a tour of inspection himself. He journeyed to the upper region, and there came upon the party in full swing. Then and there he called the roll. Not one of the platoon was missing.

They formed a hollow square around something that looked uncommonly like a beer-keg. A number of tin growlers stood beside it. The Sergeant picked up one and turned the tap. There was enough left in the keg to barely half fill it. Seeing that, the platoon followed him downstairs without a murmur.

One by one the twenty took the stand after the Sergeant had left it, and testified without a tremor that they had seen no beer-keg. In fact, the majority would not know one if they saw it. They were tired and hungry, having been held in reserve all day, when a pleasant smell assailed their nostrils.

Each of the twenty followed his nose independently to the top floor, where he was surprised to see the rest gathered about a pot of steaming chowder. He joined the circle and partook of some. It was good. As to beer, he had seen none and drunk less. There was something there of wood with a brass handle to it. What it was none of them seemed to know. They were all shocked at the idea that it might have been a beer-keg. Such things are forbidden in police stations.

The Sergeant himself could not tell how it could have got in there, while stoutly maintaining that it was a keg. He scratched his head and concluded that it might have come over the roof, or, somehow, from a building that is in course of erection next door. The chowder had come in by the main door. At least one policeman had seen it carried upstairs. He had fallen in behind it immediately.

When the Commissioner had heard this story told exactly twenty times the platoon fell in and marched off to the elevated station. When he can decide what punishment to inflict on a policeman who does not know a beer-keg when he sees it, they all will be fined accordingly, and a doorman who has served a term as a barkeeper will be sent to the East One Hundred and Fourth Street station to keep the police there out of harm's way.

DIFFICULTIES OF A DEACON

It is my firm opinion that newspaper men should not be deacons. Not that there is any moral or spiritual reason why they should abstain—not that; but it doesn't work; the chances are all against it. I know it from experience. I was a deacon myself once.

It was at a time when they were destroying gambling tools at Police Headquarters. I was there, and I carried away as a memento of the occasion a pocketful of red, white, yellow, and blue chips. They were pretty, and I thought they would be nice to have around. That was the beginning of the mischief. I was a very energetic deacon, and attended to the duties of the office with zeal. It was a young church; I had helped to found it myself; and at the Thursday night meetings I was rarely missing. The very next week it was my turn to lead it, and I started in to interpret the text to the best of my ability, and with much approval from the brethren.

I have a nervous habit, when talking, of fingering my watch, keys, knife, or whatever I happen to fish out of my pocket first. It happened to be the poker chips this time. Now, I have never played poker. I don't know the game from the smallpox. But it seems that the congregation did. I could not at first account for the enthusiasm of the brethren as I laid down the law, and checked off the points successively on a white, a red, and a yellow chip, summing the argument up on a blue. I was rather flattered by my success at presenting the matter in a convincing light; and when the dominie leaned over and examined the chips attentively, I gave him a handful for the baby, cheerfully telling him that I had plenty more at home.

The look of horror on the good man's face remained a puzzle to me until some of the congregation asked me on the train in the morning, in a confidential kind of way, where the game was, and how high was the ante. The explanation that ensued was not a success. I think that it shook the confidence of the brethren in me for the first time.

It occurs to me now, looking back, that the fact that I had a black eye on that occasion may have contributed in a measure to this result. Yet it was as innocent an eye as those chips; in fact, it was distinctly an ecclesiastical black eye, if I may so call it. I was never a fighter, any more than I was a gambler. Only once in my life was I accused of fighting, and then most unjustly. It was when a man who had come into my office with a hickory club to punish me for a wrong, as he insisted upon considering it,—while in reality it was an act of strictest justice to him,—happened to fall out of a window, taking the whole sash with him. The simple fact was that I didn't strike a blow. He literally fell out. However, that is another story, and a much older one.

This black eye was a direct outcome of my zeal as deacon. Between the duties it imposed upon me, and my work as a newspaper man, I was getting very much in need of exercise of some sort. The doctor recommended Indian clubs; but the boys in the office liked boxing, and it seemed to me to have some advantages. So we clubbed together, and got a set of gloves, and when we were not busy would put them on and have a friendly set-to. It was inevitable that our youthful spirits should rise at these meetings, and with them occasionally certain lumps, which afterward shaded off into various tints bordering more or less on black until we learned to keep a leech on hand for emergencies. You see, what with the spirit of the contest, the tenderness of our untrained flesh, and certain remembered scores which were thus paid off in an entirely friendly and Christian manner, leaving no bad blood behind,—especially after we had engaged the leech,—this was not only reasonable, but inevitable. But the brethren knew nothing of this, and couldn't be persuaded to listen to it; and, in fairness, it must be owned that the spectacle of a deacon with a black eye and a handful of poker chips expounding the text in prayer-meeting was—well, let us say that appearances were against me.

Still, I might have come through it all right had it not been for Mac. Mac was the dog. It never rains but it pours; and just at this time midnight burglars took to raiding our suburban town, and dogs came into fashion. Mac came into it with a long jump. He had been part of the outfit of a dog pit in a low dive on the East Side which the police had broken up. Sergeant Jack had heard of my need, and gave him to me for old acquaintance' sake, warranting him to keep anybody away from the house. Upon this point there was never the least doubt. We might just as well have lived on a desert island while we had him. People went around the next block to avoid our house. It was not because Mac was unsociable; quite the contrary. He took to the town from the first, especially to the other dogs. These he generally took by the throat, to the great distress of their owners. I have never heard that bulldogs as a class have theories, and I am not prepared to discuss the point. I know that Mac had. He was an evolutionist, with a firm belief in the principle of the survival of the fittest; and he did all one dog could do to carry it into practice. His efforts eventually brought it down to a question between himself and a big long-haired dog in the next street. I think of this with regret, because it was the occasion of my one real slip. The dog led me into temptation.

If it only had not been Sunday, and church time, when the issue became urgent, and the long-haired one accepted our invitation for a walk in the deep woods! In this saddening reflection I was partly comforted, while taking the by-paths for home afterward,—with Mac limping along on three legs, and minus one ear,—by the knowledge that our view of the case had prevailed. The long-haired one troubled us no more thereafter.

Mac had his strong points, but he had also his failings. One of these was a weakness for stale beer. I suppose he had been brought up on it in the dog pit. The pure air of Long Island, and the usual environment of his new home, did not wean him from it. He had not been long in our house before he took to absenting himself for days and nights at a time, returning ragged and fagged out, as if from a long spree. We found out, by accident, that he spent those vacations in a low saloon a mile up the plank road, which he had probably located on one of his excursions through the country to extend his doctrine of evolution. It was the conductor on the horse-car that ran past the saloon who told me of it. Mac had found the cars out, too, and rode regularly up and down to the place, surveying the country from the rear platform. The conductor prudently refrained from making any remarks after Mac had once afforded him a look at his jaw. I am sorry to say that I think Mac got drunk on those trips. I judged, from remarks I overheard once or twice about the "deacon's drunken dog," that the community shared my conviction. It was always quick to jump at conclusions, particularly about deacons.

Sober second thought should have acquitted me of all the allegations against me, except the one matter of the Sunday discussion in the woods, which, however, I had forgotten to mention. But sober second thought, that ought always and specially to attach itself to the deaconry, was apparently at a premium in our town. I had begun to tire of the constant explanations that were required, when the climax came in a manner wholly unforeseen and unexpected. The cashier in the office had run away, or was under suspicion, or something, and it became necessary to overhaul the accounts to find out where the office stood. When that was done, my chief summoned me down town for a private interview. Upon the table lay my weekly pay-checks for three years back, face down. My employer eyed them and me, by turns, curiously.

"Mr. Riis," he began stiffly, "I'm not going to judge you unheard; and, for that matter, it is none of my business. I have known you all this time as a sober, steady man; I believe you are a deacon in your church; and I never heard that you gambled or bet money. It seems now that I was never more mistaken in a man in my life. Tell me, how do you do it, anyhow? Do you blow in the whole of your salary every week on policy, or do you run a game of your own up there? Look at those checks."

He pointed to the lot. I stared at them in bewilderment. They were my own checks, sure enough; and underneath my name, on the back of each one, was the indorsement of the infamous blackleg whose name had been a byword ever since I could remember as that of the chief devil in the policy blackmail conspiracy that had robbed the poor and corrupted the police force to the core.

I went home and resigned my office as deacon. I did not explain. We were having a little difficulty at the time, about another matter, which made it easy. I did not add this straw, though the explanation was simple enough. My chief grasped it at once; but then, he was not a deacon. I had simply got my check cashed every week in a cigar-store next door that was known to be a policy-shop for the special accommodation of Police Headquarters in those days, and the check had gone straight into the "backer's" bank-account. That was how. But, as I said, it was hopeless to try to explain, and I didn't. I simply record here what I said at the beginning, that it is no use for a newspaper man, more particularly a police reporter, to try to be a deacon too. The chances are all against it.

FIRE IN THE BARRACKS

The rush and roar, the blaze and the wild panic of a great fire filled Twenty-third Street. Helmeted men stormed and swore; horses tramped and reared; crying women, hurrying hither and thither, stumbled over squirming hose on street and sidewalk.

The throbbing of a dozen pumping-engines merged all other sounds in its frantic appeal for haste. In the midst of it all, seven red-shirted men knelt beside a heap of trunks, hastily thrown up as for a breastwork, and prayed fervently with bared heads.

Firemen and policemen stumbled up against them with angry words, stopped, stared, and passed silently by. The fleeing crowd hailed and fell back. The rush and the roar swirled to the right and to the left, leaving the little band as if in an eddy, untouched and serene, with the glow of the fire upon it and the stars paling overhead.

The seven were the Swedish Salvation Army. Their barracks were burning up in a blast of fire so sudden and so fierce that scant time was left to save life and goods.

From the tenements next door men and women dragged bundles and feather-beds, choking stairs and halls, and shrieking madly to be let out. The police struggled angrily with the torrent. The lodgers in the Holly-Tree Inn, who had nothing to save, ran for their lives.

In the station-house behind the barracks they were hastily clearing the prison. The last man had hardly passed out of his cell when, with a deafening crash, the toppling wall fell upon and smashed the roof of the jail.

Fire-bells rang in every street as engines rushed from north and south. A general alarm had called out the reserves. Every hydrant for blocks around was tapped. Engine crews climbed upon the track of the elevated road, picketed the surrounding tenements, and stood their ground on top of the police station.

Up there two crews labored with a Siamese joint hose throwing a stream as big as a man's thigh. It got away from them, and for a while there was panic and a struggle up on the heights as well as in the street. The throbbing hose bounded over the roof, thrashing right and left, and flinging about the men who endeavored to pin it down like half-drowned kittens. It struck the coping, knocked it off, and the resistless stream washed brick and stone down into the yard as upon the wave of a mighty flood.

Amid the fright and uproar the seven alone were calm. The sun rose upon their little band perched upon the pile of trunks, victorious and defiant. It shone upon Old Glory and the Salvation Army's flag floating from their improvised fort, and upon an ample lake, sprung up within an hour where yesterday there was a vacant sunken lot. The fire was out, the firemen going home.

The lodgers in the Holly-Tree Inn, of whom there is one for every day in the year, looked upon the sudden expanse of water, shivered, and went in. The tenants returned to their homes. The fright was over, with the darkness.

WAR ON THE GOATS

War has been declared in Hell's Kitchen. An indignant public opinion demands to have "something done ag'in' them goats," and there is alarm at the river end of the street. A public opinion in Hell's Kitchen that demands anything besides schooners of mixed ale is a sign. Surer than a college settlement and a sociological canvass, it foretells the end of the slum. Sebastopol, the rocky fastness of the gang that gave the place its bad name, was razed only the other day, and now the police have been set on the goats. Cause enough for alarm.

A reconnaissance in force by the enemy showed some foundation for the claim that the goats owned the block. Thirteen were found foraging in the gutters, standing upon trucks, or calmly dozing in doorways. They evinced no particularly hostile disposition, but a marked desire to know the business of every chance caller in the block. This caused a passing unpleasantness between one big white goat and the janitress of the tenement on the corner. Being crowded up against the wall by the animal, bent on exploring her pockets, she beat it off with her scrubbing-pail and mop. The goat, thus dismissed, joined a horse at the curb in apparently innocent meditation, but with one leering eye fixed back over its shoulder upon the housekeeper setting out an ash barrel.

Her back was barely turned when it was in the barrel, with head and fore feet exploring its depths. The door of the tenement opened upon the housekeeper trundling another barrel just as the first one fell and rolled across the sidewalk, with the goat capering about. Then was the air filled with bad language and a broomstick and a goat for a moment, and the woman was left shouting her wrongs.

"What de divil good is dem goats anyhow?" she said, panting. "There's no housekeeper in de United Shtates can watch de ash cans wid dem divil's imps around. They near killed an Eyetalian child the other day, and two of them got basted in de neck when de goats follied dem and didn't get nothing. That big white one o' Tim's, he's the worst in de lot, and he's got only one horn, too."

This wicked and unsymmetrical animal is denounced for its malice throughout the block by even the defenders of the goats. Singularly enough, he cannot be located, and neither can Tim. If the scouting party has better luck and can seize this wretched beast, half the campaign may be over. It will be accepted as a sacrifice by one side, and the other is willing to give it up.

Mrs. Shallock lives in a crazy old frame-house, over a saloon. Her kitchen is approached by a sort of hen-ladder, a foot wide, which terminates in a balcony, the whole of which was occupied by a big gray goat. There was not room for the police inquisitor and the goat too, and the former had to wait till the animal had come off his perch. Mrs. Shallock is a widow. A load of anxiety and concern overspread her motherly countenance when she heard of the trouble.

"Are they after dem goats again?" she said. "Sarah! Leho! come right here, an' don't you go in the street again. Excuse me, sor! but it's all because one of dem knocked down an old woman that used to give it a paper every day. She is the mother of the blind newsboy around on the avenue, an' she used to feed an old paper to him every night. So he follied her. That night she didn't have any, an' when he stuck his nose in her basket an' didn't find any, he knocked her down, an' she bruk her arrum."

Whether it was the one-horned goat that thus insisted upon his sporting extra does not appear. Probably it was.

"There's neighbors lives there has got 'em on floors," Mrs. Shallock kept on. "I'm paying taxes here, an' I think it's my privilege to have one little goat."

"I just wish they'd take 'em," broke in the widow's buxom daughter, who had appeared in the doorway, combing her hair. "They goes up in the hall and knocks on the door with their horns all night. There's sixteen dozen of them on the stoop, if there's one. What good are they? Let's sell 'em to the butcher, mamma; he'll buy 'em for mutton, the way he did Bill Buckley's. You know right well he did."

"They ain't much good, that's a fact," mused the widow. "But yere's Leho; she's follying me around just like a child. She is a regular pet, is Leho. We got her from Mr. Lee, who is dead, and we called her after him, Leho [Leo]. Take Sarah; but Leho, little Leho, let's keep."

Leho stuck her head in through the front door and belied her name. If the widow keeps her, another campaign will shortly have to be begun in Forty-sixth Street. There will be more goats where Leho is.

Mr. Cleary lives in a rear tenement and has only one goat. It belongs, he says, to his little boy, and is no good except to amuse him. Minnie is her name, and she once had a mate. When it was sold, the boy cried so much that he was sick for two weeks. Mr. Cleary couldn't think of parting with Minnie.

Neither will Mr. Lennon, in the next yard, give up his. He owns the stable, he says, and axes no odds of anybody. His goat is some good anyhow, for it gives milk for his tea. Says his wife, "Many is the dime it has saved us." There are two goats in Mr. Lennon's yard, one perched on top of a shed surveying the yard, the other engaged in chewing at a buck-saw that hangs on the fence.

Mrs. Buckley does not know how many goats she has. A glance at the bigger of the two that are stabled at the entrance to the tenement explains her doubts, which are temporary. Mrs. Buckley says that her husband "generally sells them away," meaning the kids, presumably to the butcher for mutton.

"Hey, Jenny!" she says, stroking the big one at the door. Jenny eyes the visitor calmly, and chews an old newspaper. She has two horns.

"She ain't as bad as they lets on," says Mrs. Buckley.

The scouting party reports the new public opinion of the Kitchen to be of healthy but alien growth, as yet without roots in the soil strong enough to stand the shock of a general raid on the goats. They recommend as a present concession the seizure of the one-horned Billy that seems to have no friends on the block, if indeed he belongs there, and an ambush is being laid accordingly.

HE KEPT HIS TRYST

Policeman Schultz was stamping up and down his beat in Hester Street, trying to keep warm, on the night before Christmas, when a human wreck, in rum and rags, shuffled across his path and hailed him:—

"You allus treated me fair, Schultz," it said; "say, will you do a thing for me?"

"What is it, Denny?" said the officer. He had recognized the wreck as Denny the Robber, a tramp who had haunted his beat ever since he had been on it, and for years before, he had heard, further back than any one knew.

"Will you," said the wreck, wistfully—"will you run me in and give me about three months to-morrow? Will you do it?"

"That I will," said Schultz. He had often done it before, sometimes for three, sometimes for six months, and sometimes for ten days, according to how he and Denny and the justice felt about it. In the spell between trips to the island, Denny was a regular pensioner of the policeman, who let him have a quarter or so when he had so little money as to be next to desperate. He never did get quite to that point. Perhaps the policeman's quarters saved him. His nickname of "the Robber" was given to him on the same principle that dubbed the neighborhood he haunted the Pig Market—because pigs are the only ware not for sale there. Denny never robbed anybody. The only thing he ever stole was the time he should have spent in working. There was no denying it, Denny was a loafer. He himself had told Schultz that it was because his wife and children put him out of their house in Madison Street five years before. Perhaps if his wife's story had been heard it would have reversed that statement of facts. But nobody ever heard it. Nobody took the trouble to inquire. The O'Neil family—that was understood to be the name—interested no one in Jewtown. One of its members was enough. Except that Mrs. O'Neil lived in Madison Street, somewhere "near Lundy's store," nothing was known of her.

"That I will, Denny," repeated the policeman, heartily, slipping him a dime for luck. "You come around to-morrow, and I will run you in. Now go along."

But Denny didn't go, though he had the price of two "balls" at the distillery. He shifted thoughtfully on his feet, and said:—

"Say, Schultz, if I should die now,—I am all full o' rheumatiz, and sore,—if I should die before, would you see to me and tell the wife?"

"Small fear of yer dying, Denny, with the price of two drinks," said the policeman, poking him facetiously in the ribs with his club. "Don't you worry. All the same, if you will tell me where the old woman lives, I will let her know. What's the number?"

But the Robber's mood had changed under the touch of the silver dime that burned his palm. "Never mind, Schultz," he said; "I guess I won't kick; so long!" and moved off.

The snow drifted wickedly down Suffolk Street Christmas morning, pinching noses and ears and cheeks already pinched by hunger and want. It set around the corner into the Pig Market, where the hucksters plodded knee-deep in the drifts, burying the horse-radish man and his machine and coating the bare, plucked breasts of the geese that swung from countless hooks at the corner stand with softer and whiter down than ever grew there. It drove the suspender-man into the hallway of a Suffolk Street tenement, where he tried to pluck the icicles from his frozen ears and beard with numb and powerless fingers.

As he stepped out of the way of some one entering with a blast that set like a cold shiver up through the house, he stumbled over something, and put down his hand to feel what it was. It touched a cold face, and the house rang with a shriek that silenced the clink of glasses in the distillery, against the side door of which the something lay. They crowded out, glasses in hand, to see what it was.

"Only a dead tramp," said some one, and the crowd went back to the warm saloon, where the barrels lay in rows on the racks. The clink of glasses and shouts of laughter came through the peep-hole in the door into the dark hallway as Policeman Schultz bent over the stiff, cold shape. Some one had called him.

"Denny," he said, tugging at his sleeve.

"Denny, come. Your time is up. I am here." Denny never stirred. The policeman looked up, white in the face.

"My God!" he said, "he's dead. But he kept his date."

And so he had. Denny the Robber was dead. Rum and exposure and the "rheumatiz" had killed him. Policeman Schultz kept his word, too, and had him taken to the station on a stretcher.

"He was a bad penny," said the saloon-keeper, and no one in Jewtown was found to contradict him.

ROVER'S LAST FIGHT

The little village of Valley Stream nestles peacefully among the woods and meadows of Long Island. The days and the years roll by uneventfully within its quiet precincts. Nothing more exciting than the arrival of a party of fishermen from the city, on a vain hunt for perch in the ponds that lie hidden among its groves and feed the Brooklyn waterworks, troubles the every-day routine of the village. Two great railroad wrecks are remembered thereabouts, but these are already ancient history. Only the oldest inhabitants know of the earlier one. There hasn't been as much as a sudden death in the town since, and the constable and chief of police—probably one and the same person—haven't turned an honest or dishonest penny in the whole course of their official existence. All of which is as it ought to be.

But at last something occurred that ought not to have been. The village was aroused at daybreak by the intelligence that a robbery had been committed overnight, and a murder. The house of Gabriel Dodge, a well-to-do farmer, had been sacked by thieves, who left in their trail the farmer's murdered dog. Rover was a collie, large for his kind, and quite as noisy as the rest of them. He had been left as an outside guard, according to Farmer

Dodge's awkward practice. Inside, he might have been of use by alarming the folks when the thieves tried to get in. But they had only to fear his bark; his bite was harmless.

The whole of Valley Stream gathered at Farmer Dodge's house to watch, awe-struck, the mysterious movements of the police force as it went tiptoeing about, peeping into corners, secretly examining tracks in the mud, and squinting suspiciously at the brogans of the bystanders. When it had all been gone through, this record of facts bearing on the case was made:—

Rover was dead.

He had apparently been smothered.

With the hand, not a rope.

There was a ladder set up against the window of the spare bedroom.

That it had not been there before was evidence that the thieves had set it up.

The window was open, and they had gone in.

Several watches, some good clothes, sundry articles of jewellery, all worth some six or seven hundred dollars, were missing and could not be found.

In conclusion, the constable put on record his belief that the thieves who had smothered the dog and set up the ladder had taken the property.

The solid citizens of the village sat upon the verdict in the store, solemnly considered it, and agreed that it was so. This point settled, there was left only the other: Who were the thieves? The solid citizens by a unanimous decision concluded that Inspector Byrnes was the man to tell them.

So they came over to New York and laid the matter before him, with a mental diagram of the village, the house, the dog, and the ladder at the window. There was just the suspicion of a twinkle in the corner of the inspector's eye as he listened gravely and then said:—

"It was the spare bedroom, wasn't it?"

"The spare bedroom," said the committee, in one breath.

"The only one in the house?" queried the inspector, further.

"The only one," responded the echo.

"H'm!" pondered the inspector. "You keep hands on your farm, Mr. Dodge?"

Mr. Dodge did.

"Sleep in the house?"

"Yes."

"Discharged any one lately?"

The committee rose as one man, and, staring at each other with bulging eyes, said "Jake!" all at once.

"Jakey, b'gosh!" repeated the constable to himself, kicking his own shins softly as he tugged at his beard. "Jake, by thunder!"

Jake was a boy of eighteen, who had been employed by the farmer to do chores. He was shiftless, and a week or two before had been sent away in disgrace. He had gone no one knew whither.

The committee told the inspector all about Jake, gave him a minute description of him,—of his ways, his gait, and his clothes,—and went home feeling that they had been wondrous smart in putting so sharp a man on the track he would never have thought of if they hadn't mentioned Jake's name. All he had to do now was to follow it to the end, and let them know when he had reached it. And as these good men had prophesied, even so it came to pass.

Detectives of the inspector's staff were put on the trail. They followed it from the Long Island pastures across the East River to the Bowery, and there into one of the cheap lodging-houses where thieves are turned out ready-made while you wait. There they found Jake.

They didn't hail him at once, or clap him into irons, as the constable from Valley Stream would have done. They let him alone and watched awhile to see what he was doing. And the thing that they found him doing was just what they expected: he was herding with thieves. When they had thoroughly fastened this companionship upon the lad, they arrested the band. They were three.

They had not been locked up many hours at Headquarters before the inspector sent for Jake. He told him he knew all about his dismissal by Farmer Dodge, and asked him what he had done to the old man. Jake blurted out hotly, "Nothing" and betrayed such feeling that his questioner soon made him admit that he was "sore on the boss." From that to telling the whole story of the robbery was only a little way, easy to travel in such company as Jake was in then. He told how he had come to New York, angry enough to do anything, and had "struck" the Bowery. Struck, too, his two friends, not the only two of that kind who loiter about that thoroughfare.

To them he told his story while waiting in the "hotel" for something to turn up, and they showed him a way to get square with the old man for what he had done to him. The farmer had money and property he would hate to lose. Jake knew the lay of the land, and could steer them straight; they would take care of the rest. "See?" said they.

Jake saw, and the sight tempted him. But in his mind's eye he saw also Rover and heard him bark. How could he be managed?

"He will come to me if I call him," pondered Jake, while his two companions sat watching his face, "but you may have to kill him. Poor Rover!"

"You call the dog and leave him to me," said the oldest thief, and shut his teeth hard. And so it was arranged.

That night the three went out on the last train, and hid in the woods down by the gatekeeper's house at the pond, until the last light had gone out in the village and it was fast asleep. Then they crept up by a back way to Farmer Dodge's house. As expected, Rover came bounding out at their approach, barking furiously. It was Jake's turn then.

"Rover," he called softly, and whistled. The dog stopped barking and came on, wagging his tail, but still growling ominously as he got scent of the strange men.

"Rover, poor Rover," said Jake, stroking his shaggy fur and feeling like the guilty wretch he was; for just then the hand of Pfeiffer, the thief, grabbed the throat of the faithful beast in a grip as of an iron vice, and he had barked his last bark. Struggle as he might, he could not free himself or breathe, while Jake, the treacherous Jake, held his legs. And so he died, fighting for his master and his home.

In the morning the ladder at the open window and poor Rover dead in the yard told of the drama of the night.

The committee of farmers came over and took Jake home, after congratulating Inspector Byrnes on having so intelligently followed their directions in hunting down the thieves. The inspector shook hands with them and smiled.

HOW JIM WENT TO THE WAR

Jocko and Jim sat on the scuttle-stairs and mourned; times were out of joint with them. Since an ill wind had blown one of the recruiting sergeants for the Spanish War into the next block, the old joys of the tenement had palled on Jim. Nothing would do but he must go to the war.

The infection was general in the neighborhood. Even base-ball had lost its savor. The Ivy nine had disbanded at the first drum-beat, and had taken the fever in a body. Jim, being fourteen, and growing "muscle" with daily pride, "had it bad." Naturally Jocko, being Jim's constant companion, developed the symptoms too, and, to external appearances, thirsted for gore as eagerly as a naturally peace-loving, long-tailed monkey could.

Jocko had belonged to an Italian organ-grinder in the days of "the persecution," when the aldermen issued an edict, against monkeys. Now he was "hung up" for rent, unpaid. And, literally, he remained hung up most of the time, usually by his tail from the banisters, in which position he was able both to abet the mischief of the children, and to elude the stealthy grabs of their exasperated elders by skipping nimbly to the other side.

The tenement was one of the old-fashioned kind, built for a better use, with wide, oval stairwell and superior opportunities for observation and escape. Jocko inhabited the well by day, and from it conducted his raids upon the tenants' kitchens with an impartiality which, if it did not disarm, at least had stayed the hand of vengeance so far.

That he gave great provocation not even his stanchest boy friend could deny. His pursuit of information was persistent. The sight of Jocko cracking stolen eggs on the stairs to see the yolk run out and then investigating the empty shell with grave concern was cheering to the children, but usually provoked a shower of execrations and scrubbing-brushes from the despoiled households.

When the postman's call was heard in the hall, Jocko was on hand to receive the mail. Once he did receive it, the impartial zeal with which he distributed the letters to friend and foe brought forth more scrubbing-brushes, and Jocko retired to his attic aerie, there to ponder with Jim, his usual companion when in disgrace, the relation of eggs and letters and scrubbing-brushes in a world that seemed all awry to their simple minds.

The sense was heavy upon them this day as they sat silently brooding on the stairs, Jim glum and hopeless, with his arms buried to the elbow in his trousers pockets, Jocko, a world of care in his wrinkled face, humped upon the step at his shoulder with limp tail. The rain beat upon the roof in fitful showers, and the April storm rattled the crazy shutters, adding to the depression of the two.

Jim broke the silence when a blast fiercer than the rest shook the old house. "'Tain't right," he said dolefully, "I know it ain't, Jock! There's Tom and Foley gone off an' 'listed, and them only four years older nor me. What's four years?" This with a sniff of contempt.

Jocko gazed straight ahead. Four years of scrubbing-brushes and stealthy grabs at his tail on the stairs! To Jocko they were a long, long time.

"An' dad!" wailed Jim, unheeding. "I hear him tell Mr. Murphy himself that he was a drummer-boy in the war, and he won't let me at them dagoes!"

A slightly upward curl of Jocko's tail testified to his sympathy.

"I seen 'em march to de camp with their guns and drums." There was a catch in Jim's voice now. "And Susie's feller was there in soger-clo'es, Jock—soger-clo'es!"

Jim broke down in desolation and despair at the recollection. Jocko hitched as close to him as the step would let him, and brought his shaggy side against the boy's jacket in mute compassion. So they sat in silence until suddenly Jim got up and strode across the floor twice.

"Jock," he said, stopping short in front of his friend, "I know what I'll do. Jock, do you hear? I know what I'm going to do!"

Jocko sat up straight, erected his tail into a huge interrogation point, cocked his wise little head on one side, and regarded his ally expectantly. The storm was over, and the afternoon sun sent a ray slanting across the floor.

"I'm going anyhow! I'll run away, Jock! That's what I'll do! I'll get a whack at them dagoes yet!"

Jim danced a gleeful breakdown on the patch of sunlight, winding up by making a grab for Jocko, who evaded him by jumping over his head to the banister, where he became an animated pinwheel in approval of the new mischief. They stopped at last, out of breath.

"Jock," said the boy, considering his playmate approvingly, "you will make a soldier yourself yet. Come on, let's have a drill! This way, Jock, up straight! Now, attention! Right hand—salute!" Jocko exactly imitated his master, and so learned the rudiments of the soldier's art as Jim knew it.

"You'll do, Jock," he said, when the dusk stole into the attic, "but you can't go this trip. Good-by to you. Here goes for the soger camp!"

There was surprise in the tenement when Jim did not come home for supper; as the evening wore on the surprise became consternation. His father gave over certain preparations for his reception which, if Jim had known of them, might well have decided him to stick to "sogering," and went to the police station to learn if the boy had been heard of there. He had not, and an alarm which the Sergeant sent out discovered no trace of him the next day.

Jim was lost, but how? His mother wept, and his father spent weary days and nights inquiring of every one within a distance of many blocks for a red-headed boy in "knee-pants" and a base-ball cap. The grocer's clerk on the corner alone furnished a clew. He remembered giving Jim two crackers on the afternoon of the storm and seeing him turn west. The clew began and ended there. Slowly the conviction settled on the tenement that Jim had really run away to enlist.

"I'll enlist him!" said his father; and the tenement acquiesced in the justice of his intentions and awaited developments. And all the time Jocko kept Jim's secret safe.

Jocko had troubles enough of his own. Jim's friendship and quick wit had more than once saved the monkey; for despite of harum-scarum ways, the boy with the sunny smile was a general favorite. Now that he was gone, the tenement rose in wrath against its tormentor; and Jocko accepted the challenge.

All his lawless instincts were given full play. Even of the banana man at the street stand who had given him peanuts when trade was good, or sold them to him in exchange for pilfered pennies, he made an enemy by grabbing bananas when his back was turned. Mrs. Rafferty, on the second floor rear, one of his few champions, he estranged by exchanging the "war extra" which the carrier left at the door for her, for the German paper served to Mrs. Schultz, her pet aversion on the floor below. Mrs. Rafferty upset the wash-tub in her rage at this prank.

"Ye imp," she shrieked, laying about her with a wet towel, "wid yer hathen Dootch! It's that yer up to, is it?" and poor Jocko paid dearly for his mistake.

As he limped painfully to his attic retreat, his bitterest reflection might have been that even the children, his former partners in every plot against the public peace, had now joined in the general assault upon him. Truly, every man's hand was raised against Jocko, and in the spirit of Ishmael he entered on his crowning exploit.

On the top floor of the rear house was Mrs. Hoffman, a quiet German tenant, who had heretofore escaped Jocko's unwelcome attentions. Now, in his banishment to the upper regions, he bestowed them upon her with an industry to which she objected loudly, but in vain. Shut off from his accustomed base of supplies, he spent his hours watching her kitchen from the fire-escape, and if she left it but for a minute, he was over the roof and, by way of the shutter, in her flat, foraging for food.

In the battles that ensued, when Mrs. Hoffman surprised him, some of her spare crockery was broken without damage to the monkey. Vainly did she turn the key of her ice-box and think herself safe. Jocko had watched her do it, and turned it, too, on his next trip, with results satisfactory to himself. The climax came when he was discovered sitting at the open skylight, under which Mrs. Hoffman and her husband were working at their tailoring trade, calmly puffing away at Mr. Hoffman's cherished meerschaum, and leisurely picking the putty from the glass and dropping it upon the heads of the maddened couple.

The old German's terror and emotion at the sight nearly choked him. "Jocko," he called, with shaking voice, "you fool monkey! Jocko! Papa's pet! Come down mit mine pipe!"

But Jocko merely brandished the pipe, and shook it at the tailor with a wicked grin that showed all his sharp little teeth. Mrs. Hoffman wanted to call a policeman and the board of health, but the thirst for vengeance suggested a more effective plan to the tailor.

"Wait! I fix him! I fix him good!" he vowed, and forthwith betook himself to the kitchen, where stood the ice-box.

From his attic lookout Jocko saw the tailor take from the ice-box a bottle of beer, and drawing the cork with careful attention to detail, partake of its contents with apparent relish. Finally the tailor put back the bottle and went away, after locking the ice-box, but leaving the key in the lock.

His step was yet on the stairs when the monkey peered through the window, reached the ice-box with a bound and turned the key. There was the bottle, just as the tailor had left it. Jocko held it as he had seen him do, and pulled the cork. It came out easily. He held the bottle to his mouth. After a while he put it down, and thoughtfully rubbed the pit of his stomach. Then he took another pull, following directions to the letter.

The last ray of the evening sun stole through the open window as Jocko arose and wandered unsteadily toward the bedroom, the door of which stood ajar. There was no one within. On the wall hung Mrs. Hoffman's brocade shawl and Sunday hat. Jocko had often watched her put them on. Now he possessed himself of both, and gravely carried them to his attic.

In the early twilight such a wail of bereavement arose in the rear house that the tenants hurried from every floor to learn what was the matter. It was Mrs. Hoffman, bemoaning the loss of her shawl and Sunday hat.

A hurried search left no doubt who was the thief. There was the open window, and the empty bottle on the door by the ice-box. Jocko's hour of expiation had come. In the uproar that swelled louder as the angry crowd of tenants made for the attic, his name was heard coupled with direful threats. Foremost in the mob was Jim's father, with the stick he had peeled and seasoned against the boy's return. In some way, not clear to himself, he connected the monkey with Jim's truancy, and it was something to be able to avenge himself on its hairy hide.

But Jocko was not in the attic. The mob ranged downstairs, searching every nook and getting angrier as it went. The advance-guard had reached the first floor landing, when a shout of discovery from one of the boy scouts directed all eyes to the wall niche at the turn of the stairs.

There, in the place where the Venus of Milo or the winged Mercury had stood in the days when wealth and fashion inhabited Houston Street, sat Jocko, draped in Mrs. Hoffman's brocade shawl, her Sunday hat tilted rakishly on one side, and with his tail at "port-arms" over his left shoulder. He blinked lazily at the foe and then his head tilted forward under Mrs. Hoffman's hat.

"Saints presarve us!" gasped Mrs. Rafferty, crossing herself. "The baste is drunk!"

Yes, Jocko was undeniably tipsy. For one brief moment a sense of the ludicrous struggled with the just anger of the mob. That moment decided the fate of Jocko. There came a thunderous rap at the door, and there stood a policeman with Jim, the runaway, in his grasp.

"Does this boy—" he shouted, and stopped short, his gaze riveted upon the monkey. Jim, shivering with apprehension, all desire to be a soldier gone out of him, felt rather than saw the whole tenement assembled in judgment, and he the culprit. He raised his tear-stained face and beheld Jocko mounting guard. Policeman, camp, failure, and the expected beating were all alike forgotten. He remembered only the sunny attic and his pranks with Jocko, their last game of soldiering.

"Attention!" he piped at the top of his shrill voice. "Right hand—salute!"

At the word of command Jocko straightened up like a veteran, looked sleepily around, and raising his right paw, saluted in military fashion. The movement pushed the hat back on his head, and gave a swaggering look to the forlorn figure that was irresistibly comical.

It was too much for the spectators. With a yell of laughter, the tenement abandoned vengeance. Peal after peal rang out, in which the policeman, Jim, and his father joined, old scores forgotten and forgiven.

The cyclone of mirth aroused Jocko. He made a last groping effort to collect his scattered wits, and met the eyes of Jim at the foot of the stairs. With a joyful squeal of recognition he gave it up, turned one mighty, inebriated somersault and went flying down, shedding Mrs. Hoffman's garments to the right and left in his flight, and landed plump on Jim's shoulder, where he sat grinning general amnesty, while a rousing cheer went up for the two friends.

The slate was wiped clean. Jim had come home from the war.

A BACKWOODS HERO

I had started out to explore the Magnetawan River from our camp on Lake Wahwaskesh toward the Georgian Bay, thirty miles south, but speedily found my way blocked by the canal rapids. The river there rushes through a deep and narrow cañon strewn with sharp rocks, a perilous pass at all times for the most expert canoeist. We did not attempt it, but, making a landing in Deep Bay, took the safer portage around. At the end of a two-mile tramp we reached a clearing at the foot of the cañon where the loggers had camped at one time. Black bass and partridge go well together when a man is hungry, and there was something so suggestive of birds about the place that I took a turn around with my gun, while Aleck looked after the packs. Poking about on the edge of the clearing, in the shadow of some big pines which the lumbermen had spared, I came suddenly upon the most unlikely thing of all in that wilderness, miles from any human habitation—a burying-ground! Two mounds, each with a weather-beaten board for a headstone, were all it contained; just heaps of sand with a few withered shrubs upon them. But a stout fence of cedar slabs, roughly fashioned into pickets, to keep prowling animals away, hedged them in—evidence that some one had cared. "Ormand Morden," I read upon one of the boards, cut deep to last with a jack-knife. The other, nailed up in the shape of a cross, bore the name "M. McDonald." The date under both names was the same: June 8, 1899.

What tragedy had happened here in the deep woods a year before? Even while the question was shaping itself in my mind, it was answered by another discovery. Slung on the fence at the foot of one grave was a pair of spiked shoes; at the foot of the other the dead man's shoepacks with sand and mud in them. Two river-drivers, then; drowned in the rapids probably. I remembered the grave on Deadman's Island, hard by the favorite haunt of the bass, which was still kept up after thirty years, even as the memory of its lonely tenant lived on the lake where another generation of woodsmen had replaced his. But what was the old black brier-wood pipe doing on the head-rail between the two graves? I looked about me with an involuntary start as I noticed that the ashes of the last smoke were still in the bowl, expecting I hardly knew what in the ghostly twilight of the forest.

Over our camp fire that evening Aleck set my fears at rest and told me the story of the two graves, a tale of every-day heroism of the kind of which life on the frontier has many to tell, to the credit of our poor human nature. He was "cadging" supplies to the camp that winter and was a witness at first hand of what happened.

Morden and "Mike" McDonald were "bunkies" in a gang of river-drivers that had been cutting logs on the Deer River near its junction with the Magnetawan. Morden was the older, and had a wife and children in the settlements "up north." He had been working his farm for a spell and had gone back reluctantly to shantying because he needed the money in a slack season. But he could see his way ahead now. When at night they squatted by the fire in their log hut and took turns at the one pipe they had between them, he spoke hopefully to his chum of the days that were coming. Once this drive of logs was in, that was the end of it for him. He would live like a man after that with the old woman and the kids. Mike listened and smoked in silence. He was a man of few words. But there was between them a strong bond of sympathy, despite the disparity in their age and belief. McDonald was a Catholic and single. Younger by ten years than the other, he was much the stronger and abler, the athlete of a camp where there were no weaklings.

The water was low and the drive did not get through the lake until spring was past and gone. It was a good week into June before the last logs had gone over the canal rapids. The gang was preparing to follow, to pitch camp on the spot where we were then sitting. Whether because they didn't know the danger of it, or from a reckless determination to take chances, the foreman with five of his men started to shoot the rapids in the cook's punt. McDonald and Morden were of the venturesome crew. They had not gone halfway before the punt was upset, and all six were thrown out into the boiling waters. Five of them clung to the slippery rocks and held on literally for life. Morden alone could not swim. He went under, rose once, and floated head down past McDonald, who was struggling to save himself. He put out a hand to grasp him, but only tore the shirt from his back. The doomed man was whirled down to sure death.

Just beyond were the most dangerous rocks with a tortuous fall, in which the strongest swimmer might hardly hope to live. Nothing was said; no words were wasted. Looking around from his own perilous perch, the foreman saw Mike let go his hold and make after his bunkie, swimming free with powerful strokes. The next moment the fall swallowed both up. They were seen no more.

Three days they camped in the clearing, searching for their dead. On the fourth, just as dynamite was coming from the settlement to stir up the river bottom with, they recovered the body of McDonald in Trout Lake, some miles below. A team was sent to the nearest storehouse for planks to make a coffin of. As they were hammering it together, the body of his lost bunkie rose in the eddy just below the rapids, in sight of the camp. So they made two boxes and buried them on the hill, side by side. In death, as in life, they bunked together. Their shoepacks they left at the foot of their graves, as I had found them, and the pipe they smoked in common, to show that they were chums.

There was no priest and no time to fetch one. The rough woodsmen stood around in silence, with the sunset glinting through the dark pines on their bared heads. A swamp-robin in the brush made the responses. The older men threw a handful of sand into each open grave. The one Roman Catholic among them crossed himself devoutly: "God rest their souls." "Amen!" from a score of deep voices, and the service was over. The men went back to their perilous work, harder by so much to all of them because two were gone.

The shadows were deepening in the woods; the roar of the rapids came up from the river like a distant chant of requiem as Aleck finished his story. Except that the drivers sent Morden's wife his month's pay and raised sixty dollars among themselves to put with it, there was nothing more to tell. The two silent mounds under the pines told all the rest.

"Come," I said, "give me your knife;" and I cut in the cross on McDonald's grave the letters I. H. S.

"What do they stand for?" asked Aleck, looking on. I told him, and wrote under the name, "Greater love hath no man than this, that a man lay down his life for his friends."

Aleck nodded. "Ay!" he said, "that's him."

JACK'S SERMON

Jack sat on the front porch in a very bad humor indeed. That was in itself something unusual enough to portend trouble; for ordinarily Jack was a philosopher well persuaded that, upon the whole, this was a very good world and Deacon Pratt's porch the centre of it on week-days. On Sundays it was transferred to the village church, and on these days Jack received there with the family. If the truth were told, it would probably have been found that Jack conceived the services to be some sort of function specially designed to do him honor at proper intervals, for he always received an extra petting on these occasions. He sat in the pew beside the deacon through the sermon as decorously as befitted a dog come to years of discretion long since, and wagged his tail in a friendly manner when the minister came down and patted him on the head after the benediction. Outside he met the Sunday-school children on their own ground, and on their own terms. Jack, if he didn't have blood, had sense, which for working purposes is quite as good, if not so common. The girls gave him candy and called him Jack Sprat. His joyous bark could be heard long after church as he romped with the boys by the creek on the way home. It was even suspected that on certain Sabbaths they had enjoyed a furtive cross-country run together; but by tacit consent the village overlooked it and put it down to the dog. Jack was privileged and not to blame. There was certainly something, from the children's point of view, also, in favor of Jack's conception of Sunday.

On week-day nights there were the church meetings of one kind and another, for which Deacon Pratt's house was always the place, not counting the sociables which Jack attended with unfailing regularity. They would not, any of them, have been quite regular without Jack. Indeed, many a question of grave church polity had been settled only after it had been submitted to and passed upon in meeting by Jack. "Is not that so, Jack?" was a favorite clincher to arguments which, it was felt, had won over his master. And Jack's groping paw cemented a treaty of good-will and mutual concession that had helped the village church over more than one hard place. For there were hard heads and stubborn wills in it as there are in other churches; and Deacon Pratt, for all he was a just man, was set on having his way.

And now all this was changed. What had come over the town Jack couldn't make out, but that it was something serious nobody was needed to tell him. Folks he used to meet at the gate, going to the trains of mornings, on neighborly terms, hurried past him without as much as a look. And Deacon Jones, who gave him ginger-snaps out of the pantry-crock as a special bribe for a hand-shake, had even put out his foot to kick him, actually kick him, when he waylaid him at the corner that morning. The whole week there had not been as much as a visitor at the house, and what with Christmas in town—Jack knew the signs well enough; they meant raisins and goodies that came only when they burned candles on trees in the church—it was enough to make any dog cross. To top it all, his mistress must come down sick, worried into it all, as like as not, he had heard the doctor say. If Jack's thoughts could have been put into words as he sat on the porch looking moodily over the road, they would doubtless have taken something like this shape, that it was a pity that men didn't have the sense of dogs, but would bear grudges and make themselves and their betters unhappy. And in the village there would have been more than one to agree with him secretly.

Jack wouldn't have been any the wiser had he been told that the trouble that had come to town was that of all things most worrisome, a church quarrel. What was it about and how did it come? I doubt if any of the men and women who strove in meeting for principle and conscience with might and main, and said mean things about each other out of meeting, could have explained it. I know they all would have explained it differently, and so added fuel to the fire that was hot enough already. In fact, that was what had happened the night before Jack encountered his special friend, Deacon Jones, and it was in virtue of his master's share in it that he had bestowed the memorable kick upon him. Deacon Pratt was the valiant leader of the opposing faction.

To the general stress of mind the holiday had but added another cause of irritation. Could Jack have understood the ethics of men he would have known that it strangely happens that:

"Forgiveness to the injured does belong,
But they ne'er pardon who have done the wrong,"

and that everybody in a church quarrel having injured everybody else within reach for conscience's sake, the season of good-will and even the illness of that good woman, the wife of Deacon Pratt, admittedly from worry over the trouble, practically put a settlement of it out of the question. But being only a dog he did not understand. He could only sulk; and as this went well enough with things as they were in general, it proved that Jack was, as was well known, a very intelligent dog.

He had yet to give another proof of it, that very day, by preaching to the divided congregation its Christmas sermon, a sermon that is to this day remembered in Brownville; but of that neither they nor he, sitting there on the stoop nursing his grievances, had at that time any warning.

It was Christmas Eve. Since the early Lutherans settled there, away back in the last century, it had been the custom in the village to celebrate the Holy Eve with a special service and a Christmas tree; and preparations had been going forward for it all the afternoon. It was noticeable that the fighting in the congregation in no wise interfered with the observance of the established forms of worship; rather, it seemed to lend a keener edge to them. It was only the spirit that suffered. Jack, surveying the road from the porch, saw baskets and covered trays carried by, and knew their contents. He had watched the big Christmas tree going down on the grocer's sled, and his experience plus his nose supplied the rest. As the lights came out one by one after twilight, he stirred uneasily at the unwonted stillness in his house. Apparently no one was getting ready for church. Could it be that they were not going; that this thing was to be carried to the last ditch? He decided to go and investigate.

His investigations were brief, but entirely conclusive. For the second time that day he was spurned, and by a friend. This time it was the deacon himself who drove him from his wife's room, whither he had betaken him with true instinct to ascertain the household intentions. The deacon seemed to be, if anything, in a worse humor than even Jack himself. The doctor had told him that afternoon that Mrs. Pratt was a very sick woman, and that, if she was to pull through at all, she must be kept from all worriment in an atmosphere which fairly bristled with it. The deacon felt that he had a contract on his hands which might prove too heavy for him. He felt, too, with bitterness, that he was an ill-used man, that all his years of faithful labor, in the vineyard went for nothing because of some wretched heresy which the enemy had devised to wreck it; and all his humbled pride and his pent-up wrath gathered itself into the kick with which he sent poor Jack flying back where he had come from. It was clear that the deacon was not going to church.

Lonely and forsaken, Jack took his old seat on the porch and pondered. The wrinkles in his brow multiplied and grew deeper as he looked down the road and saw the Joneses, the Smiths, and the Allens go by toward the church. When the Merritts had passed, too, under the lamp, he knew that it must be nearly time for the sermon. They always came in after the long prayer. Jack took a turn up and down the porch, whined at the door once, and, receiving no answer, set off down the road by himself.

The church was filled. It had never looked handsomer. The rival factions had vied with each other in decorating it. Spruce and hemlock sprouted everywhere, and garlands of ground-ivy festooned walls and chancel. The delicious odor of balsam and of burning wax-candles was in the air. The people were all there in their Sunday clothes and the old minister in the pulpit; but the Sunday feeling was not there. Something was not right. Deacon Pratt's pew alone of them all was empty, and the congregation cast wistful glances at it, some secretly behind their hymn-books, others openly and sorrowfully. What the doctor had said in the afternoon had got out. He himself had told Mrs. Mills that it was doubtful if the deacon's wife got around, and it sat heavily upon the conscience of the people.

The opening hymns were sung; the Merritts, late as usual, had taken their seats. The minister took up the Book to read the Christmas gospel from the second chapter of Luke. He had been there longer than most of those who were in the church to-night could remember, had grown old with the people, had loved them as the shepherd who is answerable to the Master for his flock. Their griefs and their troubles were his. If he could not ward them off, he could suffer with them. His voice trembled a little as he read of the tidings of great joy. Perhaps it was age; but it grew firmer as he proceeded toward the end:—

"And suddenly there was with the angel a multitude of the heavenly host praising God and saying, 'Glory to God in the highest, and on earth peace, good-will toward men.'"

The old minister closed the Book and looked out over the congregation. He looked long and yearningly, and twice he cleared his throat, only to repeat, "on earth peace, good-will toward men." The people settled back in their seats, uneasily; they strangely avoided the eye of their pastor. It rested in its slow survey of the flock upon Deacon Pratt's empty pew. And at that moment a strange thing occurred.

Why it should seem strange was, perhaps, not the least strange part of it. Jack had come in alone before. He knew the trick of the door-latch, and had often opened it unaided. He was in the habit of attending the church with the folks; there was no reason why they should not expect him, unless they knew of one themselves. But somehow the click of the latch went clear through the congregation as the heavenly message of good-will had not. All eyes were turned upon the deacon's pew; and they waited.

Jack came slowly and gravely up the aisle and stopped at his master's pew. He sniffed of the empty seat disapprovingly once or twice—he had never seen it in that state before—then he climbed up and sat, serious and attentive as he was wont, in his old seat, facing the pulpit, nodding once as who should say, "I'm here; proceed!"

It is recorded that not even a titter was heard from the Sunday-school, which was out in force. In the silence that reigned in the church was heard only a smothered sob. The old minister looked with misty eyes at his friend. He took off his spectacles, wiped them and put them on again, and tried to speak; but the tears ran down his cheeks and choked his voice. The congregation wept with him.

"Brethren," he said, when he could speak, "glory to God in the highest, and on earth peace, good-will toward men! Jack has preached a better sermon than I can to-night. Let us pray together."

It is further recorded that the first and only quarrel in the Brownville church ended on Christmas Eve and was never heard of again, and that it was all the work of Jack's sermon.

SKIPPY OF SCRABBLE ALLEY

Skippy was at home in Scrabble Alley. So far as he had ever known home of any kind it was there in the dark and mouldy basement of the rear house, farthest back in the gap that was all the builder of those big tenements had been able to afford of light and of air for the poor people whose hard-earned wages, brought home every Saturday, left them as poor as if they had never earned a dollar, to pile themselves up in his strong box. The good man had long since been gathered to his fathers: gone to his better home. It was in the newspapers, and in the alley it was said that it was the biggest funeral—more than a hundred carriages, and four black horses to pull the hearse. So it must be true, of course.

Skippy wondered vaguely, sometimes, when he thought of it, what kind of a home it might be where people went in a hundred carriages. He had never sat in one. The nearest he had come to it was when Jimmy Murphy's cab had nearly run him down once, and his "fare," a big man with whiskers, had put his head out and angrily called him a brat, and told him to get out of the way, or he would have him arrested. And Jimmy had shaken his whip at him and told him to skip home. Everybody told him to skip. From the policeman on the block to the hard-fisted man he knew as his father, and who always had a job for him with the "growler" when he came home, they were having Skippy on the run. Probably that was how he got his name. No one cared enough about it, or about the boy, to find out.

Was there anybody anywhere who cared about boys, anyhow? Were there any boys in that other home where the carriages and the big hearse had gone? And if there were, did they have to live in an alley, and did they ever have any fun? These were thoughts that puzzled Skippy's young brain once in a while. Not very long or very hard, for Skippy had not been trained to think; what training the boys picked up in the alley didn't run much to deep thinking.

Perhaps it was just as well. There were one or two men there who were said to know a heap, and who had thought and studied it all out about the landlord and the alley. But it was very tiresome that it should happen to be just those two, for Skippy never liked them. They were always cross and ugly, never laughed and carried on as other men did once in a while, and made his little feet very tired running with the growler early and late. He well remembered, too, that it was one of them who had said, when they brought him home, sore and limping, from under the wheels of Jimmy Murphy's cab, that he'd been better off if it had killed him. He had always borne a grudge against him for that, for there was no occasion for it that he could see. Hadn't he been to the gin-mill for him that very day twice?

Skippy's horizon was bounded by the towering brick walls of Scrabble Alley. No sun ever rose or set between them. On the hot summer days, when the saloon-keeper on the farther side of the street pulled up his awning, the sun came over the housetops and looked down for an hour or two into the alley. It shone upon broken flags, a mud-puddle by the hydrant where the children went splashing with dirty, bare feet, and upon unnumbered ash barrels. A stray cabbage leaf in one of those was the only green thing it found, for no ray ever strayed through the window in Skippy's basement to trace the green mould on the wall.

Once, while he had been lying sick with a fever, Skippy had struck up a real friendly acquaintance with that mouldy wall. He had pictured to himself woods and hills and a regular wilderness, such as he had heard of, in its green growth; but even that pleasure they had robbed him of. The charity doctor had said that the mould was bad, and a man scraped it off and put whitewash on the wall. As if everything that made fun for a boy was bad.

Down the street a little way, was a yard just big enough and nice to play ball in, but the agent had put up a sign that he would have no boys and no ball-playing in his yard, and that ended it; for the "cop" would have none of it in the street either. Once he had caught them at it and "given them the collar." They had been up before the judge; and though he let them off, they had been branded, Skippy and the rest, as a bad lot.

That was the starting-point in Skippy's career. With the brand upon him he accepted the future it marked out for him, reasoning as little, or as vaguely, about the justice of it as he had about the home conditions of the alley. The world, what he had seen of it, had taught him one lesson: to take things as he found them, because that was the way they were; and that being the easiest, and, on the whole, best suited to Skippy's general make-up, he fell naturally into the *rôle* assigned him. After that he worked the growler on his own hook most of the time. The "gang" he had joined found means of keeping it going that more than justified the brand the policeman had put upon it. It was seldom by honest work. What was the use? The world owed them a living, and it was their business to collect it as easily as they could. It was everybody's business to do that, as far as they could see, from the man who owned the alley, down.

They made the alley pan out in their own way. It had advantages the builder hadn't thought of, though he provided them. Full of secret ins and outs, runways and passages not easily found, to the surrounding tenements, it offered chances to get away when one or more of the gang were "wanted" for robbing this store on the avenue, tapping that till, or raiding the grocer's stock, that were A No. 1. When some tipsy man had been waylaid and "stood up," it was an unequalled spot for dividing the plunder. It happened once or twice, as time went by, that a man was knocked on the head and robbed within the bailiwick of the now notorious Scrabble Alley gang, or that a drowned man floated ashore in the dock with his pockets turned inside out. On such occasions the police made an extra raid, and more or less of the gang were scooped in; but nothing ever came of it. Dead men tell no tales, and they were not more silent than the Scrabbles, if, indeed, these had anything to tell.

It came gradually to be an old story. Skippy and his associates were long since in the Rogues' Gallery, numbered and indexed as truly a bad lot now. They were no longer boys, but toughs. Most of them had "done time" up the river and come back more hardened than they went, full of new tricks always, which they were eager to show the boys, to prove that they had not been idle while they were away. On the police returns they figured as "speculators," a term that sounded better than thief, and meant, as they understood it, much the same; viz. a man who made a living out of other people's labor. It was conceded in the slums, everywhere, that the Scrabble Alley gang was a little the boldest that had for a long time defied the police. It had the call on the other gangs in all the blocks around, for it had the biggest fighters as well as the cleverest thieves of them all.

Then one holiday morning, when in a hundred churches the pæan went up, "On earth peace, good-will toward men," all New York rang with the story of a midnight murder committed by Skippy's gang. The saloon-keeper whose place they were sacking to get the "stuff" for keeping Christmas in their way had come upon them, and Skippy had shot him down while the others ran. A universal shout for vengeance went up from outraged Society.

It sounded the death-knell of the gang. It was scattered to the four winds, all except Skippy, who was tried for murder and hanged. The papers spoke of his phenomenal calmness under the gallows; said it was defiance. The priest who had been with him in his last hours said he was content to go to a better home. They were all wrong. Had the pictures that chased each other across Skippy's mind as the black cap was pulled over his face been visible to their eyes, they would have seen Scrabble Alley with its dripping hydrant, and the puddle in which the children splashed with dirty, bare feet; the dark basement room with its mouldy wall; the notice in the yard, "No ball-playing allowed here"; the policeman who stamped him as one of a bad lot, and the sullen man who thought it had been better for him, the time he was run over, if he had died. Skippy asked himself moodily if he was right after all, and if boys were ever to have any show. He died with the question unanswered.

They said that no such funeral ever went out of Scrabble Alley before. There was a real raid on the undertaker's where Skippy lay in state two whole days, and the wake was talked of for many a day as something wonderful. At the funeral services it was said that without a doubt Skippy had gone to a better home. His account was squared.

*** **

Skippy's story is not invented to be told here. In its main facts it is a plain account of a well-remembered drama of the slums, on which the curtain was rung down in the Tombs yard. There are Skippies without number growing up in those slums to-day, vaguely wondering why they were born into a world that does not want them; Scrabble Alleys to be found for the asking, all over this big city where the tenements abound, alleys in which generations of boys have lived and died—principally died, and thus done for themselves the best they could, according to the crusty philosopher of Skippy's set—with nothing more inspiring than a dead blank wall within reach of their windows all the days of their cheerless lives. Theirs is the account to be squared—by justice, not vengeance. Skippy is but an item on the wrong side of the ledger. The real reckoning of outraged society is not with him, but with Scrabble Alley.

MAKING A WAY OUT OF THE SLUM

One stormy night in the winter of 1882, going across from my office to the Police Headquarters of New York City, I nearly stumbled over an odd couple that crouched on the steps. As the man shifted his seat to make way for me, the light from the green lamp fell on his face, and I knew it as one that had haunted the police office for days with a mute appeal for help. Sometimes a woman was with him. They were Russian Jews, poor immigrants. No one understood or heeded them. Elbowed out of the crowd, they had taken refuge on the steps, where they sat silently watchful of the life that moved about them, but beyond a swift, keen scrutiny of all who came and went, having no share in it.

That night I heard their story. Between what little German they knew and such scraps of their harsh jargon as I had picked up, I found out that they were seeking their lost child—little Yette, who had strayed away from the Essex Street tenement and disappeared as utterly as if the earth had swallowed her up. Indeed, I often thought of that in the weeks and months of weary search that followed. For there was absolutely no trace to be found of the child, though the tardy police machinery was set in motion and worked to the uttermost. It was not until two years later, when we had long given up the quest, that little Yette was found by the merest accident in the turning over of the affairs of an orphan asylum. Some one had picked her up in the street and brought her in. She could not tell her name, and, with one given to her there, and garbed in the uniform of the place, she was so effectually lost in the crowd that the police alarm failed to identify her. In fact, her people had no little trouble in "proving property," and but for the mother love that had refused to part with a little gingham slip her lost baby had worn, it might have proved impossible. It was the mate of the one which Yette had on when she was brought into the asylum, and which they had kept there. So the child was restored, and her humble home made happy.

That was my first meeting with the Russian Jew. In after years my path crossed his often. I saw him herded with his fellows like cattle in the poorest tenements, slaving sullenly in the sweat-shop, or rising in anger against his tyrant in strikes that meant starvation as the price of his vengeance. And always I had a sense of groping in the memories of the past for a lost key to something. The other day I met him once more. It was at sunset, upon a country road in southern New Jersey. I was returning with Superintendent Sabsovich from an inspection of the Jewish colonies in that region. The cattle were lowing in the fields. The evening breathed peace. Down the sandy road came a creaking farm wagon loaded with cedar posts for a vineyard hard by. Beside it walked a sunburned, bearded man with an axe on his shoulder, in earnest conversation with his boy, a strapping young fellow in overalls. The man walked as one who is tired after a hard day's work, but his back was straight and he held his head high. He greeted us with a frank nod, as one who meets an equal.

The superintendent looked after him with a smile. To me there came suddenly the vision of the couple under the lamp, friendless and shrinking, waiting for a hearing, always waiting; and, as in a flash, I understood. I had found the key. The farmer there had it. It was the Jew who had found himself.

It is eighteen years since the first of the south Jersey colonies was started.[4] There had been a sudden, unprecedented immigration of refugees from Russia, where Jew-baiting was then the orthodox pastime. They lay in heaps in Castle Garden, helpless and penniless, and their people in New York feared prescriptive measures. What to do with them became a burning question. To turn those starving multitudes loose on the labor market of the metropolis would make trouble of the gravest kind. The alternative of putting them back on the land, and so of making producers of them, suggested itself to the Emigrant Aid Society. Land was offered cheap in south Jersey, and the experiment was made with some hundreds of families.

It was well meant; but the projectors experienced the not unfamiliar fact that cheap land is sometimes very dear land. They learned, too, that you cannot make farmers in a day out of men who have been denied access to the soil for generations. That was the set purpose of Russia, and the legacy of feudalism in western Europe, which of necessity made the Jew a trader, a town dweller. With such a history, a man is not logically a pioneer. The soil of south Jersey is sandy, has to be coaxed into bearing paying crops. The colonists had not the patient skill needed for the task. Neither had they the means. Above all, they lacked the market where to dispose of their crops when once raised. Discouragements beset them. Debts threatened to engulf them. The trustees of the Baron de Hirsch Fund, entering the field eleven years later, in 1891, found of three hundred families only two-thirds remaining on their farms. In 1897, when they went to their relief, there were seventy-six families left. The rest had gone back to the city and to the Ghetto. So far, the experiment had failed.

The Hirsch Fund people had been watching it attentively. They were not discouraged. In the midst of the outcry that the Jew could not be made a farmer, they settled a tract of unbroken land in the northwest part of Cape May County, within easy reach of the older colonies. They called their settlement Woodbine. Taught by the experience of the older colonists, they brought their market with them. They persuaded several manufacturing firms to remove their plants from the city to Woodbine, agreeing to furnish their employees with homes. Thus an industrial community was created to absorb the farmer's surplus products. The means they had in abundance in the large revenues of Baron de Hirsch's princely charity, which for all purposes amounts to over $6,000,000. There was still lacking necessary skill at husbandry, and this they set about supplying without long delay. In the second year of the colony, a barn built for horses was turned into a lecture-hall for the young men, and became the nucleus of the Hirsch Agricultural School, which to-day has nearly a hundred pupils. Woodbine, for which the site was cleared half a dozen years before in woods so dense that the children had to be corralled and kept under guard lest they should be lost, was a thriving community by the time the crisis came in the affairs of the older colonies.

The settlers were threatened with eviction. The Jewish Colonization Association, upon the recommendation of the Hirsch Fund trustees, and with their coöperation, came to their rescue. It paid off the mortgages under which they groaned, brought out factories, and turned the tide that was setting back toward the cities. The carpenter's hammer was heard again, after years of silence and decay, in Rosenhayn, Alliance, and Carmel. They built new houses there. Nearly $500,000 invested in the villages was paying a healthy interest, where before general ruin was impending. As for Woodbine, Jewish industry had raised the town taxes upon its 5300 acres of land from $72 to $1800, and only the slow country ways kept it from becoming the county-seat, as it is already the county's centre of industrial and mental activity.

It was to see for myself what the movement of which this is the brief historical outline was like that I had gone down from Philadelphia to Woodbine, some twenty-five miles from Atlantic City. I saw a straggling village, hedged in by stunted woods, with many freshly painted frame-houses lining broad streets, some of them with gardens around in which jonquil and spiderwort were growing, and the peach and gooseberry budding into leaf; some of them standing in dreary, unfenced wastes, in which the clay was trodden hard between the stumps of last year's felling. In these lived the latest graduates from the slum. I had just come from the clothing factory hard by the depot, in which a hundred of them or more were at work, and had compared the bright, clean rooms with the traditional sweat-shop of the city, wholly to the disadvantage of the latter. I had noticed the absence of the sullen looks that used to oppress me. Now as I walked along, stopping to chat with the women in the houses, it interested me to class the settlers as those of the first, the second, and the third year's stay and beyond. The signs were unmistakable. The first year was, apparently, taken up in contemplation of the house. The lot had no possibilities. In the second, it was dug up. A few potato-vines were planted, perhaps a peach tree. There were the preliminary signs of a fence. In the third, under the stimulus of a price offered by the management, a garden was evolved, with, necessarily, a fence. At this point the potato became suddenly an element. It had fed the family the winter before without other outlay than a little scratching of the ground. Its possibilities loomed large. The garden became a farm on a small scale. Its owner applied for more land and got it. That was the very purpose of the colony.

A woman, with a strong face and shrewd, brown eyes, rose from an onion bed she had been weeding to open the gate.

"Come in," she said, "and be welcome." Upon a wall of the best room hung a picture of Michael Bakounine, the nihilist. I found it in these colonies everywhere side by side with

Washington's, Lincoln's, and Baron de Hirsch's. Mrs. Breslow and her husband left home for cause. He was a carpenter. Nine months they starved in a Forsyth Street tenement, paying $15 a month for three rooms. This cottage is their own. They have paid for it ($800) since they came out with the first settlers. The lot was given to them, but they bought the adjoining one to raise truck in.

"*Gott sei dank*," says the woman, with shining eyes, "we owe nothing and pay no rent, and are never more hungry."

Down the street a little way is the cottage of one who received the first prize for her garden last year. Fragrant box hedges in the plot. A cow with crumpled horn stands munching corncobs at the barn. Four hens are sitting in as many barrels, eying the stranger with half-anxious, half-hostile looks. A topknot, tied by the leg to the fence, struggles madly to escape. The children bring dandelions and clover to soothe its captivity.

The shadows lengthen. The shop gives up its workers. There is no overtime here. A ten-hour day rules. Families gather upon porches—the mother with the sleeping babe at her breast, the grandfather smoking a peaceful pipe, while father and the boys take a turn tending the garden. Theirs is not paradise. It is a little world full of hard work, but a world in which the work has ceased to be a curse. Ludlow Street, with its sweltering tenements, is but a few hours' journey away. For these, at all events, the problem of life has been solved.

Strolling over the outlying farms, we came to one with every mark of thrift and prosperity about it. The vineyard was pruned and trimmed, the fields ready for their crops, the outbuildings well kept, and the woodpile stout and trim. A girl with a long braid of black hair came from the house to greet us. An hour before, I had seen her sewing on buttons in the factory. She recognized me, and looked questioningly at the superintendent. When he spoke my name, she held out her hand with frank dignity, and bade me welcome on her father's farm. He was a clothing-cutter in New York, explained my guide as we went our way, but tired of the business and moved out upon the land. His thirty-acre farm is to-day one of the finest in that neighborhood. The man is on the road to substantial wealth.

Labor or lumber—both, perhaps—must be cheaper even than land in south Jersey. This five-room cottage, one of half a hundred such, was sold to the tenant for $500; the Hirsch Fund taking a first mortgage of $300, the manufacturer, or the occupant, if able, paying the rest The mortgage is paid off in monthly instalments of $3.75. Even if he had not a cent to start with, by paying less than one-half the rent for the Forsyth Street flat of three cramped rooms, dark and stuffy, the tenant becomes the absolute owner of his home in a little over eight years. I looked in upon a score of them. The rooms were large by comparison, and airy; oil-painted, clean. The hopeless disorder, the discouragement of the slum, were nowhere. The children were stout and rosy. They played under the trees, safe from the shop till the school gives up its claim to them. Superintendent Sabsovich sees to it that it is not too early. He is himself a school trustee, elected after a fight on the "Woodbine ticket," which gave notice to the farmers of the town that the aliens of that settlement are getting naturalized to the point of demanding their rights. The opposition retaliated by nicknaming the leader of the victorious faction the "Czar of Woodbine." He in turn invited them to hear the lectures at the Agricultural School. His text went home.

"The American is wasteful of food, energies—of everything," he said. "We teach here that farming can be made to pay by saving expenses." They knew it to be true. The Woodbine farm products, its flowers and chickens, took the prizes at the county fair. Yet in practice they did not compete. The Woodbine milk was dearer than the neighboring farmers'. If in spite of that it was preferred because it was better, that was their lookout. The rest must come up to it then. So with the output of the hennery, the apiary, the blacksmith-shop in the place. On that plan Woodbine has won the respect of the neighborhood. The good-will will follow, says its Czar, confidently.

He, too, was a nihilist, who dreamed with the young of his people for a better day. He has lived to see it dawn on a far-away shore. Concerning his task, he has no illusions. There is no higher education, no "frills," at Woodbine. Its scheme is intensely practical. It is to make, if possible, a Jewish yeomanry fit to take their place with the native tillers of the soil, as good citizens as they. With that end in view, everything is "for present purposes, with an eye on the future." The lad is taught dairying with scientific precision, because on that road lies the profit in keeping cows. He is taught the commercial value of extreme cleanliness in handling milk and making butter. He learns the management of the poultry-yard, of bees, of pigeons, and of field crops. He works in the nursery, the greenhouse, and the blacksmith-shop. If he does not get to know the blacksmith's trade, he learns how to mend a broken farm wagon and "save expense." So he shall be able to make farming pay, to keep his grip on the land. His native shrewdness will teach him the rest.

The vineyards were budding, and the robins sang joyously as we drove over the twenty-four-mile stretch through the colonies of Carmel, Rosenhayn, Alliance, and Brotmansville. Everywhere there were signs of reawakened thrift. Fields and gardens were being got ready for their crops; fence-corners were being cleaned, roofs repaired, and houses painted. In Rosenhayn they were building half a dozen new houses. A clothing factory there that employs seventy hands brought out twenty-four families from New York and Philadelphia, for whom shelter had to be found. Some distance beyond the village we halted to inspect the forty-acre farm of a Jew who some years ago kept a street stand in Philadelphia. He bought the land and went back to his stand to earn the money with which to run it. In three years he moved his family out.

"I couldn't raise the children in the city," he explained. A son and two daughters now run the adjoining farm. Two boys were helping him look after a berry patch that alone would "make expenses" this year. The wife minded the seven cows. The farm is free and clear save for $400 lent by the Hirsch people to pay off an onerous mortgage. Some comment was made upon the light soil. The farmer pointed significantly to the barnyard.

"I make him good," he said. Across the road was a large house with a pretentious dooryard and evergreen hedges. A Gentile farmer with many acres lived in it. The lean fields promised but poor crops. The neighborhood knew that he never paid anything on his mortgage; claimed, in fact, that he could not.

"Ah!" said Mr. Sabsovich, emerging from a wrangle with his client about matters agricultural, "he has not learned to 'make him good.' Come over to the school, and I will show you stock. You can't afford to keep poor cows. They cost too much."

The other shook his head energetically. "Them's the seven finest cows in the country," he yelled after us as we started. The superintendent laughed a little.

"You see what they are—stubborn; will have their way in an argument. But that fellow will be over to Woodbine before the week is out, to see what he can learn. He is not going to let me crow if he can help it. Not to be driven, they can be led, though it is not always easy. Suspicious, hard at driving a bargain as the Russian Jew is, I sometimes think I can see his better nature coming out already."

As we drove along, I thought so, too, more than once. From every farm and byway came men to have a word with the superintendent. For me they had a sidelong look, and a question, put in Hebrew. To the answer they often shook their heads, demanding another. After such a conference, I asked what it was about.

"You," said Mr. Sabsovich. "They are asking, 'Who is he?' I tell them that you are not a Jew. This is the answer they give: 'I don't care if he is a Jew. Is he a good man?'"

Over the supper table that night, I caught the burning eyes of a young nihilist fixed upon me with a look I have not yet got over. I had been telling of my affection for the Princess Dagmar, whom I knew at Copenhagen in my youth. I meant it as something we had in common; she became Empress of Russia in after years. I forgot that it was by virtue of marrying Alexander III. I heard afterward that he protested vehemently that I could not possibly be a good man. Well for me I did not tell him my opinion of the Czar himself! It was gleaned from Copenhagen, where they thought him the prince of good fellows.

At Carmel I found the hands in the clothing factory making from $10 to $13 a week at human hours, and the population growing. Forty families had come from Philadelphia, where the authorities were helping the colonies by rigidly enforcing the sweat-shop ordinances. Inquiries I made as to the relative cost of living in the city and in the country brought out the following facts: A contractor with a family of eight paid shop rent in Sheriff Street, New York, $20 per month; for four rooms in a Monroe Street tenement, $15; household expenses, $60. Here he pays shop rent (whole house), $6; dwelling on farm, $4; household, $35. This family enjoys greater comfort in the country for $50 a month less. A working family of eight paid $11 for three rooms in an Essex Street tenement, $35 for the household; here the rent is $5, and the household expenses $24—better living for $17 less a month.

Near the village a Jewish farmer who had tracked us from one of the other villages caught up with us to put before Mr. Sabsovich his request for more land. We halted to debate it in the road beside a seven-acre farm worked by a Lithuanian brickmaker. The old man in his peaked cap and sheepskin jacket was hoeing in the back lot. His wife, crippled and half blind, sat in the sunshine with a smile upon her wrinkled face, and listened to the birds. They came down together, when they heard our voices, to say that four of the seven acres were worked up. The other three would come. They had plenty, and were happy. Only their boy, who should help, was gone.

It was the one note of disappointment I heard: the boys would not stay on the farm. To the aged it gave a new purpose, new zest in life. There was a place for them, whereas the tenement had none. The young could not be made to stay. It was the old story. I had heard it in New England in explanation of its abandoned farms; the work was too hard, was without a break. The good sense of the Jew recognizes the issue and meets it squarely. In Woodbine strenuous efforts were being made to develop the social life by every available means. No opportunity is allowed to pass that will "give the boy a chance." Here on the farms there were wiser fathers than the Lithuanian. Let one of them speak for himself.

His was one of a little settlement of fifteen families that had fought it out alone, being some distance from any of the villages. In the summer they farmed, and in the winter tailoring for the Philadelphia shops helped them out. Radetzky was a presser in the city ten years. There were nine in his house. "Seven to work on the farm," said the father, proudly, surveying the brown, muscular troop, "but the two little ones are good in summer at berry-picking." They had just then come in from the lima-bean field, where they had planted poles. Even the baby had helped.

"I put two beans in a hill instead of four. I tell you why," said the farmer; "I wait three days, and see if they come up. If they do not, I put down two more. Most of them come up, and I save two beans. A farmer has got to make money on saving expenses."

The sound of a piano interrupted him. "It is my daughter," he said. "They help me, and I let them have in turn what young people want—piano, music lessons, a good horse to drive. It pays. They are all here yet. In the beginning we starved together, had to eat corn with the cows, but the winter tailoring pulled us through. Now I want to give it up. I want to buy the next farm. With our 34 acres, it will make 60, and we can live like men, and let those that need the tailoring get it. I wouldn't exchange this farm for the best property in the city."

His two eldest sons nodded assent to his words.

Late that night, when we were returning to Woodbine, we came suddenly upon a crowd of boys filling the road. They wore the uniform of the Hirsch School. It was within ten minutes of closing-time, and they were half a mile from home. The superintendent pulled up and asked them where they were going. There was a brief silence, then the hesitating answer:—

"It is a surprise party."

Mr. Sabsovich eyed the crowd sharply and thought awhile.

"Oh," he said, remembering all at once, "it is Mr. Billings and his new wife. Go ahead, boys!"

To me, trying vainly to sleep in the village hotel in the midnight hour with a tin-pan serenade to the newly married teacher going on under the window, there came in a lull, with the challenge of the loudest boy, "Mr. Billings! If you don't come down, we will never go home," an appreciation of the Woodbine system of discipline which I had lacked till then. It was the Radetzky plan over again, of giving the boys a chance, to make them stay on the farm.

If it is difficult to make the boy stay, it is sometimes even harder to make the father go. Out of a hundred families picked on New York's East Side as in especial need of transplanting to the land, just seven consented when it came to the journey. They didn't relish the "society of the stumps." The Jews' colonies need many things before they can hope to rival the attraction of the city to the man whom the slum has robbed of all resources. They sum themselves up in the social life of which the tenement has such unsuspected stores in the closest of touch with one's fellows. The colonies need business opportunities to boom them, facilities for marketing produce in the cities, canning-factories, store cellars for the product of the vineyards—all of which time must supply. Though they have given to hundreds the chance of life, it cannot be said for them that they have demonstrated yet the Jews' ability to stand alone upon the land, backed as they are by the Hirsch Fund millions. In fact, I have heard no such claim advanced. But it can at least be said that for these they have solved the problem of life and of the slum. And that is something!

Nor is it all. Because of its being a concerted movement, this of south Jersey, it has been, so to speak, easier to make out. But already, upon the experience gained there, 700 families, with some previous training and fitness for farming, have been settled upon New England farms and are generally doing well. More than $2,000,000 worth of property in Massachusetts, Connecticut, and their sister states is owned by Jewish husbandmen. They are mostly dairy-farmers, poultrymen, sheep breeders. The Russian Jew will not in this generation be fit for what might be called long-range farming. He needs crops that turn his money over quickly. With that in sight, he works hard and faithfully. The Yankee, as a rule, welcomes him. He has the sagacity to see that his coming will improve economic conditions, now none too good. As shrewd traders, the two are well matched. The public school brings the children together on equal terms, levelling out any roughness that might remain.

If the showing that the Jewish population of New England has increased in 17 years from 9000 to 74,000 gives anybody pause, it is not at least without its compensation. The very need of the immigrant to which objection is made, plus the energy that will not let him sit still and starve, make a way for him that opens it at the same time for others. In New York he *made* the needle industry, which he monopolized. He brought its product up from $30,000,000 to $300,000,000 a year, that he might live, and founded many a great fortune by his midnight toil. In New England, while peopling its abandoned farms, in self-defence he takes up on occasion abandoned manufacturing plants to make the work he wants. At Colchester, Connecticut, 120 Jewish families settled about the great rubber-works. The workings of a trust shut it down after 40 years' successful operation, causing loss of wages and much suffering to 1500 hands. The Christian employees, who must have been in overwhelming majority, probably took it out in denouncing trusts. I didn't hear that they did much else, except go away, I suppose, in search of another job. The Jews did not go away. Perhaps they couldn't. They cast about for some concern to supply the place of the rubber-works. At last accounts I heard of them negotiating with a large woollen concern in Leeds to move its plant across the Atlantic to Colchester. How it came out, I do not know.

The attempt to colonize Jewish immigrants had two objects: to relieve the man and to drain the Ghetto. In this last it failed. In 18 years 1200 families had been moved out. In five months just before I wrote this 12,000 came to stay in New York City. The number of immigrant Jews during those months was 15,233, of whom only 3881 went farther. The population of the Ghetto passed already 250,000. It was like trying to bail out the ocean. The Hirsch Fund people saw it and took another tack. Instead of arguing with unwilling employees to take the step they dreaded, they tried to persuade manufacturers to move out of the city, depending upon the workers to follow their work.

They did bring out one, and built homes for his hands. The argument was briefly that the clothing industry makes the Ghetto by lending itself most easily to tenement manufacture. The Ghetto, with its crowds and unhealthy competition, makes the sweat-shop in turn, with all the bad conditions that disturb the trade. To move the crowds out is at once to kill the Ghetto and the sweat-shops, and to restore the industry to healthy ways. The argument is correct. The economic gains by such an exodus are equally clear, provided the philanthropy that starts it will maintain a careful watch to prevent the old slum conditions being reproduced in the new places and unscrupulous employers from taking advantage of the isolation of their workers. With this chance removed, strikes are not so readily fomented by home-owners. The manufacturer secures steady labor, the worker a steady job. The young are removed from the contamination of the tenement. The experiment was interesting, but the fraction of a cent that was added by the freight to the cost of manufacture killed it. The factory moved back and the crowds with it.

Very recently, the B'nai B'rith has taken the lead in a movement that goes straight to the heart of the matter. It is now proposed to head off the Ghetto. Places are found for the immigrants all over the country, and they are not allowed to stop in New York on coming over, but are sent out at once. Where they go others follow instead of plunging into the city maelstrom and being swallowed up by it. Soon, it is argued, a rut will have been made for so much of the immigration to follow to the new places, and so much will have been diverted from the cities. To that extent, then, a real "way out" of the slum will have been found.

Footnote 1: My exclamation on finding myself so suddenly translated back to Denmark was an impatient "Why, don't you understand me?" His answer was, "Lord, yes, now I do, indeed."

Footnote 2: Written in 1898.

Footnote 3: Rooney wore the Bennett medal for saving the life of a woman at the disastrous fire in the old "World" building, on January 31, 1882. The ladder upon which he stood was too short. Riding upon the topmost rung, he bade the woman jump, and caught and held her as she fell.

Footnote 4: This was written in 1900.

Made in the USA
Las Vegas, NV
06 July 2023